NOTHING

TO

CHANCE

This book is dedicated to my children,
Katie and Tommy.

Anything is possible.

NOTHING

TO

CHANCE

A novel by Mark D Swailes

Prologue

Grier

A blindside right cross to the temple finally felled him. It was a punch thrown with a sober ferocity. Knowing that helped him with his decision to stay down. The other fists had been easy to see, easy to absorb, easy to parlay into his act. Big, fat bombs hanging in the air like drunken balloons. For the last three hours he'd watched his quarry, how they moved, how they spoke, how they behaved, as a group and alone. Later, away from this place, he'd watch it again on video but for now... for now it was done; he lay on the floor holding his hands to his face, moaning. Playing the part. He'd let them toss him outside. Let them go back to their vices. Let them live the last moments of their miserable lives in the intoxicated blur of indulgence and revelry.

"Sleep it off!" cursed Kyle Braissen as he and his brother Freddy pushed him through the front doors of the old tavern.

Grier stumbled down the stairs, falling convincingly at the end. He heard one of the brothers snort a pile of phlegm into his mouth for the final insult and was relieved to hear the smack of spit in the puddle to his left.

"Ah, shit," scowled Kyle as his brother pulled him towards the door.

"He's done already."

Grier lay patiently in the long grass and weeds, listening to the music and the voices inside. When he was sure he could rise without suspicion, he stood up slowly, dusted off his coat and pants and walked through the crowded parking lot to his car. Slipping into the shrouded interior of the backseat, he let himself sink into the leather and sighed into the darkness.

"We good, Grier?" came a low voice from the front.

"Didn't see it coming, must be losing my touch." Grier confessed. "Pass me the monitor."

Grier grabbed the tablet and scanned the scene inside. Moving the camera, Grier zoomed in on the two brothers who had tossed him out. They sat in a large, oversized booth with several others, drinking and laughing, yelling and cursing.

"They've got no idea," Grier sneered.

Hours later, when the rain started, only a few cars remained. Grier could hear the hiss of the neon sign as droplets of water filtered through the porous overhang of the Hammerhead's entranceway. The dashboard clock glowed 3:58 am, and his screen showed most of the group passed out in the booth, attempting through either choice or necessity to purge themselves of their particular poisons. The interstate had been quiet until now. A vehicle approached, its headlights illuminating the downpour. As it turned into the parking lot, the headlights went dark and the driver pulled in beside Grier and his crew. The truck was here. It was time.

"Remember, nothing in the hands or the head," Grier ordered.

"We'll get it done. Ready boys?"

The car filled with sound, shotguns loading, the jangle of bullets sliding into position, of weapons clicking, safeties off. Then the three men in Grier's vehicle stepped out into the rain; from a car to the right, four other men stepped out of their car, black and silver metal glinting off the glare of the old neon. Quietly, quickly the men gained entrance. As the front door swung closed Grier sat back and watched. In moments, the gang inside was assembled: Freddy and Kyle Braissen, Clay and Keith Mallory, Sebastian Rayne, Will Jeffries, and a few others who had made the mistake of sleeping over. For them it was quick, single shots. With three dead, the six he could see were pleading now,

2

begging for clemency, stripped of their importance. Their pleas earned them nothing. Except, perhaps, a sense of justice for the ghosts of their victims: the tortured and the dead. Grier couldn't help but smile. It wasn't that he enjoyed the suffering; it was the idea that his plan was starting to form, that his genius would finally be tested. He smiled, knowing that their deaths would breathe the first wisps of life into his vision.

The boys made quick work of them. Merciful ends to meaningless lives. The bodies folded agreeably into their bags and as the sacks came out of the front door, orange and red fingers of flame rose from the center of the dilapidated roadhouse. Once the cargo were secured in the truck, everyone returned to their vehicles, like the patrons of some bizarre sporting event that had run its course. Home team zero, visitors nine.

The engine came to life; the truck and the other car turned onto the interstate. It was 4:26 am and although the sky should have been brightening, the storm clouds thickened, resolved to slow the coming dawn.

"Just like you said, Grier."

"Good work," he acknowledged, smiling out the window at the last snapshot of the Hammerhead Bar and Grill.

"Genius," he thought, feeling the first piece of the perfect plan fall into place.

Chapter 1

SOUTH ON THE I-17
APPROACHING I-10, PHOENIX, ARIZONA
FRIDAY, APRIL 29, 2005
10:18 AM

Grier

Grier pulled down the sunshade and stole a quick glance at his companions in the mirror. The scene was surreal. Dead men; all of them, living and breathing like they'd never left this world. His gaze lingered, tuning in to their conversation.

"How do I look?" Pete asked Simon.

"You look just like him. Like a killer." Simon confirmed.

"I don't feel like him."

"How would you know?"

"I guess I wouldn't. Not really. Guess I'm feeling it."

"We all are, Pete. Just stick to the script and you'll be fine. Looking the part is the gig here; besides, that guy you don't feel like, he's dead and he isn't feeling anything any more."

"I hadn't thought of that. Guess I'm more him now than he'll ever be."

"That's right. You get to write the final chapter of his life as far as the rest of the world is concerned."

"I do? Yeah, I guess I do."

Grier closed the mirror, but not before taking a look at his own reflection. Clay Mallory stared back at him. The make-up flawlessly captured the contours and shadows of the man. Carl, in the driver's seat, looked even more the part, as his physical form matched Sebastian Rayne in both size and scope.

"Everything is looking good," Carl offered.

"Kayla and Alan will be on the move," Grier answered.

"What are the chances that Alan will call it off?" Pete asked from the back.

"No chance. I have that feeling. It's gonna be on," Grier assured him.

"I don't feel anything 'cept my nerves; is that bad?" Pete asked.

"No. Not bad. It'll come, Pete, when we arrive. It'll come. Simon, you're pretty quiet back there; everything all right?"

Simon's disguise as Keith Mallory fit him well. It was the mannerisms and choppy gait that threw him off. Although Simon had come aboard late he'd somehow managed to befriend the entire crew. So much so that Grier had come to resent the bonds Simon had forged in a few short weeks. Especially with Kayla. Grier remained oddly distant from her, even after months of living and training together. The price for genius, he surmised.

"Just running it through in my head."

"Running it through in your head?"

"I gotta be ready for everything."

"That you do," Grier whispered.

"This is it, our exit. Ten minutes out," Carl intervened.

The minivan slid off the interstate, quietly joining the parade of vehicles looking to complete their daily commutes. Pete and Simon ran through the equipment. Glocks, clips, knives, watches, all ready. The laptop, an epic design of code-breaking technology, a back-up should there be a need. Finally, the bomb. Detonator-rigged military grade plastic coupled with an incendiary liquid meant to vaporize. Enough to give those CSI guys a run for their money. In the back, two more cases, attaché style, black, nondescript. Inside, the thawing remains of Grier's earlier work. The genetic last stand of their alter egos. The last case Grier

5

trusted to no one. In it, the source of everyone's absolution. Except for Simon. His destiny lay along a different path.

"We've got our spot," Carl said, sliding into a parking space outlined by city traffic cones.

"Eyes on the prize. Look for Alan's signal."

Even with the air conditioning on maximum, the temperature in the van climbed. Outside it was nuclear. Phoenix sat in the grip of an early spring heat wave that had broken every record not only for Arizona, but for the whole of the United States for as long as they'd been keeping records. And this time, the dryness of the heat was no reprieve from its lethargy-inducing embrace. Stepping out into the haze of the morning would mean instant sweat: an enemy of their complex disguises. They would have to move quickly.

"Nothing, Grier," Carl noted as he spread a large sunscreen across the front windshield. Grier nodded to Carl, who worked some numbers into a cell phone. "It's done."

Pete handed each man his equipment. A silent proficiency to each of their movements. Grier could feel the rush starting to come over him. The injection of adrenaline invigorated him. He could feel his perceptions extending. This was what he had been waiting for. This was what he craved. The rush flowed into him and through him like a tidal wave of energy, pulsating with power.

Grier's voice dropped into a monotone bass. "Let's do this."

They left the van: Grier, career criminal mob man, as Clay Mallory; Carl, ex-con preacher, as Sebastian Rayne, Pete, brilliant psychotic, as Will Jeffries; and Simon, retired thief, as Keith Mallory.

They made their way across the four-lane street and up twenty feet to the target. People moved by them, taking no notice. Four men, dressed casually, moving in twos, attracted little attention. Pete thumbed open the shoulder carrying case and removed a rectangular sheet of hard plastic. The entranceway consisted of two sets of double doors, and only as they approached the first set of glass doors, Grier in the front followed by Simon, then Carl and Pete, did Grier spare a glance at Simon and realize the magnitude of what he had done.

Chapter 2

Simon

"You up?" Kayla's voice. Soft and sweet.

"Been waiting for you," Simon lied, turning on his reading lamp.

"Don't do that."

"Do what?"

"That."

"That bullshit guy thing?"

"Yeah, that."

"Sorry K, just putting up the walls."

"Isn't it strange?"

"How do ya mean?"

"I'm tearing mine down, your putting 'em up."

"Come on. Sit down. What's on your mind?"

"My daughter. My choices. You," she said, gliding into the room.

"It's the beginning of the end, is it?"

"Listen Simon. Just watch your back, OK?"

"Always."

"You think we gotta chance?"

"More than a chance, a future."

"God… I wish I had your optimism."

"Not optimism. This is going to be the one. When everything goes according to plan. I can feel it."

"Everything?"

"Everything."

"I'm holding out hope for one small deviation."

"Me too K, me too." Simon whispered. "Somewhere down the line, we'll see if this thing is real."

"Promise?"

"On my life."

"Don't say that."

"OK, OK. On my word."

"OK."

Kayla sat on the end the bed, Simon sat beside her. She reached out her hand to him and he took it in his own. Both held firmly, sighing into the dimly lit emptiness of the room.

"You gonna me tell now? How it went down with you and Grier?"

"Why not. Can't sleep anyway."

He'd kept the story to himself. No sense in telling it. Simon doubted he could make it sound like anything other than what it was – dark and insidious. Base coercion. But here, the night before the day, with Kayla, the radiant jewel he'd found in the middle of all this shit, here it seemed safe. Here it seemed right.

"He found me outside of Phuket; I've got a nice house there on the beach, you'd love it."

She laughed. He smiled.

"Said he wanted to meet for drinks, talk about the old times. Of course I'd heard things, mostly that he'd become a made man, you know? Connected to the mob, so I knew I had to be careful. When he cruised in, it was exactly what I'd hoped for. We sat around, got drunk, hit a few nightspots, and crashed at my place. In the morning, I stumbled across the newspaper clipping, the one about Jason."

"You didn't know?"

"No. But as soon as I read the article, I knew what was coming; the whole reunion vibe came crashing down. And Grier knew it. He came outta the guest room just as I finished reading it. He didn't hold back any of his true intentions from that point on."

"And you just went along?"

"Of course not. I told him I was too long gone from the work. I told him I wasn't looking for another hit, that I'd retired. I told him I'd help to find a replacement for Jason."

"But time was of the essence."

"He fed me all the bullshit, like I was some newbie novice. Kept saying 'you're the best' and 'I need you.' I keep a shotgun in my closet. I'm not a violent man but I considered ending him. I knew the mob would be keeping tabs on him, that they'd come for me, or worse, for my family in the States if he went missing. They'd want to protect their investment."

"So you had to agree."

"He tried to make it feel like I was returning a favor I owed him, but no, we both knew his presence was cold and calculated. Six years I worked with him."

"He's a different guy now."

"You're right, he is. There's only a shadow of his old self left."

"That first morning, after you'd arrived at the farmhouse, I thought you were such an asshole!"

"Come on, how was I supposed to know that stuff was yours?"

"You could have asked!" she insisted.

Simon remembered the Detroit farmhouse where, far away from prying eyes, they had honed their tactical abilities. Weapons and explosives training, backstory review and in an old barn on the property, a mock-up of the target. He'd arrived weeks after they'd begun. First day of school. In a new town. In a new country. He was a fish out of water.

"Listen, it's your fault for having the only thing remotely edible in the fridge."

Simon had promptly acknowledged Jason's death, telling them how sorry he was for their loss. Jason was a fireball of personality; it was impossible not to be swept up by his extroverted energy and enthusiasm. Simon knew Grier would be incapable of sharing sympathies with the crew so he filled the void. The response had been immediate. They brought him in. They gave him a chance. He'd read them and the situation perfectly.

"You're blaming me for having good taste?" She kissed him playfully.

"Drinking your smoothie is my one great regret."

"Ha-ha."

"Grier forced me in. It's not all bad, we'll always have the road trip."

A week later, they packed up and travelled to the Warehouse. The trip from Detroit to Phoenix had afforded Kayla and Simon more time together, travelling as a vacationing couple in an old RV. Instead of a cooler full of food they had handguns, and instead of smuggling clothes or shoes from state to state, they were moving explosives. Somewhere in that journey they'd felt the stirrings of something meaningful. Life had been poured back into him. Each day, bringing him up, out of his self-pity.

"I know the rest of the story."

"That you do."

"For what it's worth, I'm glad you came."

"I wouldn't trade this part of it for a thousand Thai sunsets."

Simon reached up to Kayla's face and pulled her into a kiss. Lips lingered against each other; she put her arms around his face and he hers. Together on the end of his bed they felt the whisper of potential uncover itself. Kayla rose quietly, tussling Simon's hair and winking before she turned and left.

"Night," she whispered.

Simon let her final word hang in the air, breathing in the melodic tone of it, letting it bounce and tumble around his room before silence returned.

Simon lay back down, pulling the covers up over his legs and turning out the light. Sleep. It was a hundred years away. Too many thoughts. Too many possibilities. He ripped off the covers and rolled onto the ground. Push-ups always helped. He knocked out a quick set of twenty. What did she mean, watch his back? And a few days earlier, that uncomfortable silence he'd stumbled upon in the kitchen with Grier, Carl and Alan. What was that about? So many things were wrong about this job. The fact that he replaced a dead man. Jason Westing killed in a motorcycle accident. Jason. His student. Simon had taught him all the tricks, the tells and look fors. He was an excellent apprentice with a gift for the work. Jason had done well with Grier, filling the void when he had decided that enough was enough. Coming into the fray so late meant it would be harder to make connections with the others. Simon knew that. And he'd worked hard to break through.

Carl Smith was the first egg he'd cracked. An enigmatic ex-con who'd found the Lord. His steadfast approach to their training grounded everyone. He pushed the group to do it better, faster, smoother, acknowledging effort and ignoring failures. Carl empowered them to do what needed to be done. His talent in explosives was derived from work in an Alabama coal mine. Hard living for the two-hundred-pound black man, that he spoke very little of, except to say his subsequent incarceration was a welcome reprieve from the darkness of the mines. In prison he'd found the Lord, he studied the scriptures and altered his path. When he got out, he found his considerable talents were in demand. His one stipulation, the effects of his inclusion must harm corporate America. *"It's time for a new world order,"* he was fond of sermonizing. And when Grier needed some high-grade explosives and a man to work them, Carl got the call.

No one in the group was more drawn to Carl and his confident positivity than Peter "Pete" Milloy. With his awkwardness and social dysfunctions, Pete's computational mind and his heightened anxiety made everyone uneasy. Carl's influence balanced him. They spent long hours talking, the two of them, and over the course of their prep, Pete's erratic behaviors came less frequently.

Pete had technical abilities that Simon could barely comprehend. He had never attended college but had an Ivy League IQ. He'd surrounded himself with computers and had created hundreds of programs that he loved to discuss in all of their tiniest and most technical bits should opportunity arise. Simon learned quickly to steer clear of tech talk with Pete. Hacking into security systems and encryption code-breaking, these were the areas where Pete shone. When things didn't go well, Pete would lose control. He destroyed a parking lot vending machine when it failed to produce the cold beverage of his choice. Nineteen stitches later, Grier made sure Carl accompanied Pete on all his other excursions. But there were no other incidents. Pete stabilized under Carl's care. Simon would need to remain guarded during the job, Pete's capacity for explosive mood swings still lay simmering just under the surface.

In stark contrast to Pete's social ineptitude, Alan Turnbull was the perfect neighbor. He was friendly and cordial to everyone, but close to none. He filled awkward silences with humorous stories; he always asked, *"How you doin?"* Then hung around to hear the answer. He also played the part of the class clown, providing comic relief when the tension rose. He was quick and capable. A weapons specialist, he guided them in the use of the Glocks, with suppressors and without. Simon was intrigued at how differently the gun handled with the silencer on. Alan trained them in unarmed combat. He had a multitude of skills from a variety of disciplines and was a patient and attentive teacher. He would prepare the target for their infiltration, taking out the first line of defense with fluidity and grace. Alan's military background made him an excellent choice. Grier loved barking out orders and having them expedited in a timely fashion. If Simon could stay in touch with any of the guys after this job, it would be Alan. He was a great guy to meet at the pub and watch the game with, or to have your back in a dark alley. Scenarios that were sometimes only hours apart. There was no doubt in Simon's mind that he would perform his task with the skill and aptitude of a professional.

Kayla had been the last, best one to unravel. She'd kept to herself, almost entirely. Her frequent departures with Grier in the mid-mornings led to obvious conclusions about their relationship. But there was something else Simon discovered. A daughter in England. A little chickadee that Grier had used to manipulate Kayla into his world. Grier would drop her at a local Internet cafe so she could Skype with her daughter. He'd do what he needed to do, meet with his contacts, acquire a needed piece of equipment or report to the higher-ups about their progress.

Had it only been two days since she had opened herself up to him? It felt so thick with emotion, the time belied the intensity of their connection. But she knew, of course she knew, that Simon needed that extra push. She saw it in the final stages. Simon was distant, he was still running through the motions, but he was getting bogged down in the anger and frustration of his situation. So she'd opened up, told him about her life, a failed designer, pregnant to a fashion editor, abandoned by the industry and shunned by her family. And then her joy, Kasia, a daughter. She knew he'd respond. She saw the humanity in him when he told the group about his relationship with Jason. When Simon said he would try to do justice to his memory. And he meant it. She had hoped that telling Simon would refocus him. But there had been more, an attraction, immediate and polarizing. Physical, yes, that was to be expected, but the emotional connection, that had been a surprise to them both.

Simon smiled to himself, reliving the memory of their first kiss. He was invested now. Fully and completely. He would get her back to her daughter, no question about it. A yawn came. Then another. Satisfied, Simon climbed back into bed and closed his eyes. He went over the plan, one last time.

Kayla would eliminate the senior bank officials in the president's office as they salivated over her multi-million dollar stock portfolio. Alan would take out the security guards and scout the bank for other potential security risks. Off-duty cops, ex-military personnel, that sort of thing. He would signal the rest of them if anything was amiss. Carl would drive them to the bank. Disguised as their alter egos, Grier, Carl, Pete and Simon would take the bank from the front at 10:58 am. Kayla and Alan would get 'loaded' and then slip away. He would be in charge of the main room, while the others completed their jobs. Once the payloads were secure they would begin negotiations with the police, allowing their faces to be seen. It was imperative that the police identified them as the Mallory boys. Grier's disguise as Clay Mallory would force the police to back down. He'd set off two of the biggest explosions in American criminal history. Once they had him ID'ed as the man calling the shots, they'd give them whatever they wanted in the hope of avoiding civilian bloodshed and extensive damage. Of course, the cops would never get the chance. The drama of the groups' betrayal, all for the eyes and ears of the hostages, would commence in earnest. The scripted-out conflicts that would lead the Mallory's into killing their own members would culminate with the detonation of the bomb. Having shed their disguises, each of them would escape into the crowd, just another hostage who managed to survive. After the explosion and in the confusion, they would melt away into the city. It was a good plan. The video footage and the forensic evidence they planned to leave behind would solidify their anonymity. Grier really had thought of everything. Before sleep took him, Simon envisioned the faces of Kayla and Kasia, of Carl, sure and steady with Pete bouncing around him, of Alan, laughing loudly, and finally of Grier... cold and impersonal, standing on a Thai beach with that smirk, callous and dark. Would Grier let him go after this job? He thought he knew the answer, but he pushed it down, out of the way, somewhere quiet. Simon drifted off knowing that tomorrow, for better or worse, would change things. How? He wasn't sure. The future moved hypnotically behind a translucent pane of glass. Impossible to see. Impossible to escape.

Chapter 3

Grier

There was something in Simon's eyes that made Grier stop, a realization, if but for an instant, that this man that he had wronged despised him. He hadn't seen it before now, but there it was, plain and open. Hate. Grier smirked, even more pleased with himself and his plan. When he stepped through the doorway into the bank, his professionalism returned and although somewhere in the remotest corner of his soul he felt a twinge of guilt, he moved on, driven by the need for power and domination. This was business, pure and simple.

Simon

The National Bank was populated by two tellers, a man and a woman; several customers, three men and four women; and two security guards, who milled about near the entranceway. The manager, executive director and president were nowhere to be seen, meaning Kayla had done her job with the skill and precision that was expected of her. They would be fully subdued, restrained and secured. Simon was pleased with the number of customers:

seven was a palatable number. Get in, get out. It was a struggle to rein in his revulsion of Grier. He began to realize that those years in Thailand were a facade. Had he ever really been free of this?

Alan

The security guards, Harry and Bill by the names on their ID tags, looked briefly at each other as the four came through the second set of double doors. Their entrance drew little attention from any of the bank employees or customers. Alan moved silently from behind the two security guards, quickly and quietly putting them down. A perfectly aligned fist to the windpipe silenced Bill's instinct to yell for help. Alan placed the loop of a flex cuff around Bill's right hand as he struggled for breath and twisted his arm backwards, grabbing the left arm and moving it quickly and precisely into the remaining space of the plastic tie behind his back. As he pulled it tight, Alan stepped forward and delivered a harsh knee blow into Harry's diaphragm, sending him to his knees gasping for air. Harry had turned to check the great circular clock above the teller's stations. He was due for his lunch break in twenty minutes. The lapse in attention had cost him any hope of responding to the attack. Carl, having stuffed Bill's mouth with a folded piece of cloth and laid it over with a generous portion of black duct tape, performed the same exacting, practiced routine on Harry as he knelt, still winded from the knee to the gut. Carl, completing his responsibilities, bent over their incapacitated bodies and removed their weapons, while Alan slid Harry's left hand into the loop of plastic and pulled his hands tight behind his back. Kayla, in her wig, high-cut dress and heels, moved out from her position in the president's office, having neutralized her objectives just as Alan had done.

Kayla

She had gained access to the desk, professing the need to see something on their computer regarding her fictitious account.

Commenting on the luxurious look of the office, complimenting the executives on their professionalism, she'd displaced them away from the alarm system. Then she'd pulled out her gun. Kayla had the senior-most executive, the bank's president, secure the plastic slide ties around the wrists of his subordinates. He had the most to lose and would be the easiest to control physically if he decided to resist. Simon had taught her that. Once the last of them was bound, she gagged them. With the alarms secured she'd left them locked in the office closet, in the dark with the banker's boxes. She eliminated them efficiently and effectively. A quick 15-minute, 2-million-dollar job.

The length of the main banking room, and the speed with which the guards were disposed of, created the illusion for the customers who faced away from the entrance and the tellers who worked diligently to assist them, that this was still a day like any other.

Kayla, who'd moved into position behind the tellers, threw a set of keys across the bank floor to Pete, who thumbed through them quickly, moving back towards the lobby doors. The movement and sound of the keys disrupted the flow of the morning for the unfortunate souls in the bank, cueing Simon to begin his loosely rehearsed dialogue.

Simon

"Everybody down! On the ground, NOW!" His voice cut like a razor across the stunned silence of the room. As the reaction was understandably and predictably slow, Simon moved forward, his handgun brought high for all to see, and pistol-whipped the closest man, who fell to the ground with a bloody but superficial wound to the cheek.

"Down now!" Simon commanded. Everyone hit the floor in a hurry.

"That's it, got it," said Pete as the tumbler of the lock slid into the groove.

Pete turned and assisted Alan in pulling the security guards away from the windows of the lobby entrance.

Grier had moved purposefully to the gate where the employees enter the teller area. His painstaking study of the wiring, blueprints and security systems yielded results: as he quickly disconnected the circuits that enabled the alarms. Kayla, from her position behind the two tellers acted as a safety just in case they tried to act on a life-shortening loyalty. As it was, they were both so stunned and surprised by the quickness and impossibility of the events that were unfolding that neither of them made a move to activate the alarms.

"You, put this on your cheek," Simon said, handing the man he had bloodied a red and white bandana. Simon kept three such bandanas on his person for precisely this purpose. Dusty habits from a distant life.

"Now you, you and you get on your hands and knees and move over there through the employee entrance. Now!" Simon moved the three men who happened to be in the same area of the bank, in front of the stock ticker, behind the half wall of the teller booths.

Kayla and Grier moved the tellers away from the stalls and onto the open floor behind the booths, out of sight from the lobby doors, between the teller cubicles and the hallway that led to the vault. Carl supervised the remaining four women and Alan kept a close eye on the guards where they lay beside, but out of sight of, the lobby entrance. Pete flipped open his briefcase and moved intently to the network hub for the security cameras. To the broadcast video cable he attached a small hard drive with recorded footage from the bank from two months ago. Grier had returned with the device one evening, after meeting with the "Investors." The picture was remarkably unaltered, with the exception of a small willowy plant that appeared in the video but was no longer present in the bank. It presented a small risk to their plan; however, they could not procure more recently recorded video. The stolen footage would be what Kronos Security, the security agency that monitored this bank and several other banks in the downtown area, would be watching for the next few hours if need be. The timing of the breach was perfectly coordinated with a shift change at Kronos. But Grier was not satisfied and insisted that the time period from takedown to upload would need to be covered, and so Alan and Grier had planted an incendiary device that Carl had fit with a wireless transmitter behind one of the electrical outlets in Kronos Security's main monitoring room. Carl had detonated it in the van from his cellphone. The monitoring room would be vacated this morning and before anyone knew anything, it would be over.

It had been fifty-five seconds since they had entered the bank. The cameras would have recorded and stored the entrance of Grier and his crew, would have caught very clearly the faces of those involved; that too was all part of the master plan.

"OK, now you ladies, up on your hands and knees and crawl through the teller's gate," Simon said firmly. One of the women began to whimper, the kind of sound that could spark fear and panic in the others. He knew that he needed to quiet her. Quickly, painlessly. Her body twitched, like electrical jolts were passing through her hands and feet, the former being slick with sweat. Her panic was consuming her. Simon leaned down, touched her hand with his own, and said very softly, "If you want to live, do as I say; I haven't the patience for anything else."

She rolled quickly onto her stomach and moved through the tellers' gate, still whimpering but compliant. Direct instruction, Simon knew, got results. Give them something to do and they'll do it – anything to take them away from this reality.

Everything had gone according to plan. Kayla had removed the tellers' jackets and now that the last of the customers and tellers had been cuffed, she and Simon slid the dark navy blazers on. The large jacket was passable. Kayla's jacket read "Margaret" and seemed a good fit.

Just then the first set of double doors swung open and two businessmen, talking about the game the night before, or the oppressive heat, or how expensive it was to live in the city, made their way into the lobby and the second set of double doors that would lead them into the bank. Less than three feet away, the security guards lay gagged and bound.

Grier, Carl and Pete quickly hid themselves as Alan, kneeling from his position just inside the doors where the men stood, removed his Glock and placed the muzzle against Harry's temple, making sure that Bill took stock of the consequences that movement or noise would bring. Both Harry and Bill, wide-eyed, lay still, listening helplessly to the conversation of the two men in the small bank lobby.

"Did you see that basket in the second half? I mean, that was unbelievable," said the taller of the two men.

Kayla and Simon busied themselves at one of the terminals, looking confused and frustrated.

The shorter man tried the door. It pulled against the lock. He drew back, surprised. Could the bank be closed? In the middle of the morning? The other man stepped forward and pulled. Both men looked at each other and then leaned forward to peer through the glass. Simon and Kayla pretended to work at their computers. Looking down, the men noticed the plastic sign hanging from the doors.

NATIONAL BANK NOTICE
We apologize for any inconvenience this disruption to service creates for our valued customers. Please use the banking machines on the corner while we attend to some minor technical and computer system related repairs. Your business is important to us and we hope to have the problem fixed quickly.
Thank-you for your understanding,
Management

Noticeably annoyed, but apparently satisfied, they turned back towards the entrance. As the first man pushed open the door and conversation resumed about the basketball game, a city police officer opened the other door to the main entrance. Sunlight spilled splendidly into the front foyer of the bank. A conversation, one too distant, too insulated to hear, began between the two departing businessmen and the officer. Kayla and Simon looked tensely at each other. It was too soon for the involvement of the police; they had barely begun. If the officer knocked on the door, what would they do? The businessmen moved on. The cop moved into the lobby. He peered through the windows. Two tellers worked at the computer terminals, not a customer in sight. No security guards either. Maybe with the doors locked they would have been allowed to take a break in the back. It had been a point of contention and debate for several days, whether or not the sign should be posted on the outside or the inside set of doors. In the end, the risk of some random passerby seeing them place the sign on the doors in the critical minute where they took over the bank was too great. Strategically, Simon looked up from the computer terminal and made eye contact with the cop. Grier stuck the point of his gun into Simon's lower leg in protest from his hiding place below the counter. Without looking down, Simon opened his palm below the counter indicating to Grier that he had the situation in hand. Simon shrugged his shoulders and mouthed the word, "Sorry." The policeman gave a brief wave of acknowledgement and retreated from the lobby, moving off in the direction of the two suits towards the banking machines on the corner.

They collectively exhaled. The tension lessened, marginally, as they set about their business. The business of thieves. Simon became aware of the heavy breathing of the panicked woman. Looking over to her, he could see that she was starting to convulse. Short, sporadic, spastic movements. Simon quickly walked over for an assessment. Her pupils were wide, filled with a blank terror, her arms and legs twitched, but she had no Medic Alert bracelet. Sweat beaded visibly on her forehead. She was in the throes of a serious panic attack. There was nothing to be done about it. As disturbing as it would be for the others to witness, he would have to leave her. She would either pass out or calm herself. It wouldn't make Simon's job any easier, that's for damned sure.

"We're heading into the back, Keith," stated Grier. He moved forward with the plan, either confident that Simon could handle the situation or callously indifferent to the woman's plight. Given the timeline, Simon nodded his understanding.

"No problem; how many hostages we got altogether, Clay? Including the ones in the back." Simon's voice trailed off as he partially padded the woman's head with one of the bandanas he had in his pocket.

Grier picked up the briefcase and took a step towards the vault, "We've got eighteen, with the suits and the rent-a-cops."

Simon removed his Glock and pointed it menacingly around the room at the hostages.

"Let's frag a few of these fuckers! How the hell am I supposed to keep an eye on all of them?" He spit the words out like a seething volcano.

Grier stopped and turned.

"Stow it!" he barked. "We may need them later on, if anything goes wrong."

Simon cocked the gun, dramatically putting a bullet in the chamber.

"Right, Clay. Later on, don't forget bro, I'm your man. Just like Carolina."

Kayla handed her teller's jacket to Simon, then moved quickly down the narrow hallway that led to the vault with Grier, Alan and Pete. The dialogue, as contrived as it felt after so many rehearsals, had the desired effect. The hostages now all knew the names Clay and Keith. They knew something happened in Carolina. They knew how many hostages there were. Most importantly for now, they knew that Keith was volatile and eager for violence. This would help Simon control the group. Unfortunately for the panic-stricken woman, it drove her into a quivering seizure. Simon could see blood starting to run on her wrists; the plastic had bitten into her skin from the strain. Simon quickly moved over to her and, removing his knife, sliced off her flex cuff. He then tied the bandana that had been under her head around her cut wrist. It was a superficial wound, but one that needed to be dealt with. The woman calmed some as Simon administered aid.

While Simon worked, Carl made his way to each of the hostages, taping their mouths shut and then placing a lightweight breathable hood over each of them. They had all made sufficient eye contact and could no doubt ID them from police photos. Carl was about to tape the mouth of a composed thirty-something man, when the man mentioned to him that he could help the woman regain her composure. Carl nodded but applied the tape anyway. Then he hooded the man. When he finished with the last few hostages Carl stepped over to Simon, who stood over the woman assessing his makeshift bandaging. Carl quietly told Simon about the offer. Simon looked over at the man. First thought? Off-duty cop. Somehow that didn't fit. He hadn't had much luck with the woman, and the last thing he wanted was a full-on seizure. Simon knew he'd have to be careful.

Carl took up his position, to the side of the main room, with a clear visual line to the front doors of the bank and a blanket view of all the hostages. Customers entered the bank frequently. Reading the sign, they'd exit quietly. Every now and then someone would peer through the windows, but their investigative instinct would fade as quickly as it came. The heat of the day was helping to keep them moving.

Simon stepped over to the man who had spoken to Carl. He had a slight frame. Conservatively dressed. No wedding band. Simon saw the bulge of a wallet. He removed it and examined the contents. Forty dollars, some credit cards. School ID. A teacher. Patrick Jornan. From the looks of him, Simon would guess English, maybe History. Simon gauged the man and his offer. An offer made either of considerable empathy or one of opportunistic courage. If it was the latter, Simon would have to ascertain that before removing the tie. Simon bent down and removed the hood. Patrick was scared but in control; he looked calmly and quietly into Simon's eyes. No, not this man, Simon concluded. Just a good man. A man of ethics and morals. Simon held up his Glock. Patrick understood.

"My associate tells me you can help the woman?" Simon asked.

Patrick nodded.

23

"I'm going to remove the tape from your mouth; you will tell me your name and quickly how you can help," Simon said sharply.

Once again the man nodded.

Simon reached across and pulled the tape with one hand; his other hand held the Glock. Ready.

"My name is Patrick. Breathing techniques. I think I can talk her down."

Simon paused. Letting this man help would send a message that they didn't want anyone to be harmed. It was a good message to send. It would keep them in check as they awaited an end to this ordeal. He removed his knife and sliced cleanly through the plastic cuffs.

"Roll onto your hands and knees and crawl over to her."

Patrick moved onto his hands and knees.

"If I end up regretting this, you'll be dead. Understand?" Simon whispered to Patrick as he turned over.

Patrick nodded his head and made his way through the maze of hostages over to the convulsing woman. In a couple of minutes he had her in a semi-sitting position, arms extended over her head, breathing rhythmically and without the muscle spasms that her anxiety had caused. Simon, having returned to the teller's station, was impressed with the speed of her recovery. The woman seemed to be completely recomposed. Simon walked over to them and re-cuffed each. He taped Patrick and the woman, then hooded them both. She looked exhausted. Simon was amazed by Patrick's selflessness. There was something in the eyes. Something deep and meaningful. Something familiar to Simon, that brought him back to the knowledge that he had a happy, contented life waiting for him on distant shores when this day was done.

"You did good, Patrick," Simon muttered as he stood, returning to his position at the teller's stations. His watch read 11:12 am.

In total, fourteen minutes had passed since they entered the bank and now that the woman's panic attack had been dealt with, Simon shared a brief smile with Carl. The job was progressing just as they'd planned. Customers were moving down to the bank machine or back onto the street with regularity. The four team

24

members in the vault would be well on their way to securing their payloads. Both of them knew that if the next ten minutes went as smoothly as the first ten minutes they would be hitting their exit strategies and out of the state by dinner.

Patrick

Behind the covering of his hood, Patrick listened quietly in the corner, hoping that he'd done the right thing. They hadn't killed the woman. That had to be a good sign. Hadn't it?

Chapter 4

OSTLENDA RESIDENCE
1320 EL SERENO CRES., MESA, ARIZONA
FRIDAY, APRIL 29, 2005
8:22 AM

Patrick

Sunlight slanted in through the windows. The hum of the air conditioner was periodically interrupted by the ticking ding of metal on metal. The unit was being taxed this week, in the midst of this ridiculous heat wave. Sensing his wakefulness, Khan, a beast of a Retriever, jumped onto the bed for a visit.

"What? No paper?" Patrick chided.

Khan sniffed Patrick's face, who scratched him lovingly behind the ears. As Khan went for a lick, Patrick pulled away.

"Not with your morning breath, mister."

Patrick slid out of bed, making his way to the toilet, when the phone rang. He balanced his options in the doorway of the bathroom, pee or phone, pee or phone... Sighing, he turned back towards the bed and the end table which was littered with books, his water bottle and the phone. Reaching for the receiver, he knocked over his water bottle.

"Shit..." He muttered wearily before placing the phone to his ear. "Good morning," he stammered, attempting to sound more awake than he was.

"Hello Patrick? It's Mel," came the soft, feminine response.

"Who?"

"Mel." The voice on the other end repeated. "It's Melissa."

He'd heard it the first time. Of course he had. Somewhere in the back of his brain came a searing heat. His heart beat faster, his skin flushed. He'd heard it. Finally. A smile broke his tanned face and any remnant of sleep fell away as he repeated the name, "Melissa Mackenzie."

It seemed almost impossible to him that this could be happening but at the same time, deep inside, he recognized that this is what he had been waiting for, all along, all these years.

"My God, how are you? How have you been?"

It had been eleven years since they were last together. They had been deeply in love for a time. Sweethearts through the last two years of high school, they ended up continuing their relationship through college, though friends often speculated that it was destined to end sooner or later. They survived the evolution of the relationship, as new experiences and people were thrust upon them, with the kind of candid honesty that belied their ages. Certainly hers was the richest soul he had ever encountered, and somewhere in the passing years he had ended up losing himself in her. It was shortly after the realization of this that he had pushed for marriage and a family. She wasn't ready. In hindsight, neither was he. Eventually in the dying summer of 94, in the glorious canals of Venice, she had ended the relationship and he'd not heard from her since. He was devastated. After the truth came fully to bear that she was gone, he had tried to find her, but she had disappeared into the ever-changing ocean of Europe. Two weeks later, in Kiev, he gave up the search and flew home to pick up the pieces of his life. One year after their parting he received a postcard from her, the words of which he'd read over and over, a thousand times, never truly satisfied with his interpretation of her meaning. He moved on, alone. Patrick realized that in all his ensuing relationships he would never again be able to capture the love the two of them had shared.

"I'm fine." She too seemed flustered by the sudden rush of emotion that came from this impossible conversation.

"I know this might be asking a lot, but is there any chance we can meet up today?"

"You mean you're in town?"

"Yes, I'm here."

"I'd love to get together… how does lunch sound?"

Could this be happening? Eleven years and the sound of her voice was still velvet. He wanted to see her now! But many years had passed, and in those years many things would have changed. Both of them had new lives, although his plans seemed to always make room for her, subconsciously. He'd be committing emotional suicide if he ever acknowledged it. Was that fear and anxiety that he was sensing in her words? Was she in trouble, is that why she'd returned after so many years?

"Do you remember where Gladview Deli is?"

She hesitated. "Gladview Deli, on 4th Avenue, right?"

She'd always had an excellent memory. He recalled the time she'd tormented him about the color of her prom dress, suggesting that his forgetfulness was a sign of his selfishness. She had been teasing, but he felt horrible all the same. So much so that he had hunted down the old "Wishing Well" photo in the dusty archives of his parent's basement.

"That's the one. The Deli got closed down by the City Health Inspectors a few years ago and the new Italian place is very good."

"That sounds great."

"I'll call ahead. It's called the Piazza Petrullio. You still like Italian?"

She responded with a strained chuckle. He hadn't meant to touch a nerve, but why then did he pick that restaurant of the many that he knew?

"*Idiot!*"

The pause on the line was audible. Patrick waited for the click and the dial tone that would reverberate in his ears until his dying day.

"Patrick, I really need to talk to you face to face." Her voice sounded thready and his heart sank within its own callousness.

He attempted to change the tone of the conversation. "Certainly… those were different times, different lives. But I'd be lying if I didn't tell you that I don't still think about it, about you."

What the hell was wrong with him? Like he could contain this regret for eleven years and then in one three-minute phone call have it completely unravel. It was too late to take the words back, but inwardly his heart was thankful for the chance. If she hung up now, at least he'd have that.

"Are you back for long?" he pushed forward, not wishing to place her too long in an uncomfortable position.

"I'm excited about the future, Patrick, about being back, about what that could mean, but I want to save it for our lunch date, OK?"

Had she said date? What did that mean? He felt like he was in high school again, guilty and liberated all at once.

"Yes, lunch. You're absolutely right. Lunch sounds great. How's 1:00 work for you? I have some appointments this morning I can't miss."

"1:00 is excellent!"

"And how many should I make the reservation for?" This was it. If she's married or has a family then I'll find out here and save myself the surprise when I arrive for lunch, thought Patrick. Besides, it'll take some time to adjust to the thought of Melissa with a family.

"Just the two of us. I hope…?" Her voice trailed off in a question, so gentle.

He caught himself from celebrating.

"Right then, reservation for two. I'll see you at one."

"Yes, I'll be there."

"Bye, Mel." He'd said the same words years and years ago.

"Bye, Patrick." She seemed to want to say more and lingered at the other end of the line for a few seconds before the call ended.

Patrick hung up the phone. He felt like screaming. So he did.

"WOOHOO!!"

Khan stood up and, wagging his tail, went to visit this strange new morning Patrick person that was so excited and energized. Patrick rubbed his head happily, yelling, "Holy shit! Melissa fucking Mackenzie! It never rains but it pours!"

Patrick looked at his dresser and shook his head at the five-by-seven picture of an attractive woman in a red dress that graced its top.

"A beauty," he thought, *"but not the one."*

He reached down to the bottom drawer of the dresser, opened it, and pulled out a small cash box. Turning the combination lock caused the small lid to flip open. Patrick studied the contents for a moment, then reached in and fished out a ring box. He palmed the box from hand to hand nervously, then tossed it up into the air. Khan barked. Patrick caught it and opened it. Inside was the diamond engagement ring he'd purchased for their trip together to Europe, never finding the right moment to ask the ultimate question. Simple but elegant. Just like Mel. He spilled the remaining contents of the cash box onto his bed. Pictures of Melissa, of them together, at the parties, at graduation, on summer vacations, all the way back to the two of them in high school. There too amongst the fading images lay the postcard she had sent all those years ago. The ink had faded some but it remained legible. It wouldn't have mattered anyway. Her poignant message had been etched into his memory.

He rose, grabbed a towel from behind the bedroom door, and made his way to the shower, pausing just long enough to let Khan outside for his morning routine and turn the radio on.

"It's going to be another scorcher today as the city heat wave continues. The temperature is expected to hit a record-breaking 124 degrees today; right now it's a sweltering 108..."

Out of the shower, clad only in his drying towel, Patrick opened his wardrobe. What does one wear for the greatest day of their lives? He couldn't decide. He dropped the towel and closed the mirrored wardrobe doors. He looked good naked. Without the responsibilities of family and long-term relationships, he was able to take care of himself, staying fairly fit and trim. Turning from angle to angle and shifting from side to side, he thought that he could have looked better, but he wasn't unsatisfied with what he saw. At thirty-six this year, he was in a hell of lot better shape than most of his friends.

He wondered what she might look like now. She'd been a cloaked bombshell, hiding the emerging curves of her body in sweatshirts and jackets, baggy pants and over-sized athletic shorts through the entirety of high school. Except for Prom. He remembered the envious looks he received from guys like Charlie Thompson, an athletic, popular and successful student, that smacked of self-centered narcissism. As if he needed that idiot's approval to date Melissa, easily the most beautiful girl in the school. Time had a way of changing people. He didn't care. She could have put on a hundred pounds in a Swiss cheese factory, it wouldn't matter. It had always been the complex caverns of her mind and her heart that took possession of his own, not her physical features, as radiant as they'd been.

After dressing, he grabbed a glass of orange juice and a yogurt from the fridge in the kitchen. He flicked off the stereo and heard the whine of Khan at the door. Snapping his fingers, he let Khan back inside, then back-tracked into the kitchen where he filled Kahn's bowl with water from the tap.

"Have a good day, buddy," Patrick told Khan.

Everything had changed for him this morning. Melissa Mackenzie. The name itself seemed to be suddenly uncovered like some ancient treasure. And now that it was he found that he could think of nothing else except the possibilities that this day might afford him. He was a dreamer. Had always been. But now he was also a realist. He felt ready to face his dream in either the realization of its truth or the loss of its illusion.

Once he was down the steps of his loft apartment, he pulled open the garage and climbed into his two-year-old VW Passat, a sleek black coupe that he spoiled like a child. Turning the engine over he drove slowly out towards the street. His apartment sat on the top of a large three-car garage to the rear of a gorgeous Georgian home which belonged to his landlady and friend, Beatrice Ostlenda. She had rented him the apartment at considerably less than it was worth as he had agreed to do as many landscaping and yard duties as she could dream up. Looking to the front door he could see Beatrice struggling with her keys, her door and two arms full of groceries. Patrick quickly stopped his car and jumped out to lend a hand. As expected, Beatrice yelled at him in an attempt to fend him off as if he were trying to steal her purse.

"You get on now, Patrick; I've got everything under control," she shouted as the apples went spilling over one of her grocery bags.

"Nonsense, chivalry is not dead, my lady, and let me offer forth the proof," he professed as he started to collect the apples from the ground.

She looked at him fondly for a moment and, with a sigh, resigned herself to his kindness and generosity. It was exactly what she should have expected from him, she knew, but his selflessness always seemed to awe her, reminding her very deeply of her late husband's giving disposition.

Finally, after wrangling the door open and capturing those more mobile items from their temporary freedom, she released him from his knightly vows, adding, "We'll certainly miss these good turns you afford us here."

He particularly enjoyed it when Beatrice included her Mod Squad of pets as her extended family and referred to the lot of them as "us" or "we." Three cats, a parrot and a tortoise kept her sufficiently entertained.

"You're sure to miss those little treasures my dog leaves in your backyard too," Patrick offered jokingly.

"You're one of a kind Patrick, no matter how you twist it. Get on to your business now. It's going to be another scorcher today I'm afraid."

"It certainly feels that way already, doesn't it?" Patrick acknowledged, wiping a droplet of sweat from his cheek. "A very good day to you, Mrs. O." He bowed slightly before he made his way to his car. Effortlessly gliding back into his Passat, Patrick slipped it into gear and moved purposefully towards the city center.

With all the excitement of this morning's phone call Patrick had almost forgotten about his 9:20 am appointment with his closest friend, Gordon Hooper. Gordon, a hotshot lawyer, was handling the legal end of the deal. This would be their final meeting, the papers would be signed, and a lifelong dream would be fulfilled. The old Danbury house on Lincoln Avenue would be his before noon. He'd have to scoot over to the bank before the luncheon with Mel in order to finalize the mortgage and insurance issues, but he still figured he'd have plenty of time to prepare himself for that reunion.

Patrick arrived at the Law Offices of Bernstein, Walsh and McDunna promptly at 9:18. Cathy Doyle, Gordon's longtime secretary, nodded her head towards the office door and Patrick proceeded straight inside.

Patrick winked at Cathy, a fifty-something widow, adding, "It looks like first degree murder, make sure we're not disturbed."

Cathy rolled her eyes and inspected the phone.

"Oh, looks like he's on a call right now, Patrick."

But Patrick was already closing the door. He just managed to catch himself. Gordon had a slightly panicked look on his face as he listened intently to the voice on the other end of the telephone.

Gordon "Hoops" Hooper was a tall, bronze-skinned man. Intimidatingly muscular. His body lean and quick, his movements smooth and graceful, but the power that Gordon exuded lay in his dark brown nearly black eyes. They were penetrating when need be. Always compassionate and convincing in friendship. The eyes themselves were set in a rugged face, high cheekbones framed by a squarely set jaw. It was a strange thing to admit, but Patrick felt safer when they were together.

Patrick sat down quietly in one of the high-back brown leather chairs. The kind of chairs you'd expect to find in a lawyer's office, stuffy and conservative. Gordon looked across the desk at Patrick, rolled his eyes, and then yawned dramatically in between his occasional interjections of "you're kidding" and "it'll all blow over soon enough."

Patrick had made the reservations for lunch on the way over, asking for a few special additions – fresh-cut flowers on the table and a specific Chardonnay he thought she'd enjoy. He now hoped that he wasn't doing too much, wondered whether she'd be impressed or terrified, and he made a motion to call back and cancel the extras, when Gordon hung up the phone.

"Wow. What a shit storm." He seemed flat, like he'd expended all his energy on that one phone call.

In an effort to invigorate his friend back to life, Patrick slapped him on the shoulder. "Hoops! How's the firm treating you?"

"Don't ask. We've got some serious damage control going on right now, and I've become the resident social worker."

Gordon knew that he could tell Patrick anything about the problems taking place in the firm, but he understood that Patrick was taking a big step forward with the purchase of this house and he didn't want to diminish the happiness and joy this day would bring. Besides, the seedy underside of the internal affairs investigation into the city's Chief of Police was bound to appear that evening on the local news. The corruption in the case was clear to both of the legal teams; however, the chief had mysteriously and quite brilliantly severed any and all connections between himself and those external threads of guilt. No one was talking, from paid informants to the officers allegedly involved, and that meant the firm, as the counsel for the defendant, Chief Rutherford Mills, could pressure internal affairs into pressing charges or closing the investigation. Everything seemed to be moving towards an agreeable end when early this morning the Chief had given an unauthorized, unscripted interview. The media spin was less than desirable. Patrick had already heard about it on the radio on his way over. Although the Chief did not mean to further implicate himself the angle the local news crews took went in the other direction. This had sent Kyle McDunna, lead counsel and partner at the firm, into a frenzy of slanderous remarks before organizing an official response slated to go live to air on the local news sometime before noon. Damage control was definitely the phrase of the day and, for his part, Gordon attempted to talk down the tense and anxious personalities of McDunna's staff, fellow lawyers attempting eventually to add their names to those of the firm's.

"Everyone wants to vent, and I guess I've got the biggest ears." Gordon shook his head and quickly seemed refreshed; Patrick had always envied him that. He didn't dwell; he acted.

Patrick smiled and sat up in his chair. "OK, then let's get the deed settled on the Danbury place; my apartment is shrinking by the day."

Gordon grabbed a brown file from his desk drawer and flipped it open. "Looks like all we're waiting on is your rather cryptic signature. This mortgage, house stuff isn't my bag, but I had the guys down the hall run the numbers, just to be sure. It's a done deal, buddy. Congratulations, Patrick!"

"That's great! I'm going by the bank this morning to finalize." Patrick felt the blood racing as he signed his name to the bottom of the legal pages that would make the Danbury house his very own.

"You know," Gordon offered, "you could do all of your banking right here on my computer if you wanted to."

Patrick shook his head. "This is too important to leave to a glitch in the Internet. I'm a renaissance man; besides, I've got a date for lunch." Patrick smiled, finally able to work this morning's phone call into their conversation.

"Laurie?" But Gordon knew it wasn't Laurie; Patrick looked like he was going to burst.

"Nope, not Laurie," Patrick said, pausing painfully for effect before blurting out, "Melissa's back."

"Melissa's back?" All the pieces finally fell into place for Gordon; he understood the rich tapestry of feelings and emotions that her return must have drawn out of Patrick and yet at the same time Gordon was wary. Fearful for his friend, knowing Patrick's ways, Gordon tried to make him aware of the dangers.

"Be careful, buddy. I don't know what to think or say besides that."

"Yeah, yeah, OK Dad, I'll be careful." Somewhere inside, Patrick's own thoughts echoed Gordon's concern. But he had to obey his heart; it had always been the only way.

Seeing the worry on his friend's face prompted Patrick to change the subject, "Still working out tomorrow?"

"Are you kidding? How else am I going to hear about the Big Date? Besides, I've got a few new moves to try out." Gordon laughed aloud suddenly, envisioning their last experience at the gym, which had them attempting at the bequest of his wife Deirdre an advanced spinning class. He'd made a personal note to commend his wife on her fitness level every day this week, at least until he was able to walk fully upright again.

"Still can't sit comfortably?"

"No, you?"

"I'm thinking tomorrow will be better, otherwise I'll have to get a donut."

"I can see that. Old man Hooper sitting on his donut."

"Get lost, Mr. Danbury; say hi to Melissa for me."

They smiled and joked with each other and the tension of the morning for both of them slipped away. It was what had made them friends to begin with and what would keep them friends throughout their lives.

"Alrighty then, see you at the gym and say hi to Deirdre and the girls for me." Patrick made a move to stand.

"Will do, Patrick."

They moved to the door where they embraced and shook hands before parting. Indeed they knew that they were fortunate to have found each other's friendship in the chaos of college and all those people who spin like revolving doors in and out of one's life.

The day, the rising sun in a clean blue sky, the quiet streets of suburbia, held for Patrick a fresh beauty. The Ironwood trees that lined the old streets of Stone Ridge Park seemed to reach out to him with their budding green arms and slender fingers, promising a bountiful summer. Even the lights at the intersections on his way over to the Danbury house seemed to smile at him, winking as he edged closer with their emerald eyes. It was a rare day off from the stress and tension of school and he noticed a few teenagers enjoying a Friday mid-morning rollerblade down Waterford Avenue, maximizing the pleasure of a long weekend. Teaching had been like therapy for him upon his return from Europe. His six classes and all of his two hundred plus students kept his mind on his lesson plans, on the inner workings of literature and poetry, on reading and composition. More importantly, they provided him with perspective. That first year back without Melissa, teaching High School English, had quite possibly saved his sanity.

He had since made enormous strides professionally, serving for the last three years as the Head of the English Department at Brophy College Preparatory School and publishing his master's thesis in a notable literary journal. There were dear friends on faculty who supported and nurtured his growth as well as a few loathsome enemies who despised his energy and advancement. But beyond the politics in the staff room, he felt that he could always turn to the students and his classes in order to see more clearly.

Patrick's VW rolled to a stop along Madison Avenue, just to the left of what would today, officially, be his very own driveway leading up into the separate two-car garage located at the rear of the house. For Patrick, the house possessed a rich history and a vibrant, almost tangible feeling of comfort and security. Patrick keyed the engine off and stepped out of the car, making his way slowly towards the green wooden gate, all the while coming to grips with the truth that the house was now his.

In the summer of 1986, Patrick answered a classified ad in the local newspaper: young hard-working apprentice needed, must be a quick study and handy with tools, steel-toed boots required, excellent student job opportunity. Patrick had been reluctant to call but he also had to get some money together for college. In his youthful righteousness he refused to work in fast food. Greasy slave labor for minimum wage was not his idea of a summer well spent. That was when he met Takashi Tsujiuchi, a Japanese

37

architect who spent his time traveling from place to place buying land and building houses. He remembered waiting his turn as seven other boys all around his age from all over the city interviewed with Takashi, or Tsujiuchi-san as he preferred to be called. Patrick hadn't felt confident; some of the other boys had tool belts and safety glasses and other such impressive props, which looked worn and used. No one spoke, perhaps for fear of giving up some valuable information; everyone there inspected the ground or ceiling waiting for their turn. The interview itself consisted of three quick questions.

"What is your name?" Takashi's voice was firm and engaging.

"Patrick Jornan, sir," he had answered.

"How old are you?" He asked the question like someone who wasn't really concerned with the response.

"Sixteen and a half." Patrick's voice trailed away; he was sure he wouldn't get it now; some of the other boys were definitely in their graduating year of high school.

"What would you rather be doing this summer?" His tone took on the mantle of interest and he leaned forward slightly to get a clear indication of Patrick's reaction.

Patrick suddenly couldn't remember what he expected the next question to be; suffice it to say this wasn't it. His first thought was of Melissa; spending time together through the entire summer would have been great, but she too had to work towards college. Then he thought of hanging out with some of the guys down at the mall, but they always ended up doing something stupid and getting into trouble. Slumming at home watching TV and playing video games also appealed to him, but there was no way that could keep his attention and interest for two months.

Patrick shrugged his shoulders and without any further deliberation stated, "I guess I'd like to learn something new this summer and not be stuck inside slaving over a grill in one of those fast food sweat shops."

Takashi looked at him a moment and after a slight pause said, "Tomorrow. 7:00 am. Be at this address and don't be late. Also, be prepared to work. Understood?"

"Yes sir!" Patrick beamed. "7:00 am, sir. No problem. Thank you, sir," he added before exiting. Elated.

Takashi just nodded and packed up his clipboard and notepaper.

The next morning he arrived at what would eventually become the Danbury house, then a vacant lot, or as Takashi remarked, "A space to be shaped and molded." They worked through the summer, edging ever closer to completion, and as they worked, side by side, the master and the apprentice, Patrick grew to appreciate the eye for detail and proportion that Takashi possessed. He was as skilled an architect as he was a builder and he refused to rush any element of the construction. Patrick found himself absorbed in the work: the labor he had learned through Tsujiuchi-san's precise instruction produced tangible results. It nearly became an obsession, as Patrick would often agree to work on the property through his weekends. The feelings of gratification that he experienced rivaled anything he had ever felt before.

Melissa had frequented the construction site, dropping by to see him as often as she could, and they would spend the afternoons together, during the hottest part of the day, when work was impossible. She took a particular interest in the Japanese Garden that Tsujiuchi-san was planning and even lent some time towards its completion. It was original, inventive and beautiful. And as the summer closed and the house stood extremely close to completion, Melissa had come over one last time to share lunch in the garden. They lay on the grass talking and laughing like they had always done, except something was different that day, something was making Patrick feel happier than he'd ever felt before and he didn't quite understand why. Then Patrick had looked over at Melissa and seeing her on the edge of that stone bench eating her sandwich, he knew something about himself that he needed to express. Rolling over on the grass calling to her, he braced himself against his butterflies.

"Melissa?" His voice shook. "I want to tell you something, something I just realized but I don't want you to freak out, OK?" He felt like a child; he knew what he wanted to say but he was fumbling around with the words.

39

She edged forward on the bench, acknowledging the tension in his voice with her own look of concern.

"I'd like to… I feel…" This was impossible.

Looking up into her eyes he calmed himself, "I was wondering if it would be alright… well, if it would be alright if I kissed you?"

She flew off the bench, hugging him repeatedly as they rolled part way across the lawn. They kissed, long and soft in the green sea of the garden. She pulled her face away from his own and said, "I think that would be OK." She smiled again and then once more they lost themselves in each other's arms.

Patrick shook off the memory and noticed that he'd made his way over to the garden, which had been neglected over the years. Tsujiuchi-san had left at summer's end and sold the home to a young family moving into the neighborhood, the Danburys. Patrick had kept tabs on the place through the passage of time and when his chance finally came he was frustrated that he did not have the money to make the purchase. Fortunately those in the Phoenix housing market were not looking for something unique; size was all that mattered. It was this trend that allowed him, finally, to make a move on the home. No one could appreciate the thought and the vision that had been poured into the dwelling. He had worked himself into the very fabric of the structure and found afterwards that he could not disengage himself totally from it, as he found he could not totally separate himself from Melissa. He glanced at his watch, 10:20 am. Still plenty of time to get his banking done and make the luncheon with Mel. He walked back over the lawn and climbed into his car, sparing one more glance towards the house before he drove off in the direction of the bank. He felt as if he'd been asleep for the last ten years and then suddenly awakened into a world where all of his dreams were within his grasp.

Chapter 5

Simon and Harry

The black duct tape pulled painfully at his cheeks as it was ripped off. Harry, the fat security guard, coughed uncomfortably.

"I swear no funny stuff. But I have got to go to the toilet." Harry looked into the big black man's eyes desperately. His breakfast had settled nicely on top of his dinner and something was about to give. Harry could see that it was 11:13 am. His routine had been disrupted: on a regular day, he'd be in and out of the crapper before 11:05, and the pressure that had been building since 10:00 was threatening to detonate.

The thief nodded, replaced the tape over Harry's face, and returned to his position with Simon by the teller stations. "Well, seeing what all his wiggling and shuffling was about was a good idea. He's gotta go to the can. And from the look in his eyes, I'd have to say he means it."

Simon sighed, then glanced over at Harry; he had a slick sheen to him and yet the bank's temperature was perfectly hospitable.

"Alright, I'll take him. Here, give me his hood. Keep a close eye on the rest of them," said Simon before slipping quietly through the prone bodies of the other hostages towards Harry.

"Alright, big fella. I'm gonna help you stand up; together we are going to walk into the staff lounge; once we get into the washroom I'll take your wrist guards off and you can do your business. The entire time I will have my gun on you; hopefully this won't cause stage fright because quite frankly you're not going to get another shot at this." Simon thought he saw in Harry's face a passing look of rebellion, a brilliant flash of anger, but then it was gone.

Simon leaned in closer to his face, "Nod if you understand."

Harry took exception to being called a "big fella"; this young punk was really starting to get under his collar. He felt for an instant like he could, if the moment presented itself, take this guy out, but a new wave of cramps coming from his bowels quickly brought him back to more pressing matters.

Harry nodded, swallowing his pride.

Once up and on their feet, they walked into the lounge and straight into the washroom. Simon reached down and cut away the hard plastic of the tie and stood in the doorway of the stall as Harry quickly unbuckled his belt and slid his pants and boxers around his knees, finally releasing the tension that had been building inside of him. Simon could not repress his disgust for not only the sounds of Harry's movement but also the looks and facial contortions that he displayed. They almost made the smell tolerable, but not quite, and Simon was forced to cover his nose with another bandana he had stashed away in his pocket. Thank God.

Harry was more relieved than embarrassed. Although the one time he did look up and see the face looking back at him he felt a hot piercing flash of rage. He looked down ever so briefly at the top of his left calf: there just below his crumpled pants was the small Beretta he kept in an ankle holster. The fucker who'd taken him and Bill out had done a decent job patting him down, but for once his bulk had paid off; it was a fluke that the weapon remained unchecked. Of course the broken strap he'd been meaning to replace on the holster made the gun ride up his leg out of position just behind his knee. Anyway, he felt a whole lot better knowing he still had some heat. Quickly he looked away so as to not arouse suspicion. Harry had considered drawing it but his chaperone had his gun at the ready and he could envision the weapon getting tangled in his boxers or his belt on the way up into firing position. No. Now was not the time.

Harry finished up and once again stood fully clothed, although it was a bit of a chore for him to regain his pants. Simon instructed Harry to wash and wipe his hands before Simon slipped another plastic tie around Harry's fat, sweaty wrists. As they exited the bathroom, Simon surmised that Harry was weighing in around 260, maybe more. He'd had an aunt who'd topped the scales at 300 pounds but Harry didn't look that big, not yet anyway. He seated Harry leaning up against the far side wall of the bank next to an air ventilation grill in order to keep a closer eye on the security guard. It felt cooler over by the wall, and Simon hoped it would help regulate Harry's temperature; no need stressing his heart any more than it was. Simon placed a generous portion of duct tape over Harry's mouth and then pulled the cloth hood over Harry's head, whispering, "You could have a real future in sanitation if this security guard thing doesn't work out." Harry sat motionless. Job done, Simon made a point on his way back over to his position with Carl to stop and see how Patrick was making out. He knelt down beside Patrick and lifted his hood to his forehead.

"You good?" Simon inquired, glancing down to his left where the woman who had been hyperventilating lay quietly breathing.

Patrick

Patrick nodded his head silently. He probably would have said "thanks for asking" had his mouth not been taped. Patrick knew that some time had gone by since they took the bank and he wished that they would leave soon, very soon. The longer they stayed the worse their chances were, especially if the police ended up arriving, as eventually they must. Anything he could do to expedite their departure, he would do.

Grier

In the vault of the bank, Pete, Alan and Kayla had dispensed with their disguises. The clothes of their alter egos lay on the floor beside the briefcase which housed the unarmed bomb. The molded latex of their perfect masks also lay in amongst the scattered clothing. It was an odd sight, scabs of faces peering with eyeless vision around the vault, as if the bodies of those faces had disintegrated and left only this. Grier remained fully disguised. He too would remove his mask but only at the end, given the presence of the police or otherwise.

Under their clothing each of them wore a tight black Lycra suit that extended from the neck and upper arms to the ankles. In the fabric of each suit were numerous pockets and flaps which they now worked together packing with stacks of cash. They would all leave the bank empty-handed; the money itself they would wear like a second skin under the new clothes that Kayla had brought into the bank in her two-wheeled suitcase. In the construction of each suit, anywhere from seventy-two to eighty-six pockets had been sewn, into which a single, double or triple stack of bills could be stored depending on the location of the pocket. Thanks to the obese nature of the average American, that meant more hard cold cash for the party. Given that a single stack of hundred dollar bills consisted of a hundred notes or ten thousand dollars and that there were eighty-six such pockets, each person would be carrying, including the double pockets, approximately one point four million dollars. Between the six of them, they would leave the bank with well over eight million. Quite a payday. Even before the real money: the bank notes. As a federal reserve bank, the National Bank's vault also contained bank notes worth an estimated eighty million dollars. Yes, yes. The bank notes were the real prize, and each suit had a compartment in the middle back for their safe storage and transportation. Each suit would be worth close to fifteen million. Eat your heart out, Givenchy. The kicker was the fact that their sponsors, Grier's bosses, had agreed to a measly thirty percent of their take. They wanted to destroy the insurance company that fronted the bank; they'd laughed at the scant millions Grier and his team would liberate. Their profits would be much, much higher.

"It feels a lot lighter than those weights we trained with," said Pete as he jumped up and down a little on his toes, testing his range of motion in his knees as well as his elbows.

"You're looking good, Pete; go on out and take Carl's position while I finish loading up Kayla and Alan," Grier stated as he moved towards Alan and began to load up his rear pockets, those that weren't accessible to the wearer.

"Yes, guy! It's time for the bomb talk; this is my favorite part," Pete revealed as he thumbed the final few buttons on his shirt and slapped Alan on the back on his way to the front of the bank.

Alan and Grier exchanged a glance as they watched him depart. "He'll be fine, Grier. He's just wearing his rush a little closer to the surface than you or I," Alan stated, in an effort to relieve the tension he'd seen in Grier's features.

"Yes, I'm sure he'll be fine." Grier's voice betrayed his doubt, but it was out of his hands. It was a small role that Pete was to play, but he'd screwed it up enough times in practice to give reason for Grier to pause.

"We're ahead of schedule; let's see if we can keep it that way. Alan, can you take out the 'spare parts' when you're done?" Grier said, snapping once more into his role as master and commander.

Alan spared a look at the suitcase and sighed. "Shit, this is definitely not my favorite part."

Simon

Carl and Simon could hear Pete's footfalls coming down the hallway that led to the vault. The sound preceded his appearance, and they readied themselves, especially Simon, for the information

45

that could potentially cue the hostages into a frenzy of hysteria. This would be a difficult and tense time. Simon would have to be at the height of his observational skills, watching the reaction of each person as the news of the explosive device reached their ears. When Pete entered the main banking room, he began his dialogue.

"Clay is fucking everything up back there!" shouted Pete as he approached the customer counter.

"What are you talking about?" Carl said, agitated.

"I'm telling you, he's changing the fucking plan; the bomb is hot and cooking. I mean he's turned the goddamn thing on already. He said it would help speed us up." Pete's voice was loud and clear. There could be no mistaking his words. A few of the bodies on the floor moved uncomfortably. There was a bomb in the bank and it was alive, ticking towards a destructive detonation.

Carl, his voice at the peak of his aggressive tones, chimed in, "Are you serious? What the hell are we going to doing about it, Will?" There was a brief tense pause. "Forget it, I'm heading back there. Any idea how much time before we all get blown to shit?"

"He gave it a twenty-minute heart beat, but he said he could change it without too much problem," Pete stressed.

"If you can't get results back there, just give a holler. We may have to put Clay in his place, if you know what I mean. An opportunity like this? Jesus, we've been outta commission for twelve months; he ain't gonna blow it for me, for us." Simon's voice bridged the agitation of Carl and the frustration of Pete. He brought resolution to the conversation and gave the hostages the knowledge that he and he alone was prepared to act in light of this new information. If they cooperated with him, they cooperated with life, or at least a chance at survival.

"I'll be back." And then Carl was off through the back hallway towards the vault. He removed his clothing as he walked, revealing the tight black suit that they all wore underneath their disguises.

Simon stood beside a smiling Pete, who placed the teller jacket on over his outer clothes and took up Carl's station. Looking around the room, Simon was impressed by the amount of composure that remained. Even the woman who had previously succumbed to her emotions was successfully suppressing her hysteria. Simon noted that Patrick was in close proximity to her, his presence apparently enough to contain her panic. Once again, he was assisting them. In the other direction, Simon noted that Harry sat awkwardly against the wall, moving his head from side to side, apparently stretching his neck. Simon was thankful that he had dealt with his problem before this information was revealed. The older man that he had struck earlier as well as one of the tellers made quiet whimpering noises under their hoods and through their taped mouths, but the noise level was low and it seemed to grow quieter and quieter as Simon scanned the rest of the hostages.

Harry

Harry could feel the sweat of his palms, despite the air conditioning in the bank. When he'd been seated he noticed that six inches to his right was the air ventilation grill. He'd managed to shimmy himself sideways over to it over the last few minutes, a little at a time. The metal wasn't very sharp but he'd set himself to work on it. He stretched his fingers down to feel the plastic tie where he was rubbing it against the air vent that was now directly behind him, blocked by his bulky form. He figured he was close to a quarter of the way through the plastic, still not enough to pull apart with his limited strength. The revelation concerning the bomb made him wish he were back in the bathroom fumbling for his Beretta and a chance at some payback. The sheen from his sweating head was making the hood slightly transparent; he could make out forms now and with a little more sweating, something he'd never been able to control, he would be able to make out individuals. Harry hoped he'd still have a chance to exact some justice. He knew he'd been destined for something heroic all his life; how could this not be it?

Chapter 6

Harry

The water in the shower didn't get as cold as Harry expected it to. Or needed it to, in order to beat the heat of an Arizona heat wave. Even the ground water was having a difficult time staying cool. After rinsing the soap from his back, he checked to make certain the hot water tap was off completely. Then he stuck his head under the cold stream still flowing from the faucet. It splashed off the short bristles of his hair, then ran over his belly and down his legs causing a general stir under his arms, over the top of his head, and in that space between his thighs. Those areas that were usually the first to begin sweating. The rest of his body hardly noticed at all.

The idea of a cold shower was hardly novel, but this particular technique had come to him from his older brother, John-David, who had run off to Canada to avoid the draft for Vietnam, and was still working there in a mine. Let the water get progressively colder, until you simply can't stand it any more. Apparently it helped the miners adjust to outside temperatures after a shift underground. JD had obviously forgotten that Arizona water never got that cold. Especially when it had to run up five floors of sun-baked piping. Still, it usually went a long way in deferring that moment when his body would begin to sweat, gluing up his clothes like wet newspaper.

Harry turned off the tap and stepped out onto the linoleum. On a hot day like this he'd let himself drip dry. He grabbed a towel to keep himself covered, pinching both ends of it in one hand to keep it around his waist, then stepped into the kitchen.

Over the counter he had a clear view of the living room, and the television set. It was still on. Images from an MTV video were flashing across the screen. He had obviously forgotten to turn it off last night, an easy oversight, as the sound had been muted. How kids could stand to listen to such crap was beyond him. And the videos, flashing from picture to picture so quickly you hardly had the chance to enjoy the women in them. It seemed pointless. Had there been anything else on late last night he wouldn't have bothered.

He strolled over past the sofa and checked the coffee table for the remote. It wasn't there. He must have been tired indeed, not to have put it back. He checked the other side of the couch, almost tripping over several unseen, empty beer bottles. He bent to pick them up, causing the towel to pop out from between his fingers. He let it dangle loosely in front of him as he stood, grunting from the effort.

On the way to his bedroom he deposited the bottles inside a case beside the refrigerator. There were several other empties on the counter that received like treatment. Harry swore. All this activity was causing him to sweat. And he had yet to don his uniform. He quickly made his way into the bedroom. Patsy – his eleven-year-old air conditioner, was moaning loudly in the window. On the verge of a nervous breakdown, it was all she could do to keep the room cool. Eleven years wasn't too much mileage in your average household, but for Harry, in Arizona, those were dog years for old Patsy.

Throwing his towel over the door, Harry made his way to the closet and pulled out one set of clothing. He had five uniforms – one for each day of the week. All save the ties. Only two of those, though he was now down to one, thanks to a spaghetti stain that proved too obstinate to be picked off with a fingernail. One tie was all he needed, however. And it was time to get going.

Harry felt it a real luxury not to have to think about what to wear. Deodorant first. A good thick layer. None of that anti-perspirant crap. Unnatural. Couldn't be good for you. Boxers. Loose. Comfortable. Then his socks. Black. Non-elastic. Next his undershirt. Sleeveless, like his father's. Then his white shirt. Double X-L, but still undersized, the buttons turning slightly sideways and the spaces in between stretching open when his stomach was too full. A small holster on his left calf; he was, after all, a right-handed shot. Pants next, pulled on while sitting on the bed. Belted. No suspenders. Then the tie. Clip-on. He would clip it in place just before he strolled into the bank. Not before. It was too damn hot. The jacket would go on at the same time. Not in the apartment. Even with Patsy set at full bore.

Harry slid his shoes on. They were pre-tied as well. This wasn't as much a time-saver as a simple necessity. He could no longer get at the laces to do them up. Not without a battle. He had to save his energy for more important things.

Crossing the room, he checked himself in the mirror on his dresser.

The clothes made the man. That was certain. And Harry looked sharp.

Picking up a comb, he ran it through his hair, which didn't respond at all. It didn't matter. His hair was too short to need any arranging.

He checked his eyes for burst vessels and his teeth for bits of food. Then he donned his belt. On one side his tonfa. On the other his piece. He took it out of the holster. It was a Magnum .44 Calibre. Larger than the police-issue, glock 20s. This was a man's weapon. The most powerful handgun in the world. Who'd want to argue with old Clint Eastwood on that one; no sir, from one Harry to another. He spun it around a finger and slid it back into place in his belt holster. Reaching forward, fumbling slightly with the latch on the chest of drawers, he drew out a smaller handgun, a Beretta which he attempted to place in the calf holster he'd put on before

50

his pants. It took Harry a couple of concerted efforts, but finally, feeling a sweat just starting to break on his forehead from the strain, the weapon found its home and Harry readjusted his pant leg to properly conceal it. His lower holster strap had broken two months earlier, he'd been meaning to get it fixed, the damned thing rode up his leg now and Harry had to reposition it every time he had a break or went to the can. But he'd grown fond of the idea of having a back-up. All the lethal weapons in the world wouldn't mean a thing if you didn't have the will to use them. He was sure that he did though. Damned sure.

Yes. Nothing like a man in uniform. He placed his uniform hat on his head, then drew the magnum out again, pointing it at his reflection, and practicing several expressions of intimidation he'd rehearsed, but never used. The hat came off the moment his head started to get too hot. And he placed his magnum back in its drawer; this one was his own, for personal home protection, his work gun he'd receive when he checked in for the day. Same gun, just those damned regulations stopping him from walking around town with it in his belt. Sliding the drawer closed, his magnum now safely inside, Harry noticed something was missing from the mirror above the dresser. Several pictures were wedged into the crease between the glass and the plastic frame. One of him and the boys on a hunting trip to Colorado, a rare out-of-state vacation for which he no longer had the time or energy. Phil had just nailed a buck. Everyone was smiling. Half-pissed. A picture of Max, his younger brother, about a year before he drowned in a neighbor's pool. One of his family taken at about the same time. Maybe a year before his parents split. Three brothers. His father towering over them all. His mother – tiny. Shadowed by her husband. They were all big men, the Trumans. Big and handsome. Another picture of his ex-wife in their bungalow with Jake, the dog. He kept the picture for Jake. Not Arlene. Good riddance to her. Had there been some way to cut her out...

It was Steven-Michael that was missing. His son.

Harry took a half step back from the dresser and turned his head sideways so that he could see the floor at his feet. It wasn't there. He grunted and bent to a knee to check under the bed.

And found the remote.

He must have carried it to bed and dropped it on the floor. If he hadn't looked here, it may have stayed out of sight for a week or more. What a blessing the photo had gone missing. Getting up to change channels was such a pain in the ass. How they had endured it as children was beyond him. Of course, there were far fewer shows to choose from back then. You had to watch whatever crap was on. Not like nowadays. Ninety-six channels. Whatever you like.

He stood, pushing off his knee. Quite a workout for the morning. It was making him very hungry. Not unusual when he drank as much as he had the night before. As he righted himself, he felt a little buzzing between his eardrums. He frowned and it went away. He'd certainly suffered worse. Much worse. Doctor Harterre would be pleased. Harry was following his advice and drinking much less. The diabetes and cirrhosis he'd been warned of weren't going to claim him, as they had his father. The changes were having an effect; he'd lost nearly 9 pounds in the last five months. In his mind, sure and steady progress.

He was on his way to the living room when he realized he'd forgotten about his son. Turning at the door, he spied the photo. It was sitting on top of the refuse in the wastepaper basket. The near edge of it was almost in reach. With one hand near the foot of the mirror for support, he bent and picked up the basket, then rescued the picture from inside. It was crumpled. Bent along lines that had been folded and unfolded from several such incidents. Harry straightened out the picture once again, then jammed it into place beneath Arlene and Jake the dog.

No one could push his buttons like his son. Not even his ex. He didn't understand Steven. The kid just didn't listen. And Harry knew he had been far more patient with the boy than his own father had been with him. And far more gentle. He couldn't remember throwing out the picture last night, but something about the boy must have set him off.

Of course, he was hardly a boy now. Almost twenty-two. Or was it twenty-three? No. Twenty-two. 1983. Steven was in the military now. A good thing. They'd teach him some discipline. And harden him up. That was what the boy needed. He was too soft. Harry's father had been a real disciplinarian. It had worked for his children. But kids these days had no respect. Too much television and not enough thinking. Not enough time spent in the real world. Shaking his head, Harry made his way towards the door, hat in hand, jacket over his arm. The TV was still on. He'd forgotten the remote in the bedroom. He'd have to shut it off after work. More head-shaking followed.

The same videos day after day. Didn't people have better ways to spend their time? It certainly wasn't like the old days. Everything on TV back then was good. Quality. And things were built to last. Not like today's throwaway world. A rumbling in his belly sent him quickly to the elevators. It was nearly time to eat, and Denny's was still a good 10-minute drive away.

It had been a long time since Harry had been forced to cook for himself. It was a painful inconvenience. Since Arlene left he ate almost all his meals out. It was better that way, as his lifestyle hardly afforded the time to slave over the stove. Arlene hadn't been much of a cook anyways, so his life hardly skipped a beat when she left. Not like his old man. He'd been far too dependent on his wife. Of course, she'd been equally dependent upon him. That's the way things had worked. There were roles to play. It made things easier. Better. Dinner ready the moment Dad hit the driveway. Paychecks every two weeks. Sunday dinners with the TV off. As steady as the evening news. And great meals too. Nothing like home cooking.

Harry stepped through the steel security door into the underground garage. The heat wave was less noticeable here, but he could still feel a sheen start to form on his brow. Harry waddled quickly over to his car, a late 70s caddy. V8. A true luxury machine. He opened a door that was a good three and a half feet long. Lots of steel. Heavy, like all good things.

When he started it up he set the air conditioner at maximum cool and then slid a Patsy Cline cassette into the vintage 8-track player.

Now this was music. Something a man could appreciate.

Harry backed the car out of the underground lot and got ready to take his place among those suburbanites en route to the city centre. The commute didn't bother him. It was short now that he was living in the west end. Not like the old days in the bungalow with Arlene. Like most on the highway he had suffered through years of commuting an hour to work each day. Now it was only that long if he stopped and ate in the restaurant. Work was only twenty minutes from his apartment.

Arlene had got the house, which was fair. She got the mortgage along with it. He preferred the flat. More personal space. Less crap to trip over. A place for everything and everything in its place. Not like Arlene and her plastic and porcelain knick-knacks all over the house, and her constant whining whenever he didn't put things away.

At least he hadn't been forced to suffer the indignity of alimony payments. Arlene had always been independent. Socially. Financially. He needed someone who would respect his space – who could take care of themselves. He had no desire to be saddled with someone like his mother. A clingy woman who didn't earn one red cent for her family. The patience his father must have had...

It was hot outside, too damned hot for this time of year. Harry stepped on the gas to get the car moving faster towards breakfast. The most important meal of the day. He passed the sign for the interstate and smiled. He was getting closer, the same familiar route. He hadn't been in the apartment long. Perhaps three years. But this stretch of road was one he had also traveled as a kid. One night in particular stood out in memory. It was after Max had died. With his mother gone, and his father having drunk more than usual, there was no one to stop him and John-David from stealing the old man's car and going for a cruise. It was a Caddy, not unlike the one he was driving now. But back then, underage, unlicensed, terrified and overjoyed, their ride to freedom sparked a string of wild nights, and wild summers, that made one wonder about the passage of time, and the terrible unfairness of it. The best times of his life. No question. If only Max had stayed alive. And his parents hadn't left the booze out. They were all so curious as kids. So ready to try dangerous things. He shook his head and turned off the music. His jaw grew tight. And then there was Stevie. He'd started into the same nonsense when he came of age. He had no idea what was at stake. He'd never lost a brother. If only he and Arlene had had the money to send him to boarding school. Even with two salaries, and Arlene's careful eye, there simply wasn't enough to go around. They should have saved better. Now the military would have to do the rest. Teach the boy some discipline. That's what the kid needed. A firm hand.

Harry slowed the car, signaled, and turned into the drive thru at Denny's on 51st Avenue. It was absolutely too stinking hot to be getting out of his car. To leave the air conditioning, even for a moment, at today's temperature would be a disaster. And he'd moved around enough already this morning, considering he wasn't yet at work. The National Bank. He'd be on his feet all day. Assuring the customers and employees that they were safe. Their money too.

He decided on the eggs. Pancakes made him feel dopey about a half-hour later.

He placed his order. A short time later he paid and pulled the car into a parking space. Opening the bag of food, he unwrapped an egg sandwich and spread the wax paper out over the seat beside him. Coffee went into the holder. Ketchup on the hash browns. The beans he never ate. The bacon he ought not to. Leaning sideways over the makeshift placemat, facing out the passenger window, he gulped the food down in large bites, spilling occasionally on the paper, but never on his clothes. This was never something he could have done with Arlene. Eat in such a manner.

And of course, she would have been sitting where his food was. But those were the advantages of bachelorhood. He could do what he pleased.

Harry saved himself a strip of bacon. He always finished with this. It crunched sublimely between his teeth. No matter how insistent he was that she cook it longer, Arlene was never quite able to get it as crispy as he liked it. "Cook it yourself, if you don't like the way I do it," she'd reply. He'd been sorely tempted a few times. But there wasn't room in the kitchen for two. That was Arlene's territory. Where she'd do the morning dishes and enjoy her coffee after he left for the bank. She'd follow him out the door, an hour later, walking to the store where she still worked as a manager. Perhaps he ought to drop by and see how she was doing. He hadn't spoken to her for about a week. He should have called her last night. Good for a laugh, at least. Arlene still had a knack for hitting his funny bone. A new joke every minute. And none of that well-rehearsed punch line crap. Real wit. Spontaneous and fun. It had left a real gap in his social life, when they'd split. Changed his life dramatically. He'd lost his best friend. And his home. That place his son returned to when college was out. He guessed it would hold true of the boy's military career as well. He'd have to work harder to stay in touch. Make certain that Steven felt welcome in the apartment. In three years he'd only been over a handful of times, mostly because Harry just wasn't ready to entertain. It was one of the disadvantages of bachelorhood. There was no one there to remind you that the place was sliding.

Harry took a gulp of coffee and checked his watch. It was time to finish the drive, 8:57 am. If he left now, he'd be a good ten minutes early for work. Enough time to cool off in the air-conditioned foyer before the doors were open for the clients. Harry was on mornings this week, 9:30 to 5:30; bank hours were so agreeable. He'd take his usual place by the door, greeting most of them by name as they entered. Those who didn't just use the machines down on the corner. It was important – to make everyone feel welcome. And appreciated. Like a big, happy family.

Exiting the lot, Harry turned "The Greatest Hits of Patsy Cline" back on. He'd almost forgotten about it. Thinking of his family could distract him like that. And he didn't want to be late. In 21 years – only eight to go before retirement – he'd only been late once. That was the morning Stevie was born. No other times. Despite hangovers; morning feuds with Arlene, nagging at him endlessly – Jesus, he didn't miss that; car problems; inconveniences of every kind. No. In 21 years Harry S. Truman, "Big Hank" – named for the Prez who dropped the big ones, a name chosen by his mother, God rest her soul – had just once, been late for work.

Chapter 7

Grier

In all their tests, their relentless tampering with the security system and tripping of the bank's alarm system, whether it was midday or midnight, Kronos Security had never once failed to arrive at the bank in less than fifteen minutes. In fact, in the beginning, they had arrived in less than ten. However, with the constant string of false alarms that the bank had suffered of late, their response time had dwindled, and officers who would rush the bank, at the ready, now strolled into the lobby of the bank shaking their heads and shrugging their shoulders. The last time Grier had set off the alarm, on Sunday no less, only two officers from the three squad cars that arrived even exited their vehicles, choosing instead to remain behind in their air-conditioned environments, regulations be damned. Talk on the street was that the bank was shopping around for another security company, a hefty contract that would have at least half a dozen such businesses salivating over the prospective contract. It was 11:21 am, just past the twenty-second minute. In another five, everyone would be exiting. It seemed that Kronos remained in the dark. The smoke and fire must have engaged the surveillance team at Kronos completely when they entered the bank. The plan, his baby, the one thing he had worked on for the last year, poured his soul into until it spilt off the planning table onto the open floor of the warehouse they had trained in, was nearing completion. Everyone, except for Simon, had their suits fully packed with cash and bank notes, and Grier could not resist a grin as he stared into the now nearly barren vault. Behind him, Carl and Alan loaded up the last pockets of Kayla's suit. On the ground, positioned partially in and partially out of the entrance to the vault, the bomb. Placed carefully at the sides and on top of the beautiful explosive device were recently thawed pieces of human flesh and bone, ready to be shattered and scattered through the wreckage that the blast would create. The severed hands looked unreal, like discards from a department store window display, expressionless mannequin hands touting the latest fashions lying in amongst the latex of the masks. Grier had a brief flashback to the bodies that used to be attached to those fingers, rough and scarred, broken and bloodied. The jawbones were unsettling. But they were needed, for complete success, the proof – such undeniable proof that only dental records and DNA samples could provide – was an absolute must, especially given the amount of money they were about to walk out of the bank with. Of course, there would be an unsettling lack of physical remains that could not truly be attributed to the intensity of the blast; however, the video would flawlessly match up with the faces that each of the customers would identify. Yes, who could deny the eyewitnesses, the video and the genetic proof that they would leave behind? Really, it had all gone incredibly smoothly; they could not have anticipated a better set of circumstances. Every detailed plan, every single blueprint, thought, debate and after-thought had been absolutely correct, absolutely genius. How could he not take credit for this masterpiece? He was responsible. They were all about to be rich – well, some of them were going to be rich and others were going to be richer. As for Simon, Grier wouldn't feel guilty. It's a dangerous business. If anyone understood the risks involved, it was Simon. Goodbyes and happy endings were for the delusional. Of course, there was still so much more that they had planned for –

the security force, the police, even the FBI if it came down to that. All of this had been predicted and they still had viable options for escape. No, not only escape but escape with all the money. No one would come looking for them. There would be no unexpected knock at the door several months down the road. No America's Most Wanted special. They'd all be free. He'd done that.

"Looks like we're in and out clean on this one. I'm heading up to the front to take Simon's spot. I'll send him back. Carl, you know what to do," Grier stated, looking at Kayla's ass when he turned. It was a hard sight to resist and he was never one to avert an eye, especially from such a luscious treat. There was a time in the beginning when he thought he would be bedding Kayla on a regular basis by now, but she proved to have a much more developed courting process than the girls he was used to. If a two-hundred dollar dinner and a sparkly trinket of some sort didn't get him laid, well, there were plenty of women for whom it would. Course there were those evenings when time was short and his need was great. Money those nights went straight to the purpose; in his eyes though, it was always prostitution in one form or another.

"I'll do what needs to be done, but yours is the hand that'll finish the job," said Carl as he continued to stuff the slots in the middle back of Kayla's suit with stacks of cold hard American cash.

"*Genius*," thought Grier as he walked out of the vault towards the front, "*absolutely genius.*"

Harry

The plastic for some reason still felt incredibly strong. He tried to pull at it again, straining with whatever knotted muscles remained beneath his thick fatty bulk, and still it held. He would have to continue rubbing it against the air ventilation grate before he would be freed. Inwardly, Harry told himself that had it not been under these circumstances, he would have been able to pull apart the plastic minutes ago. He was certain that he could probably pull it apart now but the risk was just too great. If he strained any harder he'd have a difficult time controlling his arms and hands as they pulled free from behind his back and the last thing he wanted to do now was draw any attention to himself. His gun would do that as soon as he liberated it from its holster. The hood was quite damp and he could make out two figures standing by the teller stations. Other than that, there were several bodies lying on the floor in the space between him and the robbers, thieves, terrorists, whatever they were called these days. He was reminded of Arlene's nagging habit of correcting him when he used ancient terms that had long ago died away. He'd called someone at work a square once and it was three days of laughing and teasing before he'd finally blurted something else out that he couldn't (thankfully) remember right now. Well, whatever it was, she'd joked and laughed at him about that for a while. What a bitch. Well, he'd show her, she'd see the kind of man he was once he busted through these plastic handcuffs. He'd show them all. She'd come running back. But he'd make her wait in line to see him.

Patrick

Patrick had heard plenty of rehearsed dialogue in his day, as the study of English was so closely tied to the performing arts. But he hadn't known or realized it was happening here until the last voice had come into play, the words about the bomb and the growing hostilities in the back. Now there was a voice for which the term over-acting could aptly apply. He doubted, given the dire circumstances, that anyone else would or could have picked up on the odd clarity and projection which the man had tried to convey, the cadence and the pacing which he nearly fumbled with, twice. No indeed, something was afoot and although he was curious, he was more interested in getting out of the bank alive. What a story he would have to tell Melissa this afternoon.

The woman next to him had been easier to calm this time. He was glad to be of some service; she reminded him a little of his mother, fair haired and fragile, an emotional woman. Inwardly, he wondered if there really was a bomb in the bank set to go off. According to the banter there was probably another ten minutes. He'd never really considered his own mortality before, apart from his desire to have children at some point. But today, when his life seemed to be on the cusp of something larger, it was like everything that had transpired in his world so far had done so for this one day; he felt a splinter of fear pierce his heart. A pang of doubt, a shadow of regret, that he might never see the realization of his dreams.

Simon

Pete shifted uneasily in his position at the teller's station, so much so that it looked to Simon as though he might bolt back into the vault or out the front doors of the bank at any moment. Simon told him to relax his shoulders and try to concentrate on the computer screen. He would comply for a few moments but then his tension and angst would take him back into his previous pose, anxious and volatile. Simon knew that Grier would be coming up to the front to relieve him at any moment and the thought, in addition to relieving him, made him shudder. Pete and Grier, as useful and intelligent as they might be, would rely on force more than persuasion should anything go amiss in his absence. If Kayla, Carl and Alan were as efficient as they had been during the many rehearsals, he'd only be absent three to four minutes. Hopefully those would be the most uneventful moments of this job.

At the front doors of the bank more customers arrived. There was an unending intermittent stream of people, men and women, most in business attire, seeking to get their banking done before the lunchtime rush. Many pulled on the second set of doors before noticing the sign hanging there. A few lingered, pressing their faces up to the glass to get a better look at the activity or lack thereof in the bank. They all left, some quickly, some reluctantly, but all of them moved on eventually.

Simon, nodding to Pete in the direction of Harry, began to move over towards the big man propped up against the far wall.

He'd noticed some movement out of the corner of his eye. Harry had probably only shifted his position, but Simon wanted to be sure. As he stepped over the prone body of one of the bank tellers, a plain-looking woman in her late thirties, he glanced down to check his footfalls and noticed the edge of a dark, deep, yellowish bruise on her upper thigh. Even her dark nylons could not mask the battered skin beneath. There would be more bruises further up the leg Simon knew; however, her skirt had hiked up her leg just enough to show this one grisly badge of abuse. Definitely an impact bruise, the kind that could only be caused by repetitive blows. No chance a fall could do that sort of damage, but Simon felt certain that that was the story this woman would tell if anyone asked. It was then that Simon noticed four people enter the lobby of the bank. They were young. Dressed in the trendy clothes of the youthful. For a moment he thought they were teenagers, but as he took a closer look, seeing the shadow of unshaven facial hair and the weathered look on their faces, he figured that they were older, probably college aged. They pulled on the doors. They looked down at the sign, one by one it seemed; they couldn't believe that the bank was indeed closed. There were three guys and a girl. The girl, her face obscured by her thick copper hair, stuck close to one of the bigger fellas, probably her boyfriend; he looked anxious and stressed. He remained in the back and as Simon stepped back towards the teller station – he'd have time for Harry when this quartet exited – he noticed that the girl was pulling at the big guy's hand, back in the direction of the doors leading to the street. The other two took up looking through the glass of the doors, spoke briefly to each other; one of them, the older one – he didn't much look like he'd ever gone to college – laughed and patted his buddy on his back. They made no motion towards the exit. This was damned peculiar. Just then, a couple of suits entered the first set of doors; the occupants turned to them and exchanged words, in loud agitated tones. Something was happening here.

Simon, looking over at Pete, said under his breath, "This could be trouble. Stay alert."

Pete, who had already taken notice of the four people now residing in the bank lobby, reached smoothly into his pants and pulled out his Glock. He then securely fastened the silencer to the barrel end of the weapon.

Simon, knowing Pete's impulse, suppressed an instinctive reflex to tell Pete to put the weapon away. No, something here was not as it should be. Offering instead of a reprimand, "If we were really tellers, we'd probably be on the phone to the police."

This had the desired effect on Pete; he smiled briefly and although his gaze never faltered from the four, his tension was temporarily checked. "As long as they keep everyone else out, hell, they're doin' us a favor," said Pete, his voice low and focused.

It was true. Another man had opened the outer doors to the bank and shared an exchange with the squatters before leaving in the direction of the bank machines on the corner. The fact that they seemed to be content inside the small air-conditioned lobby made little or no sense. Simon's head rang with warnings; the bells and whistles of his instincts were reaching new octaves of alarm. It could just be escape from the sweltering heat, he heard his mind say in an attempt to quell the feeling in the pit of his stomach that he was standing at the edge of some vast abyss. What were they doing, those two in the front? It looked like they were trying to do something to the lock of the second set of double doors. The two at the back started to bang around in the lobby, making all sorts of incoherent noise and sounds. They were trying to cover some other noise, they had to be. Unless they were strung out on drugs, yet another possibility. The hostages, hearing the commotion and perhaps sensing the proximity of some people that might be in a position to save them, began to fidget and shudder. The woman with Patrick began to weep. Others too, sensing the solidity of the tension, the electricity in the air, could not help but stir into motion and sound. Fortunately the sounds coming from the four in the lobby were drowning them out. No, no. This was not good. This was not good at all. If Simon had to guess, if he had to predict the next move, he'd have to say that somehow, those four... Who the hell were they?... Those four were trying to break into the bank.

From the angle of the teller stations, Simon could occasionally see, when the movement of the four allowed it and as the sunlight from the street streamed in through the windows, the solid steel tumbler of the lock that separated the calm interior of the bank from the chaos in the lobby. Pete's angle was not sufficient to allow him to see the lock, he could only see the twisted, worried, anxious faces of the kids spinning about wildly in the foyer. Then, for a moment, everything in the bank went still. The bodies on the floor, which were quivering, now seemed to go silent; the humming, shouting, yelling and singing coming from the lobby suddenly hit a pause; even the noise that Simon's blood made as it rushed by his ears somehow went still; and in that moment, in that impossible moment, when they stood on the edge of a great triumph, on the precipice of a miraculous accomplishment, in that moment, Simon saw and heard with unmistakable, undeniable clarity the steel tumbler of the lock, the light from outside illuminating it in perfect clarity, click, and fall away.

"Here they come," whispered Simon before the bank fell into chaos.

Chapter 8

THE JUNGLE HOUSE
23 SOUTH VENTURA DRIVE, PHOENIX, ARIZONA
FRIDAY, APRIL 29, 2005
7:06 AM

Tony

It was just after seven in the morning when Anthony Johannes Xavier sent his shoe somersaulting across the room. It tumbled awkwardly end over end like a drunken baton before slamming into the wall above his alarm clock and clunking down upon his desk. The alarm, set in concert with the previous day's exam schedule, continued to buzz, an angry horde of bees whose auditory assault would have raised the dead.

The clock had been saved for that very reason.

Swearing, Anthony rose from his bed and crossed the room, wading through several days' worth of clothes and tripping over his old Cougars helmet, a high school memento from his former days of football stardom. Moving the clock out of arm's reach had been his friend Clara's idea, a double insurance that Tony would in fact wake and stay woken for his last exam. Yesterday's blessing was today's curse. He'd forgotten to turn the damn thing off.

As he approached his desk, Conrad began thumping on the wall between their rooms, muttering something that a few inches of drywall rendered unintelligible. Sadly, the other residents of the Jungle House were gone, and so would be unable to appreciate the poetic justice that resonated from the wall with each thump of Conrad's fist.

For countless nights Conrad, the Radical One, and Screamin' Suzanne, his ignominious partner in shame, kept the house awake with a live radio play version of Behind the Green Door, an ensemble complete with squeaks, grunts and near endless thumpings throughout which Suzanne earned her namesake by screaming like a banshee. Thankfully, Screamin' Suzanne had left for the summer. Exams were difficult enough. Throw her and the bees into the mix, and you have the Jungle's best impression of a medieval dungeon. Terrible food, a ridiculous workload, insufferable sleeping conditions, and the threat of academic annihilation creeping inexorably closer like the executioner's axe.

Miraculously, this last crisis had been averted. And now exams were over, school was over, and the only impending doom for Tony was his indoctrination into the real world. With a Bachelor of Economics he was one step closer to his goal of becoming a CPA, certified public accountant. That was real-life enough. Unfortunately he was a giant leap closer to destitution. Student loans were going to hit him like a mortgage pretty soon. Ten more years of bargain brand foods and keeping a close eye on his empties. He had almost considered investing in the occasional lottery ticket. Almost.

Anthony lifted an old pizza box from the alarm clock and the sound of bees intensified. Conrad began to swear next door. Anthony let the clock buzz for a few more seconds, the beginnings of a smile at the corners of his mouth. With his housemates gone, he was left to savor this retribution alone, his only legitimate reward for being held at Arizona State until the last day of examinations.

It had always been a shared dream of the Jungle House that when their university lives ended, they would raise the roof with a party that would keep Hollywood script writers busy for millennia, but new careers, vacations or impatient girlfriends had beckoned Anthony's friends away. Only Conrad remained. So the year-end party had been a fizzle of good-byes, the house was still standing, and Anthony's last hurrah was a quiet night spent in a near empty pub, he and his few remaining friends too tired from a plethora of all-nighters to support any serious consumption. That was how life at State U had ended, not with a bang, but a whimper. Anthony let Conrad blaspheme a few more times, then silenced the hive with a push of his finger.

Awake for the day, Anthony decided to brave the kitchen for whatever breakfast food he could scrounge. Wrapping himself in a bathrobe, he hobbled down the stairs, his careful steps measured out by the clacking of his ankles and knees. His joints were always stiff in the morning, even in the warmth of early spring, though the night had been, once again, unusually hot. The heat wave continued to bake them all, slowly, methodically, like some giant Easy-Bake oven. The fans in his room and those in various other strategic locations, two in the kitchen, three in the family room and another in the upper floor bathroom, saved them from the worst of the heat. When he reached the stairs, he used the railing and the wall to take as much of his weight off his feet as his shoulders would comfortably allow, then took the steps one at a time, descending almost sideways to make the trip easier.

When he passed through the living room on his way towards the kitchen, he spied Clara asleep on the couch, her curly hair spilling over the edge of the sofa cushions like a mass of copper spires tumbled to ruin. He crept over as slowly as his body would allow and crouched down beside her head.

"I love you, Clara," he whispered in his best southern drawl, blowing gently in her ear.

Clara rolled over, covering her head with the cushion. "Piss off," she muttered pulling the light cotton sheet up over the whole arrangement of hair and pillow. The movement exposed her feet at the other end. Anthony quickly took advantage, tickling the first arch that emerged. Clara balled up like a fetus.

"Go away," she groaned.

"But ahh luvv yahhh," Anthony persisted.

Clara kicked him smartly in the thigh. "Don't joke."

A short time later Anthony returned to the couch with a bowl of stale cereal, the no-name equivalent of Fruit Loops. Clara had rolled over onto her back and was snoring softly. Anthony set his cereal on the floor, then turned and lifted Clara's legs from the couch. After sitting, he lowered them back down so that they stretched across his lap like a TV tray. He then took up his cereal and began to eat, hoping that if he filled his belly, it might forgive him for the fiasco with the bees, and let him crawl back into bed. He thought of snuggling up with Clara for a moment. No. Not worth the risk.

If she woke up in a mood she'd probably slap some colour into his face. He'd rather brave the bees again than tempt her humor. It was a terribly unfair match. He, ex-varsity football hopeful, sporting more muscle than a Clydesdale, and she, Anthropology major with a minor in women's studies, her body shaped well only from an intense paranoia about her ass becoming too big to fit into a size eight pair of jeans.

She beat him every time.

Of course, it was impossible for a man to get one up on a slaphappy woman if he was never going to hit back. And Tony never was. It made him the target of choice. When a barrage was imminent, and he sensed at least one on the menu for the day, Anthony simply steeled himself for the worst, and implored her not to hurt herself when she started dancing around, punching him with a fist so thoroughly misaligned that if she'd had any power whatsoever, she would have sprained a wrist. Anthony actually enjoyed the attention. He knew it to be the only sincere affection she directed towards anyone. At least to his knowledge.

In the four years that he'd known her, she'd never fallen in love, or even fallen into bed, with anyone. She was relationship intolerant. Intimate ones, at least. Though paradoxically, she was an excellent stand-in date when the occasion arose, and it had almost everyone in the house. It was a mystery to them all, and an assortment of girlfriends, why Clara was so willing to play this second string roll, never developing a genuine interest in anyone. It seemed she wanted neither the cow nor the milk, free or otherwise. Matt thought she was just waiting for a good time to come out of the closet, which bothered Anthony, not because she might have been a lesbian, but because if she was, she should have known well enough that he'd think no differently of her, and so should have given him the scoop sooner. Conrad had most of the house convinced that she'd been assaulted, maybe during orientation, or at high school, and just wasn't ready to be intimate with guys again. Anthony admitted that the theory had plausibility. He had always wanted to find out the answer without having to ask her for it. There were just certain questions that self-respecting men didn't ask. He'd simply work his way through her defensive barricades one layer at time until she trusted him with the truth, or he discovered it on his own. At the rate he was going it would take a century or two. It was unfortunate. She could tolerate *Star Wars*, didn't wear make-up, never dieted, knew the rules to football, and lacked those inferiority complexes that turned many intelligent women into doormats. Everything a man might want, save an interest in sex, which unfortunately was high on the priority list of every guy he'd ever known under the age of oh, a hundred and twenty.

Anthony watched her breathing while he chewed his cereal. The peaceful aesthetic of her movement was dashed by the occasional wrinkling of her face, followed after by a rattle in her throat and a snort. That was Clara, three quarters Marilyn Monroe, one quarter Olga Bonecrusher.

Anthony was halfway through his cereal when Clara rolled over, knocking the bowl from his hands with her shin, spilling the milk and soggy rings all over his face, his robe and the cushion beside him.

Anthony began to laugh. What was he expecting? Nothing good happened in The Jungle before 7:30. He should have stayed in bed.

Clara stirred awake from the ruckus and sat up beside him, accidentally placing her hand on the part of his robe that was sodden with milk. This inspired another facial warp while she wiped her hand on the sheet.

"Having trouble with your cereal?" she asked, her face full of mock concern. She flicked one of the fruit loops from his robe, part of a collective that were clinging to the fabric like burrs.

"No. Why do you ask?" Tony pulled one from his chin and popped it in his mouth.

Clara wiped a hand over her eyes and checked her watch. "You've got to be kidding!"

She then squinted out the front windows. Streams of light were exposing every streak and stain upon the glass. There were many.

"The early bird gets the worm."

"I don't want your worm." She punched his shoulder.

"Don't hurt yourself."

"You say that every time."

Clara slipped back against the armrest of the sofa. She drew the sheet up to her armpits.

"I'm concerned every time."

"Really?"

"Really."

"Well then, Mr. Concerned, try not to spill any milk on me while I'm asleep. And you could try making some decent conversation. Something a little less predictable..."

"If you didn't hit me so much, I'd have other things to say."

"Well... try not to deserve it. It wouldn't kill you to behave like a gentleman."

"And how should a gentleman behave?"

"You see? That's your problem." She rose and punched him again.

"What was that for?"

"Ignorance... And lewd thoughts."

Anthony remained silent for a spell, gathering up the spilled rings and piling them on the arm of the sofa. He then plucked a limp ring from his robe and offered it to her.

"Would you like something to eat?"

"It's too late for a peace offering," Clara replied, cocooned in the sheet once more. "Your intentions are revealed. Go back to bed. Try again, preferably after noon."

Anthony smiled. "And leave you in a puddle of milk? You could be sleeping on a nice firm mattress, you know?"

"You won't corral me into the sack that easily."

"No?"

"No."

"Guess I'm out of luck."

"Guess so."

"Everyone's gone, you know. Sharky, Dan-o, even Robbie 'the Selrac' and 'Mayhem' Mike have left. Conrad's the only one here."

"It won't improve your chances."

"No?"

"No."

"Well. There are some empty beds upstairs... If you'd rather sleep in a comfortable place. Sharky hasn't moved his furniture. Neither has Dan-o."

"Okay," Clara agreed, nuzzling her head into the pillow. "Carry me?"

Anthony stood and deliberated.

"Come on, Clark. Be a gentleman."

Clark was one of Tony's many nicknames. For some reason, they never stuck. "Clark" was Clara's: a Superman reference that reminded Tony of Clara's uniqueness amongst women.

Tony reached underneath her back and knees, then hoisted her off the cushions.

"Show off," Clara quipped.

"You're impossible to please," he jabbed.

"Hardly. All I really wanted was a bowl of fruit loops and a decent conversation."

"I could read you some poetry."

"Dr. Seuss isn't poetry."

Anthony made his way back to the stairs, his joints snapping as he hobbled across the hardwood floor.

"You should oil those," Clara suggested.

When he turned sideways to negotiate the stairs, she asked to be put down.

"No. It's all right. My joints always creak in the morning."

"This doesn't hurt your knee?"

"No more than walking."

Clara closed her eyes and remained silent until Anthony deposited her on Sharky's futon.

"Wake me up before ten and I'll never speak to you again."

"Is that a promise?"

Clara snorted, "Ouch. Walked into that one, didn't I?"

"Head first."

Tony closed the door, then walked back into his room. Conrad was there, sitting at his desk, the phone wedged between his shoulder and his ear; one leg perched across his knee, foot bouncing in agitation. There were only a few jacks in the house, and Anthony had been blessed by having one in his room, for better or for worse.

When he entered, he nodded his "what's up?" greeting to the still talking Conrad. His friend placed a finger over his mouth, then in a fit of irritation, waved for him to leave the room. Tony ignored him, and lay down quietly on his bed.

"I understand... Look, I understand. I'm a reliable... Look, I assure you... Yup. Won't be a problem. No, I'm not going anywhere; where would I go?"

Conrad looked into the receiver for a second before he hung it up.

"Who was that?"

Conrad just shook his head. "I have some calls to make." He got up to leave.

Tony waved for him to sit down. "No, no, no. Stay here. Use the phone. I'll pit out in your bed." He rose. "Let me know when you're done."

Conrad shook his head again. "No Tony. Better for me to go downstairs."

"Trouble?"

"Big trouble."

Anthony nodded. This was nothing new for Conrad Alphonsis Montgomery the fourth. The Radical One. He was a breeding pit for problems.

Conrad had flunked out of pre-med in first year, than flunked out of bio the year following. His parents thought he was still in school. Since first year, his old man had been giving him tuition

73

money, and paying his living expenses. Conrad made it back into bio a week or so ago, but he was still three terms from graduating. He hadn't told his parents yet. The plan was to say he was staying in school to get a second degree or maybe a master's. Anything to defer facing The Colonel, Dr. Conrad Wilberforce Montgomery the third. His old man, a local plastic surgeon, was as devout a worshipper of the money god as one was likely to find in the First World. He wouldn't take kindly to his son's deception, as much because of Conrad's failure and dishonesty as his wasting of a serious wad of cash. Close to eighty grand. Most of Conrad's "bursaries" had subsidized the local bars, and a few gambling trips to Vegas. If his old man ever found this out, the House joked that Conrad's organs would probably be auctioned off on the black market. The Radical One didn't think that was very funny.

"You're still in?" Anthony asked.

"Far as I know. Once they let you back in, they don't boot you out until you fail something. Different kind of trouble."

"Something I can help you with?"

"Nope."

Conrad walked to the door, then turned back. "Ahh. There is one thing." He walked over to Tony's desk and ripped the alarm clock from the wall. He swirled it around his head, a dark-haired, goateed version of Roger Daltry spinning a too fat microphone. Then he smashed it against the floor. Still holding the cord and the shattered remnants of the bees' nest, he walked to the door, handing the mess of plastic and wires to Tony as he passed.

"Sorry, Tony."

"Feel better?"

"A little."

"You know, I think this was an antique."

"Still is."

Conrad closed the door after himself as he left. Tony listened while his friend briefly stopped in his own room, then strode down the stairs taking them several at a time. Tony threw the dead clock into his wastepaper basket, then crossed the room, picked up the phone, and waited for Conrad to do likewise. Ordinarily, this would have constituted an invasion of privacy, but the Radical One had a way of slinking silently towards self-destruction that necessitated little intrusions into his life from time to time. Tony didn't want to do it, but his instincts for trouble were sound, and alarms were running amuck along those inner corridors usually reserved for bees, exams, and the late night shrieks of Screamin' Suzanne.

A few seconds after Tony raised the receiver to his ear, Conrad picked up the phone downstairs. A rapid succession of beeps followed, then several rings. A voice answered, too groggy with sleep to support a conversation that was anything but broken and lethargic.

"Stone?"

"Yeah... Who the hell is this?"

"Conrad."

"Oh, Radical. Hey brother, what's up?"

"The usual."

"That bad huh?"

"That bad."

Stone yawned. Conrad followed a second later. Tony had to cover the receiver when his turn came.

"So where were the Jungle boyz last night?" Stone asked. "Missed you at the club, man. It was quite a show."

"Yeah, always is... AJ and I took it easy. We were pretty crapped out. We had some pints down at the Hall with Timmy and Rob."

Stone grunted. "Lame excuse."

"Whatever. Look... You ready to move, or what?"

"Today?"

"Yup."

"This early?" Stone whined.

"Yup... We've got to hit my parents' place first," Conrad confirmed.

"Your old man ain't gonna kill ya?"

"He's in Port-au-Prince with his new wife."

"Oh, right." Stone paused. When he spoke again he was talking from the side of his mouth. Probably hauling on a smoke. "What did Eddie say?" he asked at last.

"Marco wants the money by Friday."

"Harsh." Stone paused to exhale. "You can't just hit the old man up for some cash?"

"No...I thought about it." Conrad sighed. "Can't tell him where it's been going. No reason to ask for more..."

"You can't invent something?" Stone suggested.

"Not this soon after hitting him up for summer school funds."

"You in summer school?"

"Nope."

"Gotta be a better way to get fifty large."

Conrad sighed again. "I can't think of one."

"Yeah… me neither... You sure you're up for this?" Stone asked.

"No choice. Can't have some ape like Eddie bustin' my skull. The old man'd find out, then I'd be doubly fucked. No… This is the only way."

"Why don't you just smash a machine?"

"No. This is better. I don't know how much money those things have... You got the stuff?" Conrad said, fed up with the small talk.

"Yup. Old man came through. Told him I locked my keys in my car and he gave me what I needed, and a few odds and ends he thought might come in handy."

"He's cool with this?"

"Must be." Stone took another puff. "Be over in ten. No, make that twenty."

"Me or you?" Conrad asked.

"Me. I'll be over in twenty."

Stone hung up the phone, and Conrad followed suit an instant later.

Tony waited to see if another call was forthcoming before he set his receiver back in the cradle. No. That was it. A conversation that sounded like the script from a bad movie. Crappy dialogue, horrible casting. Unclear plot. He didn't know who Eddie was. Marco he'd never heard of either. But Stone was enough bad news for one day. One of Conrad's friends from the Oasis, a nightclub off the strip, Stone was an automaton. One whose major aspiration was to get high. Tony worked his summers at the Oasis and still didn't know the guy's first name.

An instant later the Radical One came bounding up the steps. He must have been extremely anxious. He was never out of bed before eight in the morning, unless he had yet to go to sleep.

Tony was raising his fist to knock on the wall, hoping to start a dialogue with his friend, when Clara announced herself from the doorway.

"Having troubles with your alarm clock?" She crossed her arms and pointed her nose at the wastepaper basket beside his bed.

Tony didn't answer.

"You about to call someone?"

He covered his mouth with a finger, then crossed the room. Taking Clara by the elbow, he pulled her gently in from the hallway and edged past.

"Can you wait here for just a minute?"

"I was just going to go home."

Tony didn't respond. Backing down the hall, he simply pointed his index finger at the ceiling, repeating the "one minute" gesture until he got to Conrad's door. Tony knocked, then entered, closing the door behind him.

"Thanks for knocking." Conrad said sarcastically. He was sitting on his unmade bed, pulling on a sock. "I thought you were going back to bed."

"No. When the bees wake me up, it'd take a sledge hammer to get back to sleep."

"I'd be happy to oblige," Conrad offered.

"No thanks."

"You know, I think someone stayed here last night."

"Yeah. It was Clara," Tony confirmed.

"I think she pissed on the couch."

"No, that was me. I spilled some milk there this morning."

"Oh. Well, it stinks."

"I think it stank before." Tony watched while Conrad pulled on a pair of jeans.

"You know, I usually charge money for people to come in here and watch me change."

"Yeah. Well… It's probably a good idea. I understand you're hard up for cash."

Conrad paused, about to pull a T-shirt over his head. "Who told you?"

"You did," Tony stated, flatly.

Conrad stared at him for a moment, a look of awkward confusion.

"Last night at the pub," Tony lied.

"I don't remember."

"It's not important."

Conrad nodded slowly, then finished dressing. "Well it is important. I'm in trouble. Deep trouble. End of the line kind of trouble."

"It can't be that bad."

"Well it is. Look… I don't have time to explain. Stone's on his way over, and we have to go to my parents' place to get some shit. And I hafta call my sister."

"Oh... You gonna pawn something?"

"Do I look like I have anything to pawn?"

"No. From your dad's place," Tony suggested.

"No. My dad keeps his valuables in a safe. I wouldn't know how to move that kind of stuff anyways. Paintings, carpets, china. You've seen the place; it's full of shit. And worth a bundle, but I need some quick cash. What the hell would I do with a painting?"

Tony shook his head. His friend had obviously given this some thought. A bad sign. "Gambling debts?"

"More or less... Look, I gotta be ready to go." He checked his watch and swore, then made as if ready to leave.

Tony didn't move from in front of the door. "It's what, quarter to eight, ten to eight?"

Conrad didn't respond.

"You haven't been up before eight o'clock since the kitchen fire. That was two years ago. You gonna tell me what's goin' on, or not?" Tony said, blocking the doorway.

"You want in?" Conrad asked, incredulously.

"Yup," Tony said, knowing he needed more time with Conrad to figure out just what the hell was happening here.

"I'll explain in the car," Conrad said, moving forward towards the hallway, beyond Tony's large frame.

"You can use my phone," Tony offered, letting him move past.

The two spilled out into the hall. Clara was standing just outside Tony's threshold and waved to Conrad as he came out.

"I'd better use the phone downstairs."

Tony nodded. "I'm taking a shower." He added, "Don't leave without me."

Conrad headed down the stairs, leaving Tony and Clara alone in the corridor.

"Where you goin'?" Clara asked, leaning against the wall, her arms folded once more across her chest.

"Don't know," Tony said, his mind elsewhere.

"Big secret, huh?"

"No. I don't know what's going on. He said he'd tell me in the car."

"So you're just going to abandon me here?" Clara inquired sheepishly.

"I thought you said you were going home."

"Oh. So you were listening."

"Very funny." Tony reached around his door to unhook a towel that was hanging there

"Yeah, I'm going home. I've gotta pack," Clara said.

"We could drop you off."

"It's two blocks away."

"Just trying to be a gentleman." Tony made for the bathroom, then turned to speak over his shoulder so that he was hobbling down the hall sideways. "Could you just wait and make sure that Conrad doesn't leave without me?"

79

"It'll cost ya."
"Just put it on my tab."

Anthony never felt ready for the day until his body was invigorated with some hot water. Years of plyometrics and strength training, coupled with several sprains, pulls, bouts of tendonitis, and other afflictions, some known, others mysterious, had stiffened up his joints over the years. Walking before a shower was awkward, sometimes even painful, unless he took his time about it, and gave his body a chance to adjust to its own weight. Though he was only two hundred and twenty pounds, his frame had been designed for less. The Xavier men were all lean. His natural weight, if he'd depended on genetics alone, would have been perhaps one eighty. One eighty-five, tops. His extra weight was good weight, muscle and sinew, but the exercises he had done to ensure that he stayed quick, sprint training and the like, and the many collisions he had endured, moving faster and with more mass than God had intended him to have, had played out like a tragedy for his soft tissue. Cartilage, menisci, ligaments. Now that his football career was officially over, the torn ACL at the end his sophomore year had ripped away any chance he'd at making it to the show. The scouts vanished and he played sparingly over the last two seasons. He traded in the letters NFL for CPA. It was hard letting go of the game, the comradery. Soldiers of the gridiron, he'd give it all for the team, duty and honour demanded nothing less. But that was over now. It was time to let his body eat itself, digest a bit of muscle for the sake of his future. It would be hard to see the weight go. He'd worked so hard to put it there. But the alternative was to get old before his time. Yes. It was time to lighten the load for his poor bones and become a moderate. Start exercising for fun.

Anthony let the water spill over his head and down his back, the spray of it feeding a host of molds and other fungi that no-one in the house could be bothered scraping from the walls. Poor Conrad. If only he'd opened his eyes to the collection of organisms whose life-cycles were playing themselves out in the untamed wilds of the shower, perhaps then the spirit of biology would have taken root within him, raising him above the mundane arenas to which he currently seemed confined. Casinos, pool halls, nightclubs and frat houses. But Conrad was no more a biologist than the Jungle House was a field laboratory. Conrad was as blind to the mold in the shower as he was to the need for a lifestyle adjustment.

Tony shook his head back and forth under the faucet. It always took a while for the heat of the water to penetrate his core. It was impossible to rush the process. It wasn't like a cleansing shower. He was exorcising his stiffness. The process took about fifteen minutes.

When he was at last finished, cooled and dressed, he descended to the living room. Clara was on the sofa, reading. She never travelled without a book. Even a night out would demand that some wrinkled paperback be stowed away in her purse, usually for a next morning perusal.

"Where's Conrad?" Tony asked her.

Clara kept her eyes in her book.

"He took off with Stone."

"I thought I told you not to let him leave."

"What can I say? He's a grown man. He does what he wants."

"Shit."

Clara folded her book over a finger. "He was in a hurry," she said. "I asked him to wait, but he said he couldn't."

"Did he talk to his sister?" Tony asked, impatiently.

"He talked to someone. Look, he always needs money." Clara returned to her reading. "He's probably going to pick up a paycheck or something."

"Not this time," Tony answered, making his way over to the desk in the front hall. He began digging through a dish that housed several sets of keys, a handful of pennies, a screw, some paper clips, and several other oddities that no one could ever throw out. Tony found his car keys and slipped his finger through the ring.

"He's going to do something stupid, rob a bank or something. I don't know any of the details, but I've got to try to ground him."

Clara studied Tony's face and realized he wasn't kidding.

81

Tony held his keys aloft and jangled them back and forth. "Feel like a drive?"

Conrad's parents lived in Scottsdale, in a neighborhood so lavish the swimming pools and fountains from each estate could've kept a small African country alive; all this in the middle of the desert. Finding the place was easy. Just follow the money.

"You can't be serious about this?" Clara asked, flipping through the glove box in the car, searching for something that wouldn't weigh down the tape deck as heavily as Iron Maiden. She came up empty. Settled instead on the car's air conditioning controls. It was already scorching hot.

"Yeah, I'm serious. Would I be driving around at eight-thirty in the morning if I wasn't?"

Clara popped the tape from the deck and tried the radio.

"Is he that desperate?" she asked, disbelieving.

"It would appear so."

"This is just the stupidest thing I've ever heard. I mean the stupidest... Christ."

Tony started to laugh.

"What?" Clara slapped his arm. "What is it? Are you pulling a fast one on me?"

"No." Tony's laugh totally destroyed the credibility of his answer.

"What the hell is so funny?"

"I'm driving to Conrad's dad's place, so I can talk him out of God knows what, which is probably illegal, to pay off a debt he got by taking money from some guy named Marco." He shook his head. "And the little bastard took off without me."

"I think you're full of shit," Clara declared, hoping she was right.

"Yeah?"

"Yeah."

"So why are you coming?" Tony inquired.

"Oh, bugger off."

Tony rolled into the Montgomery compound and discovered that the green glow of the digital numbers, usually alight on the dash, had blinked out. He balled his fist and slammed it beside the clock, re-establishing the poor connection. The numbers flashed, then fizzled. Eight forty-seven.

To his relief, Conrad's car was still there. Tony pulled up beside it.

"Do you want to come in? This might get ugly," he asked with some uncertainty.

"Stupid, more like. Yeah, I want to come in. You think I drove all this way to sit in the driveway in this heat?" Clara opened the door and stood between the two cars. Though seemingly determined to go with Tony inside, she appeared content to let Tony lead the charge. He walked in without knocking.

No one greeted the two as they entered. A voice, no more than a quiet murmur, was carrying on a fragmented discourse in a room far to the left. Tony slipped off his shoes, then made his way through several of the open rooms towards the den, where he suspected the two refugees were camped out. Clara stayed behind, her eyes funneled from showpiece to showpiece in the foyer. A crystal chandelier glittered two stories above her bathing the ornate central staircase in light.

In the den, Stone was stretched out on one sofa, a magazine spread-eagled before his face. Conrad was sitting on a table behind the couch opposite, his feet resting on the seat of a chair. A phone was jammed between his ear and shoulder, and he was jotting notes on a pad of paper spread across his knee. When he saw Tony enter, he grinned and nodded, then pulled up the receiver with his pen hand just long enough to say "What'd I tell ya?" to Stone, who sat up to peer over the top of the sofa.

"Hey T, good to see ya," Stone said, folding his magazine into one hand. "Conrad said you'd be comin' over. I thought he was full of shit. Sorry we couldn't wait. Boss's orders," Stone confirmed, pointing absently towards Conrad.

Tony nodded mutely, unsure of how to corner Conrad with his wingman in the room.

"Who's he talking to?" Tony asked, tilting his head towards Conrad.

"Janey."

"Is she going to help?"

Stone seemed surprised by this question. He shrugged. "I think he's just looking for information. Say man, are you comin' on this trip?"

Tony shook his head.

"We could use a driver."

Tony's head teetered back and forth as if he was actually thinking about it, his eyes refusing to fix themselves upon anything. They finally settled on Clara, who was leaning against the divider separating the den from the dining room.

"No," he said firmly. "I think this is crazy, and I don't even know what 'this' is."

"Well, that's what I said," Stone replied, stretching out once more, his back to Clara during the dialogue. "But you know our man. Tell him it's crazy and it eggs him on."

Tony took a seat on the sofa in front of Conrad, opposite Stone, who promptly buried his face back under the magazine. Clara drifted back into the dining room, her eye caught by a painting or sculpture she'd walked past.

Tony waited for an opportunity to begin a discourse with "the boss." It took some time. When Conrad was finished on the phone, he took off, disappearing into the bowels of the mansion, returning a short time later with a duffel bag that clunked heavily on the floor when he set it down.

"You want in?" Conrad asked, his voice and his hands trembling.

"Are you out of your mind?" Tony started in. "Your shakin', man."

"Hey, screw you!" Conrad retaliated.

Tony stood up, the abrupt aggression of his movements forced his friend back a few steps.

"Easy..." Stone said, sitting up once more.

Conrad was shaking his head. "You're in or you're out. That's all I want to know."

"What are you talking about? Are you trying to throw your life away?" Tony's voice was louder than he had intended. His carefully rehearsed plan, a series of calm and meaningful questions, intended to direct his friend towards the proper course, had been blown away by Conrad's persistence.

Conrad began to pace between the twin sofas, one-two-three-four, turn, one-two-three-four, turn, speaking into the floor.

"I'm fucked if I don't."

"Bullshit. Just come clean," Tony advised, his tone softening.

"This isn't about the old man. He's an ignorant piece of shit, and I'm sure he'd pay me for the rest of my life just to stay out of his. This isn't about him. I need some cash."

"How much?" Tony asked, already knowing.

"Fifty grand."

"To who?"

"It doesn't matter," Conrad muttered.

"Sure it matters."

"Marco Golini," Stone chimed in. Conrad nodded.

"Who's that?" Tony said, turning towards Stone.

"It doesn't matter," Conrad said. "What matters is that he needs his money in five days. Five days. I can't even get *ten* G's in five days."

"What about your car?" Clara voiced, having returned to her spot by the arched entrance into the den.

"What about my car?" Conrad retorted.

"Can't you sell it?" Clara asked.

Conrad shook his head. "Already sold it."

"What?" Tony demanded.

"I sold it to Stone two weeks ago."

"For how much?" Tony needed to confirm that Stone was a hustling loser, willing to exploit and manipulate circumstances to benefit himself.

Conrad didn't answer. Tony redirected the question to Stone, who was staring at him, his hands dangling across his knees.

"Two grand." Stone answered, twisting one of his rings slowly around a finger.

"Two grand!" Tony was furious. "It's worth at least six. What the fuck is that? Two grand."

"Look." Stone stood so that he, Conrad and Tony formed a dangerously small triangle. Stone pointed two fingers at Tony's chest. "It was all I had at the time. I didn't have to help him at all. He needed the cash, so I gave it to him. If he pays me back, he can have the damned car. So get off my case, man."

Without backing up, Tony retreated with a downward glance and a sigh that doubled as an apology. "Do you have any idea what you're taking on?" he asked Conrad.

"Yeah... Yeah..." Conrad walked over to the table and retrieved his note pad. He seemed relieved to have something else to talk about. "I got layouts, information, security, schedules, the bank's procedures, police response times. I know exactly what to do." He began flipping through the sheets. Tony was mildly surprised.

"Where did you get all of this?"

"My sister. She used to work there. I told her I had a job interview coming up, and I had to make it look like I knew what I was talking about. You know, like I'd worked in a bank before. She told me everything." He waved his hand at Stone, who was taking his seat again. "We got it all worked out."

"All worked out, huh?"

"Hey it's easy, man. When my sister was there, she said it happened all the time. If you're in and out, you never get caught."

"Never?"

"Look. The police have shit to do when they get there. Secure the premises. Get information. It takes time. They never get people right away. And when they do, it's always, and I mean, like, always, because they try to do something with the money right away. Deposit it. Spend it. Some jackass made off with eighty G's a couple of years ago and tried to put it in his account the same afternoon. Can you fuckin' believe it?"

He tossed the notepad onto the coffee table between Stone and Tony, anxious to continue his monologue. "I'm not goin' to spend the money. And neither is Stone. At least not right away. A year at least, and never very much at one time. Marco gets his cash, and anything extra I can use to pay back the old man. Later. Much later."

Tony placed a palm over each eye and sat with his elbows on his knees. He ground his hands into his orbits, then let them slide over his face until they came together in front of his mouth, as if in prayer. He clapped them together several times and stared at the coffee table.

Back to plan A.

"Best case scenario. You get in. You get out. No one gets hurt. You try to pay Marco. Will he even take stolen cash? Will he try to take all of it?"

Conrad was fidgeting, but stopped momentarily as if frozen in place by the suggestion. He obviously hadn't considered it. "He'll take it." He began to pace again. "And if he doesn't, it's not my problem."

"And if he takes all of it?"

"One less thing to worry about."

"Okay." Tony ran his fingers through his hair. "Worst case scenario. One of you gets caught."

"We won't get caught," Conrad insisted.

"But if you do?"

"Look. Cashiers are trained to do exactly what they're told when a man's waving a gun in their face."

"Guns? Where the hell are you going to get guns?"

"Got them already." Conrad opened the bag and pulled out two wheel guns.

"Starting pistols," he explained. "Old ones. They don't have the red plastic in the end, so you can't tell they're fake."

"Fake guns?"

"We don't want anyone getting hurt. And you do less time if you get caught."

"I thought you weren't getting caught."

Conrad didn't answer.

"Security cameras?" Tony continued.

"We'll be wearing masks, sweatshirts and jeans. What fuckin' good will a camera do?"

"They'll see the car."

"Yeah. We thought of that. But I have some fake ID. People lose their wallets in the Oasis all the time. You know that. I've got a driver's license that even you'd swear was mine, as long as I've got the goatee on. We're going to rent a car. We'll drive a few blocks, ditch the rental and hop in the Mustang, lose the shirts, and it's back to normal-ville."

"What do you think of this?" Tony turned to address Stone. "You've seen this ID?"

"You white people all look the same to me."

"Funny... Well, they'll see you at the rental agency. What if they have cameras there?"

Conrad looked at the ground, then his hands began to swirl as if directing his thoughts on the way out. "I go in with shades and a baseball cap. I lose the goatee after the hold-up. Shit. They're goin' to start by lookin' up the guy whose ID I have anyway. They'll never know. There's no way."

"So what about him?" Tony asked.

"Who?"

"The guy whose ID you have? You're kinda screwing him over, aren't you?"

"He'll be innocent. The truth shall set him free," Conrad said, not convincingly.

Stone started to laugh.

Tony tried to ignore him. "When are you going?"

"This morning... Are you in?" Conrad asked, hopeful.

Tony shook his head. "I came here to talk you out of this."

"Well forget about that. I have no choice."

"You always have a choice," Tony suggested.

"Yeah. Well, my choice is to do this or get killed," Conrad stated.

"You don't know that."

"Tony, these people don't mess around. You don't fuck with them. I don't want to get whacked. I don't want to have my thumbs or my kneecaps broken. This is a whole god-damned world that you don't know a damn thing about."

"And you're about to dive into it head first." Tony tried to reason with him.

"No man. I'm a bartender. I'll have a BSc soon. I pay, and I'm out," Conrad explained.

"Only that Marco's going to know you robbed a bank."

"What the fuck does that mean?" Conrad asked, agitated by Tony's attempts to dissuade him.

"I don't know. Just that... I don't know. He'll have one over on ya. He'll know. It's leverage."

Conrad took a deep breath. All his energy seemed to leak out when he exhaled. "It's better than the alternative."

"Call your old man," Tony reiterated.

"No. No way."

"Tell him the truth. You don't think he'd pay fifty thou' to bail you out?"

"Bail me out of what? That's the point. I open that can, and everything spills out. If I'm in over my head with Marco, I'm in way over my head with the old man. He'll want to know what's going on. What the hell do I tell him?"

"The truth."

"He wouldn't believe it. So much the worse if he did."

"Tell him it's for me," Tony offered, trying desperately to find a way to get through to Conrad.

"Oh right, the golden boy. Sure. He'd believe that." Conrad laughed.

"Your sister?" Tony inquired. He was running out of options.

"Two kids. Single mom. She doesn't have that kind of money. You don't think I've thought about these things? What do you think I've been doing for the last two weeks?"

"Getting pissed a lot," Tony said, shaking his head.

"You would too. Look. In or out?" Conrad asked, a tone of finality in his voice.

"When are you leaving?"

"A couple of hours. I want to have time to rehearse things with Stone."

"Here?" Tony asked, his mind spinning, trying to find a hole in the reasoning Conrad had formulated. The insanity of this plan was somehow evading him.

"Yeah. No one can bother us here."

"And you need a driver."

"Yeah," Conrad acknowledged.

"Drop by on your way. I'll give you my answer then."

"You'll be at the place?" Conrad asked.

"Yeah. I gotta think about this. I'm goin' try to come up with somethin'. I don't like this," Tony stammered.

"I don't like it either," Conrad added.

Tony turned to leave.

"Tony…"

"Yeah."

"Thanks."

Tony nodded and left. He was halfway through the line of rooms when he realized Clara wasn't with him. He'd forgotten she was there. Clara was always reasonable. She probably could have helped.

Tony checked the hall. Her shoes were gone. Through the panes of glass flanking the double doors, he spied her sitting on the hood of his car, her book spread open in one hand. He opened the front door and made his way towards her.

"How did it go?" she asked, genuinely concerned.

"It could have been worse. We might have all been crushed under the weight of the stupidest idea to take root in that idiot's tangled mind since he decided to lie to his old man about failing out of school."

"That was quite a mouthful." Clara closed her book and slid from the car. "What's going on?"

"I'll tell you on the way home." Tony reached out to unlock the car. He inadvertently locked it instead, having forgotten to do so before going in.

"It's open," Clara offered. "But probably hotter than Hades inside."

"Thanks." Tony said, sliding in to start the car and flip on the air conditioner.

Tony waited until they were through the gate and clear of the drive before he asked Clara why she had left.

"I can't stand this sort of thing. Too much testosterone. Everyone's yelling. Nobody's listening..."

"It got better," Tony suggested.

"I must have missed that part," Clara said darkly.

"Well... Regardless... He's going to go ahead with it."

Clara simply shook her head, then let it slump against the seat belt. If she was surprised, it was hidden by a thick layer of disinterest.

"I'm sorry for dragging you out here," he offered in apology.

Clara smiled. "Don't worry about it, Clark. If I hadn't been at your place, I'd have just been packing at home. No fun lost there."

"Are you okay?" she asked a moment later.

Tony took a few deep breaths before he answered, his hands clasped so firmly about the wheel it was in danger of being torn from the steering column.

"I. Just. Screwed. Up. Completely." He spat the words out one at a time.

Clara simply watched him carefully, waiting for an explanation.

"I couldn't convince him not to do it."

"You tried," she consoled him.

"That, I did."

"You think he'll go through with it?"

"He's definitely going through with it. And I think he'll swing by before he does. He needs a driver."

"I don't think he'll do it. He'll chicken out," Clara said, trying to throw Tony a rope, it sounded like he was slipping on the idea of going along. She couldn't let that happen.

"I think these people mean business."

"Stone? Are you kidding?" Clara laughed.

91

"No, the people Conrad borrowed the money from. He's got until Friday to produce fifty grand or he's finished. At least, that's what he thinks," Tony explained.

"Is it true? Or is it bull?" she asked.

Tony shrugged. "He thinks it's true. That may be all that matters."

Clara nodded slowly. "I'm just glad you're not mixed up in this."

Tony wasn't sure if this was a question. He didn't respond immediately, which would have been an answer of sorts, had she not moved on to another idea.

"Should we just call the cops?" Clara suggested, hoping to shake Tony out of his funk.

"I don't know what right we have. They aren't going to hurt anyone. And they might change their minds. I have no alternatives for them. What else can I suggest to him? If we call the cops, then we're throwing him to the wolves."

"It may be the best thing for him."

Tony shook his head. "Not these people. His old man maybe. Conrad's terrified of him. But these people mean business, by the sound of things."

"Why don't you call his old man?"

"I'm not going to do that."

"Why not?" she asked.

"I'm not going to squeal to his dad. He's on vacation anyway. I have no way of getting ahold of him."

"What about his sister?" Clara continued.

"Janey. She's got no money."

"Could she call his old man?" Clara added, unwilling to let the conversation fizzle before she explored all the possibilities.

"I don't know," Tony said. "I never thought of that." He then started nodding. "Yeah. I bet she could. I'll mention it to Conrad. Maybe she could borrow the money for him. She's got a perfect excuse. Two young kids. Psycho-prick ex-husband who doesn't pay alimony. She has a restraining order and everything."

"Well it's an idea," Clara confirmed, relieved.

"Best one so far," Tony added, brightening somewhat.

"Aren't you glad you brought me?" she jibed.

"Always."

Tony let his head fall back on the old couch, wishing for a moment that he could put his feet up on the coffee table, or anesthetize his brain with a little television, neither of which was possible. Both articles were now ghosts of a previous life. Gone, along with his friends, the Jungle boys of '05, leaving him to stew in a near empty house, with only the decomposing sofa for company.

He got up. He needed to talk to Clara. She was asleep in Sharky's room, having declined the opportunity of going home to pack. Her staying wouldn't make things any easier. If Conrad didn't agree to their suggestions... Well. Clara wouldn't approve. He was sure that he could talk some sense into Conrad; fuck Stone, he was a self-serving prick. Here at the house, Tony knew, from the episode this morning in Scottsdale, that he wasn't going to get through to them. His best shot, his main play, would come at the bank, outside in the car, before they went in. That's when his words would find their mark, that's when Conrad would be most cognizant of his actions and their consequences. That would be when Tony would have to lay it all on the line. But that meant he'd have to tag along. Agree to be the driver. Telling Clara would be like biting his tongue. Painful, and once done, it was unlikely he'd get the chance to say anything further.

Breathing deeply to curtail his anxiety, Tony took the stairs slowly, uncertain how to construct an argument potent enough to keep Clara from talking him out of getting involved in the heist. A lost cause. There was only one argument he could make. Friends didn't leave friends to swing from the gallow's pole. He had to help Conrad because he was the only one left to do it. If Conrad decided to go through with things. If he hadn't found another driver. If Clara didn't say "screw you all" and blow the whistle. If... If... If.

Tony tapped gently on Sharky's door. No answer. Opening the door a crack, he saw Clara asleep on the futon, so he tiptoed in and settled down beside her. After fifteen minutes or so she rolled over, acknowledging him with a soft grunt muffled by several inches of pillow.

"Is Conrad here?" she purred.

"Not yet. Probably not for a while," he said, unable to contain the confusion in his voice.

"Could you move for a second?" Clara asked.

Tony raised himself up while Clara freed several inches of comforter pinned beneath him, edging herself into the material. Once she was finished, Tony settled back down.

"It seems cold in here. Weird, eh? You warm enough?" she asked.

"Yeah."

"You're going with him, aren't you?" she said into the room, her tone flat.

"Yeah," Tony answered.

Clara rolled over and looked straight into his eyes. Tony felt his face go limp while she prodded him with her gaze. Dark eyes framed by an expression he guessed was as unreadable as his own. He felt numb.

Clara rolled away so that her back walled him off from her words.

"Well, I'm coming too."

Uncertain as to whether he was emotionally frozen, in shock, or just overly tired from the marathon of final exams, Tony said nothing. After thinking it over for a minute, it seemed the only reasonable response. Any argument presented to dissuade her would only be tossed back in his face to dissuade him from helping Conrad in the first place. Friends never left friends...

"He might change his mind..." Tony said at last. "Right before he goes in, that's when I can turn him, that's when he'll start to fold." Tony said, adding *"I can do it. I can save him."* But only in his mind.

"Don't count on it. He wants to martyr himself. It's a no-lose situation for him."

This didn't entirely make sense. Tony said so.

"It makes perfect sense to me," Clara explained. "The guy can't tell the truth to anybody. This way he doesn't have to. If he gets the money, he's fine. If he gets caught, or worse, the truth is out there without him having to tell anyone himself. And he gets a dose of sympathy from everyone for having been so desperate. He's not going to back down." She'd been busy thinking.

"You said he might chicken out, and I'm gonna try to push his buttons so he will."

"I'd chicken out. He won't. The alternative is scarier. Telling the truth. Facing his father."

"And the mob," Tony added.

"It's his father that's the problem. He's probably friends with those other guys. The mob. They're probably just people from the club."

Tony didn't think so, but was in no mood to argue, agreeing as he did with most of what she'd said. Nodding, he rose to leave.

"Where you goin'?"

"I think I'm going to lie down. I don't know. I'm tired, but I think I'm too uptight to sleep. I might just walk around or something."

Clara mumbled into her pillow, the words barely audible to Tony as he made his exit.

"What was that?" he asked, one foot out the door.

"Don't leave without me," she repeated a little louder.

"I won't," Tony answered. He then wondered for a moment if there was some way to take that back. He rarely lied. It was one of the few things he felt he shared with Clark Kent and the man of steel. He'd refused dishonesty when it came knocking in his childhood. He conceded to omission when necessary, but lying? No. That just wasn't his style. He'd have to take her now. It was a shame. He had just committed them both to a leap of faith. He knew he could talk Conrad out of it, he just knew it, but what if he couldn't, what if it came down to that, what then? Tony didn't have the answers. Not yet, anyway.

Conrad arrived early, just after 10 am. Clara was up and reading, and Tony, trying to escape into the pages of a story as well, was fighting hopelessly with the book in his hands. He might have gotten into it eventually, had there been time. When the Radical One arrived, Tony dropped his book with relief.

Conrad didn't stop to talk. "I need a few things," he said, disappearing up the staircase.

Tony followed after, capturing Conrad in the act of looting his own room.

"Forgot my balaclava, it was a joke gift from Janey a few years back," Conrad offered by way of explanation.

"You still need a driver?" Tony was surprised he had to ask.

"No."

"You sure?" Tony pressed.

"Yup."

"Who did you find?"

"No one," Conrad stated, moving onto the next drawer in his dresser.

Tony closed the door behind him. It was his way of asking for an explanation.

"I'm not dragging you into this," Conrad said, looking down into the pile of clothes through which he was digging. An instant later he came up with his buried treasure, a black lump of material.

"You have to."

"No I don't," Conrad half snorted, half laughed.

"You agree, or you don't walk out of this room."

Conrad stopped moving. He looked at Tony with a dead expression. Neither moved for a full half minute. Then Conrad took a step backwards and slumped ass first into his desk chair.

"If something goes wrong, I don't want it on my conscience that I dragged you into this," Conrad finally admitted. Defiant. Determined.

"Well, I don't want to have to wait here all afternoon wondering if it went wrong, then find out that it did, and wonder if I might have made a difference."

"Stone is all I need. He knows the risks."

"Stone doesn't know shit. He'd follow you off the edge of a cliff for a pint of beer. He's no better at saying 'no' than you are," Tony explained, rocking slightly as he did so, attempting to dissipate his growing frustration.

"Well, I can say no to you. I can't let you drive, man. No way." Conrad's tone, flat and cold, told Tony he'd have to be more persuasive.

"I drive. Clara comes. If you get caught, we plead ignorance. We were just offering you a ride."

"In a rental car?" Conrad asked, illustrating the poor logic of Tony's plan.

"We'll take mine."

"The security cameras. The plates."

"We'll cover the plates," Tony suggested, not willing to back down.

"And the car?"

"We'll hide it at your dad's and repaint it." Tony felt Conrad's weariness; he was done listening and Tony hadn't gotten a single thing through to the thick-headed asshole.

"No." Conrad stood. "No, this wrecks the plan." He reached in front of Tony for the doorknob. "Come on. I gotta go."

Tony's hand moved so quickly Conrad only had time to stiffen in surprise and close his eyes before an open palm landed dead in the middle of his forehead. It sent him tumbling across the room to land in a tangle of clothing, his limbs draped like wet noodles over books, loose pages, and the chair that had upended him. Tony closed the space with a bound and stood seething over the arrangement of body and mess. He had thrown the switch. It wasn't actually a switch. It was more a sluice gate. His mind had told him that he was angry, and rather than consciously suppress the feeling with rational arguments about self-control, he let the heat of rage pour into his body. It was a practice developed from countless hours spent in gyms, on the track, and on the football field. In an instant he was furious enough to tear the tusks from an elephant's maw. He knew Conrad had never seen this manifestation of his personality, so he stood and watched as his friend slowly drew himself up into a ball. In a matter of seconds Tony's anger drained away, leaving his body with the awful sensation of having been expunged of everything inside it. A vacuum of shame remained. Conrad rolled over and kicked out with a foot, pushing himself through the mess and against the wall. Before he sat up, he reached in behind his back and removed something and pointed it at Tony. It was an automatic.

Stunned, Tony stood ramrod straight while Conrad slowly rose to his feet, the gun trained on his assailant. Conrad was shaking, and two diaphanous streaks of water connected his eyes, red rimmed and agitated, to his goatee.

"Get out of the way," Conrad ordered, his voice thready and coarse.

"Where did you get that?" Tony demanded, feeling the flash of rage inside him begin to boil, threatening to return.

"It's my old man's. Now get out of the way," Conrad repeated, partially regaining his composure.

"No. You'll have to shoot me." Like this whole asinine plan, Tony didn't think Conrad had it in him.

"Jesus Christ." Conrad half-turned away and bent over as though he had just landed from the ceiling. "You stubborn jackass. You would make me shoot you, wouldn't you? You stubborn jackass!"

Tony didn't move.

"Please, Tony. Get out of the way. I've got to get going." Tears were still dripping down his face.

"You're cracking up," Tony observed.

"You would too," Conrad retorted.

"Would you want to help me if I was?"

Conrad slid the gun back between his pants and his spine.

"Yes. Yes I would." He turned and righted his chair. Then he sat back down and wiped his face dry with his sleeves. After a few long minutes he rose, stalked past Tony, and opened the door. "If you're coming, let's go."

"And Clara. She'll probably call the cops if we don't let her come," Tony advised, knowing that he'd do better with her in the car than without.

"I don't care. I don't give a damn. I just want to get going. I just want this to be over." He began wiping at his face again, and headed towards the stairs.

Clara rose from the common room when Conrad headed out the door, yelling over his shoulder that he was just going to get Stone. Tony was following him.

"Is he going to call his sister?" she asked.

Tony stopped walking abruptly, as though the end of his invisible leash had just snagged a tree root. "I forgot."

"What was that?" Conrad asked, returning.

"Clara had an idea that you might want to call your sister and see if she could ask your old man for the money. And say it was for herself."

Conrad's head began to swing back and forth like he was following a tennis match on the far side of the room.

"She hasn't spoken to my father in six years. Not since Tony knocked her up."

Clara gave Tony a bewildered look.

"Not this Tony. Another Tony. She decided to keep it, and not get married. It was too much for the old guy. If she hasn't called him for two pregnancies, a wedding and a divorce, I sure as hell am not going to ask her to call him up for some cash. You don't think I've thought of this already? Come on. I'm lazy, but I'm not stupid."

Tony was about to protest. Conrad wasn't lazy, he was just undisciplined, but Stone announced himself at the door with a nod and a "wassup" ending that line of conversation.

"Make yourself comfortable," Conrad said, pointing to the sofa. "We've got two extra pairs of hands to work into the formula."

Stone looked over Tony with an approving nod. "Who else?"

Conrad pointed at Clara with his nose.

"Oh, the chick. Cool."

Conrad and Tony shared a fearful look, waiting for Clara to explode. She surprised them all by glancing over Stone without seeing him and stretching out on the sofa, leaving him an open seat at the end. He sat down, then shot up like geyser a second later, rubbing a dark spot on his ass.

"Hey man, I think someone pissed on this couch."
Tony chuckled softly. Good-ol' Clara.
"Tough break," she added.

The bank, they heard from Conrad, was essentially a great hall. From the front lobby doors, the side offices narrowed the passageway as customers entered the bank. Conrad had been to the bank three times in the last week, casing it out. Confirming much of what his sister had already told him. A large over-sized banking counter with six to ten separate areas for penning out deposits and withdrawals sat in the middle of the floor, half way from the front doors and the tellers. It was never that busy- not since banking machines and Internet banking had revolutionized the industry. A little further down the main floor of the bank, the brass poles and felt-lined runners forced customers to queue up, single-file, and wait for the next available teller. To the right was a small enclave of chairs and a stock ticker. To the left and center were the teller stations: modern, comfortable, a chest high counter over which money was exchanged along with the occasional pleasantry. Behind the half-wall were the managers' offices, the staff lounge and washrooms, and the L-shaped hallway that led to the safety deposit boxes and the vault. Of course they wouldn't be sticking around long enough to get back there, they just wanted the cash from the teller booths; it would be enough. It was a simple design and Conrad's sister had made it perfectly clear that it was every inch under surveillance. The front lobby, she'd confessed, was poorly monitored, and the camera angle she had seen of the front was good for catching only the height of the assailants. The camera placement was too high, too bird's eye, to capture faces and specific features of those coming and going.

Tony, Stone, Conrad and Clara left half an hour later, at 10:51 am. Their plans had been finalized. They were going to wear panty hose over their faces and baseball caps, as there weren't enough ski masks to go around, and it was agreed that the balaclava would also stand out to passers-by who might see into the bank, or catch a timely glance as the three left the car for the entrance. Tony was coming inside. It was Stone's suggestion. A waste of manpower otherwise. Tony felt he couldn't refuse. With Stone there, it was a matter of face. Tony also considered himself to be a true friend of Conrad's, and didn't like the idea of playing second fiddle to Stone, whom he considered to be a good-time guy, one rank higher than a drinking buddy. If Stone was going, by right, he should go too. Clara didn't say a word during the planning, she sat on the couch and listened; most often, she would look up at Tony; sometimes he would feel her gaze but only occasionally would he meet it. It was difficult for Tony to sit still during all this talk; he still planned on getting Conrad to see the insanity of the plan, the reality of his options and the clarity of his potential future. Nevertheless, Tony interjected from time to time, trying to fit in, trying to contribute. Tony knew that if Conrad left without him, it would be game over. Once everything was agreed upon, the four hopped into the rented car Stone's cousin had grabbed for them on the way over. He'd report it stolen around eleven. With their heads swimming in their youthful delusions, they took off for the National Bank, to pay off a loan shark and settle Conrad's debt with The Colonel. Tony cemented his final thoughts about their future in his mind. There was still a chance he could save them all.

Chapter 9

Grier

As Grier walked the short hall towards the main room of the bank he could sense a twinge of disappointment rising in him. His full genius would go untested if they walked out of the bank without incident. It had never been in question, that law enforcement would arrive at some point to stop them. Escaping right past them in the chaos, that was a feeling he now regretted imagining. No one would ever know... ever know if the sheer impossibility of his plan would have, could have, truly succeeded. Accompanying this feeling of loss, the emptiness that went with not being taxed to the fullest possible extent of his resources, his mind, his abilities, came the quick and regrettable adjustment of his body. He could feel the tension dissipate, the heart rate slow, the senses dull slightly back into normalcy. The "rush" was rushing away, leaving him alone and empty, frustrated and fatigued. He was no longer a young man it seemed, and the flow of adrenalin that used to go with these jobs ran empty. This heist, too smooth, too perfect, tasted bitter, like he'd gone to the well one too many times.

Even as he walked to the end of the hallway, edging closer to the front of the bank, where he would undoubtedly find that everything was in perfect order, he could hear, but only in the back of his mind, a commotion up ahead. There were strange voices in the bank. He had never been one to lose himself in reflection, not in circumstances like this, but with the realization that no demands would be made of him during this job, he had allowed himself this one introspective fancy. Self-pity. He hated it in others and had rarely indulged in it himself. And only when he felt the sharp momentary pain and pressure of the bullet enter and leave his neck, followed distantly by the sound of the weapon discharging, did he feel with his hand the hole where he had been shot, did he see the geyser-like spray of blood flowing out of him over the wall, feeling the warm viscous bath of it as he slid down the wall. His knees buckled and he fell like a rolling wave searching to break on the beach that he knew would be the green and blue marble of the floor, his eyes flashing to the walls, the ceiling; his head hit the ground with a bounce, it should have hurt he thought; his pity and conceit expelled with every beat of his heart, tumbling out of him, wet and slippery; he felt a slight chill before he closed his eyes. This isn't so bad, he thought. There were shots being fired and voices yelling now, people crying, it all sounded so far away, as if a television had been left on somewhere. It was a good plan… what the hell went wrong? They'll be lost without me. Brilliant Grier, fucking brilliant.

Clara

11:14 am. Clara sat for what seemed like an eternity in the running car just outside the entrance to the bank. She had expected that Anthony would be sitting beside her but he had shrugged off her suggestions that this… this ridiculous plan was absolute insanity. She'd been privy to this kind of male loyalty before, observing men walk through fire for each other and more often than not getting burned beyond recognition. But Anthony? Not Anthony. Oh how he had tried; they both had tried. The first five minutes in the car were the only silent ones; the rest had been intense, adamant, passionate, sometimes eloquent, sometimes primal bickering back and forth between Tony and Conrad. The end result of which she could not fully fathom. And yet, she only had to look through the car window to see that yes, it was true, it was happening, it was for real. Something stirred to life deep down inside, something she had swallowed and suppressed for the last four years was bucking and kicking against its cage, the careful constructs that her mind had placed over her emotions. And when Anthony had held her hand in the backseat of the car, only seconds ago, and they had looked briefly into each other's eyes, his look told her, something she'd felt for a long time now, if anything goes wrong, know this: *I love you.*

He had gently squeezed her fingers with his massive paw and released them to the fabric of the car seat upholstery. She saw the three of them, yes three of them, Tony included, enter the outer doors to the lobby of the bank and all of her barriers fell away in a flood, rushing all at once, starting low in her stomach then shooting up into her chest and rising still, gaining momentum until her feelings exploded in several large sobs. Tears gushed down her face steadily for several seconds before she knew what was happening. She glanced down at her fingers and remembered the fresh warm touch of Anthony's hand on her own. She looked up and saw two businessmen pull open the outer lobby doors; they exchanged some brief terse words with Stone and moved on down the street. They hadn't gone inside. Perhaps Tony was finally breaking through to Conrad. Please, God. Let him break through. She clambered over the seat and fumbled with the handle, then ran from the car, wiping the tears from her eyes, into the small lobby of the bank. All three of them turned to look at her as she entered, her hair obscuring her face, and she moved beside Anthony, taking his hand, braving in her don't F with me voice, "What's up Clark? Finally get through to these jokers?"

"The doors are locked; the sign says the bank is temporarily closed and from what we can see there are only two tellers inside." Anthony's voice was calm and low.

"We could not have gotten fuckin luckier, I mean this will be a cakewalk." Stone beamed. "Come on, let's make some noise," he said, starting to sing and dance in the front window of the lobby.

Conrad stood close to the doors, pressed up against them, fumbling with something in his hands; every few seconds the jingling of keys told Clara that he continued to work the locksmith's master key ring, attempting to break in. She looked in through the glass door and pulled Anthony back towards the street; he only slightly obliged her before standing his ground against her desire to leave.

"You should get back to the car, Lois. I don't want you here, OK?" Anthony's voice dashed her hopes that they would leave together but she couldn't bring herself to exit. The memory and taste of those feelings that she had in the car a moment ago circumvented her desire for self-preservation. Just then the outside door opened and a man in his late forties, business suit, took a step inside.

Stone turned quickly in his direction. "What the fuck do you want? The bank is closed; can't you read the fuckin' sign?"

He pointed back in the direction of the second set of doors, oblivious to the fact that Conrad's body partially covered the words on the sign as he attempted to jostle the lock while concealing, as best he could, his intentions.

"This is our pocket of air-con, close the god-damn door, it's hotter than shit out there." Stone spoke loudly and was highly animated, all of which added to his intimidating look, but it was wasted, as the man had stepped back outside at the first hint of Stone's harsh language and deranged appearance.

Clara, still grasping Anthony's hand, watched the door slide silently back in place, once more separating them from both the reality of the street and the fantasy of the bank. Here in the lobby they all stood suspended between what was to come and what had already passed. One step away from a world of regret and pain, whichever direction they chose.

Harry

11:12 am. Harry breathed a sigh of relief into his damp, semi-transparent hood. He'd come close, he knew, to being discovered. He'd over-exerted himself on his last attempt to break through the plastic tie and lost his balance, sliding over onto the floor from his propped-up position. This made the air ventilation grill behind him visible and, unfortunately, as he worked to right himself, he drew the attention of one of the thieves. It was difficult to tell, but he moved like the one who had escorted him to the bathroom – that arrogant bastard.

"*You idiot!*" thought Harry as he rolled back onto his ass from his sideways position. He could only hope that he had once again covered the grill with the sheer bulk of his form; if even a corner of the grate were visible, what probably looked like normal arm and hand adjustments behind his back, to relieve tension and relax muscles, would take on the much more accurate look of a man braving escape. Who knows what these ingrates would do to him. Kill him, or maybe they'd wound him and leave him to rot. People who dealt with bombs and hostages, they had to be prepared to kill. He'd read all about it, the mercenary camps in *Soldier of Fortune* magazine, underworld training facilities for just this sort of thing.

He noticed the man moving closer to him, stepping softly over the bodies of the hostages, but as he moved just to the side of the hallway down into the vault, something else attracted his attention and he quickly moved back into his position at the teller station with the other man who stood guard over them all. Now Harry could hear the commotion in the lobby of the bank: it didn't sound like a rescue or the security force, which Harry thought was just as well at this point. At any moment he'd be through his plastic cuffs and into his pant leg for his weapon. The tide would turn, Harry thought, and he went on listening to the ramblings of what sounded like teenagers in the bank lobby. Hell, if he were on duty, they'd be licking their wounds, makin' all that noise in his bank lobby. The disrespect was appalling.

Simon

11:16 am. As the tumbler of the lock fell away, the two young men in the front quickly pulled some nylons over their heads and donned baseball hats before pushing open the doors of the bank and stepping inside. Simon couldn't believe his eyes, and as he fumbled for the silencer of his own weapon he heard one of the two, it was impossible to tell which one, shout, "Step away from the computers and put your hands on your head!"

There was an edgy energy to the request and Simon could now see that these two had indeed drawn weapons: one looked like an automatic, the other a ridiculous wheel gun, something out of an old Cagney movie. Both however looked lethal. Simon's mind raced. This was not possible. Everything, absolutely everything had been considered. What the fuck was happening here? They were at most five minutes away from leaving the bank, totally, absolutely free. Who the hell were these kids to screw them over in a half-assed attempt at a bank robbery? He'd come so far, against his will, against his better judgment, and now, here, in the bank, in the eye of the hurricane, he was sacrificing it all for these people; everything he'd built, everything he was, every moment of his future hinged on the escapades of these deluded kids charging into the bank, women's panty hose over their heads! Simon swallowed hard. An anger was rising in him now, a full and explosive charge of rage curved up his spine, and he, for one of the few times in his life, considered killing. Shooting them all in a deadly barrage of silenced weapons fire. It was a familiar feeling: he'd felt it not long ago, but he couldn't put his finger on when or where. He'd wanted to kill someone. If they were careful to avoid the windows at the front of the bank, Simon felt certain that he and Pete could do the job. Simon closed his mind to the thought. The two moved further into the bank, passing the large banking counter, their footfalls echoing off the green marble floor, off the empty cavern that was the bank's high, impressive cathedral style ceiling, sounding out, each second, like a ticking bomb. Simon and Pete stepped slowly away from the teller stations but kept their hands low, out of the line of sight of the two who had entered.

"Move away! Hands on your head!" came the second blast of commands; it was the same from the first hooded figure, the one with the automatic.

Click, clock, each step closer brought these amateurs, these ignorant idiots, an improved angle from which to view the bank; in another few seconds they would be able to see the first of the hostages, lying hooded and bound on the cool stone floor. The other two only now entered the main room of the bank, standing dazed and uncertain just inside the second set of double doors. They hadn't drawn any weapons nor had they covered their faces, so profound was their apparent disbelief at what was happening. Simon, glancing momentarily at the face of the big guy by the door with a long curly-haired girl at his side, knew that his own face wore the same disjointed, incredulous expression. Those two, they weren't here for money. They wanted to be anywhere else but here, just like him. And that is when Simon finally snapped into action.

"Follow my lead," whispered Simon to Pete, who looked ready to pop them both at the first signal from Simon.

The two masked, would-be bank robbers finally gained the perspective that Simon had been waiting for. They stopped dead in their tracks.

"What the fuck is this?" one said to the other, the wheel gun wavering slightly.

"Holy shit… this is messed up; Stone, what the hell is going on here?" The voice behind the mask staggered away from its previous confidence; the automatic dipped momentarily.

"This…" said Simon, raising his weapon and pointing it at his target, the one clutching the automatic, "this, you absolutely unlucky shits, is a bank robbery."

Pete raised his weapon in accordance with Simon's actions and targeted the other veiled bandit, Stone.

They glanced at each other. Disbelieving. Even through the mesh of the nylon, Simon could see the flashing glaze of tears. The shoulders dropped, the weapons wavered.

Confused. Bewildered. Alone. They rocked uneasily in their shoes.

Simon stepped to the side very slowly, as they had been trained to do; Pete also took a step to the side, away from Simon. Together they were too easy to pick off should a finger slip.

"Now listen carefully." Simon eased a little more to his left; his back now faced the L-shaped hallway which led to the vault. "If you want to live, slowly put down your weapons and step through the teller's gate."

The masked men stood unmoving, unspeaking.

"Do it now," Simon's voice commanded but did not rise in volume. He needed to give them this out, this one chance to defuse the lethal reality of their predicament. If they were left with no options, then, Simon knew, they might follow that hopeless feeling they felt right now to their destruction.

Pete stood ready, now a good nine feet away from Simon's position. The half-wall that the tellers worked at still stood between them and the two hidden faces. Simon was only a step or two from the teller's gate.

"Nice and slow," said Simon, even though they had made no motion to give up their weapons.

The two at the back of the bank towards the doors could have left, but they were frozen in place. This was taking too long; at any moment another customer could try the doors, they would open now and the plan would be shot to hell.

"Do it now!" Simon yelled.

All three of them jumped, Pete included. Tears were streaming down the face of one nylon-hooded figure, pooling at the bottom of his jaw line, while the other, Stone, remained nearly motionless. Simon could see the white-knuckled grip on the automatic, the tension on the trigger. And then, finally, they began, almost in unison, to bend down very slowly at the knees. Simon and Pete kept their weapons trained following them down. Simon

109

knew they were thinking, considering their choices and possible acts of rebellion. He would be thinking the same thing, but they had to come to the same conclusion, life later was better than death now. There was, however, a desperation in the movements and look of the nameless thief, the one with the automatic. An exasperated heave of the shoulders, like this was his one shot at a better life. That sort of desperation was a dangerous prospect and Simon was careful to keep his gun trained on him through the entirety of his movements. They reached the floor and moved to place the weapons down in front of them as instructed.

Simon could hear the footfalls of someone walking down the corridor behind him, coming from the vault. Perhaps Grier had heard the strange sounds that were emanating from the front and was coming to investigate. In any case, reinforcements would help to control this explosive situation.

"Stone," said the other masked man. Automatic touching the floor but not yet released from his fingertips.

"Don't do it!" yelled Simon.

"Get out while you can!" he screamed, rolling forward to the base of the teller station. Simon's weapon discharged three times, missing his target by the narrowest of margins before losing sight of him at the base of the teller wall. Beside Simon, the air was punctured by the sound of silenced gunfire; Pete had a clear line to his target. As Stone ran and dove for the cover of the banking counter, his back exploded in several small fountains of blood. Simon knew he'd be dead before his body stopped sliding across the floor.

The other assailant, who had rolled forward and was momentarily out of view, suddenly stood bolt upright only about six feet from where Simon stood. He had crawled along the front of the teller station wall so that when he finally did come up he was well over from where Simon and Pete had expected him to be. Even before Simon could see him, he was reacting to the loud screaming sound of automatic weapons fire; the wall above him was getting popped and small pieces of wood and stone began to rain from on high. Simon dove to the left, trying to land behind a small desk next to the open hall that led towards the vault. Bullets from the automatic streamed by him into the wall. The window in the manager's office shattered in a maelstrom of glass and steel. Pete dove to his right, managing to slide over the top of the teller counter, out onto the open floor, and as he performed this feat, he tagged the masked man twice in the back of his shoulder, sending him spinning away from Simon. Pete had only a few seconds to scamper under the customer coffee table as bullets began to shred the wood. A moment later, Simon rose from his position behind the money machine, his weapon ready; the click, click, click of the empty gun being fired over and over and over again rippled through the silence. Then, pulling off his nylon mask, the young thief finally fell to the floor, bleeding heavily from his left shoulder.

It was Grier, Simon recalled. It was Grier he had considered killing. Grier…back in Thailand. A million miles from this place.

Patrick

11:21 am. Patrick could barely hear the request that was being made by Simon, so loud were the moans and groans of the hostages, the whimpers and outright bawls, as many were still wrapped in the terror that the gunfight had caused. The woman that he had been attending to had, he was quite certain, passed out, her panic becoming too much for her body to bear. There was also the possibility that she had been killed by a stray bullet during the melee, but he had found her pulse and it was strong and true. From what he could gather from the last few minutes, another group had entered the bank, not realizing that it was already being robbed, with the intention of robbing it themselves. The odds against this happening had to be astronomical, no one would ever believe this. Especially not Melissa, not at least until she saw it on the evening news. Patrick was certain that people had been shot, given the request for assistance being made.

111

"Anyone with any medical training please make yourself known." It was his "acquaintance," the robber's voice alright and for the first time since he'd heard it, Patrick sensed desperation. That tone, barely containing its urgency, told Patrick that something was terribly, terribly wrong.

He then heard, fairly close by, the hood being removed from one of the hostages as well as the twang of the plastic being cut open in order to release the hands. His "friend" was asking a volunteer if they understood that he would have to kill them if they tried anything. No other warnings were needed. He could hear them being shuffled down the corridor towards the vault.

"Margaret, let us know what you need," Patrick heard the voice say.

He remembered that one of the tellers, a demure slight woman, had a name tag which read "Margaret." It would have to be her. Patrick only remembered it because it seemed likely that she was going to be the one helping him with his transactions. That memory burned with normalcy and Patrick pushed it away: nothing from the moment the bank was taken felt at all familiar or sane. The fact that they were trying to save someone meant they were willing to risk discovery, perhaps unable to move the wounded person. There was no way that the shots being fired within the bank could not have been heard from the street. There was still the chance that no one would react, that no call would be made, but the thieves would be fools to expect that. Once the shooting had stopped the barked-out orders had come fast and furious: "Lock the doors" and "Carry him into the back" along with "These two need ties, unless one of them can do anything for him." From the sound of things, these orders were being carried out without a word; hopefully, and especially with the impending arrival of the law, this would all be over soon. One way or another.

Chapter 10

Margaret

Margaret Sawyer awoke, as usual, to the first signs of light slanting through the half opened blinds, touching the edge of the lace curtains her parents had donated to the room. She was finding it difficult to breathe as she struggled through sleep to open her eyes. There was a weight on her. It was Kevin. Slowly, her senses and memory returned. Kevin had been working the afternoon ride for the Phoenix Fire Department this week. He hated that shift. She hated it, too. Afternoons meant he finished at 11pm and had plenty of time to hit the local bar. The oppressive heat wasn't helping either, just another excuse to keep the drinks coming. She wasn't sure what time he had arrived home, nor what the damage was from his night of drink. The last thing she wanted to do was wake him. Rising early allowed her some important time to recover and prepare for the day ahead. He was a deep sleeper, even without the bottled tranquilizer he reeked of.

Slowly, Maggie slid onto the floor, leaving her snoring, intoxicated husband on the bed. She slipped on her robe and closed the blinds, leaving the room in darkness. Her hands were numb today and doing up the cord on her robe was a chore. In the bathroom she noticed a scrape on her hip and some new bruises on her thighs. She closed her eyes and rubbed her hands down her legs, as the evening's events came rushing back to her, like the release of the bulls at Pamplona, run for your life, the terror replaying painfully in her mind.

Kevin arrived home late. She vaguely remembers hearing him trip on the shoes in the foyer, but then everything was quiet and she hoped that he had simply passed out in the hall. Relaxing, she drifted again off to sleep. It was 3:57 am when he arrived at their bedroom door; he had a fresh bottle of whiskey in his hand from the stock that he kept hidden somewhere in the recesses of the house. She chose the only option available to her. She stayed still and quiet and kept her breathing slow and deep. There was always the chance that seeing her asleep would deter him from whatever he had in mind. She chanted silently to herself. A mantra that was supposed to subconsciously put him to sleep in the bed beside her without incident. *"One for sorrow, two for joy, three for a girl, four for a boy. Five for sleep, six for hold, seven for secrets, never told."* She had tried this before and the results were not perfect, but she could swear that it had worked. But, not this time.

"Whore!" he barked so loudly and suddenly that it made her jump. She struggled to maintain control of her body, frantically considering her next move. She would have to be deaf to not have heard that. Gauging his level of intoxication by the stench issuing on his breath through a single word, she decided that he was unaware of his volume and continued to feign sleep, picking up the mantra in her mind. *"Five for sleep, six for hold, seven for secrets, never told. One for sorrow..."*

Kevin lurched through the door, dropping the whiskey bottle in the process. She heard it rolling on the hardwood and the soft gurgle of the contents seeping into the cracks. He didn't notice and she heard him fumbling with his clothes, groaning and cursing under his breath. Buttons hit the floor like distant gunshots. Perhaps he was getting ready for bed. Breathe. In. Out. In 2, 3, 4. Out 2, 3, 4.

While struggling with his pants, Kevin fell heavily onto the bed, narrowly missing her leg, and causing the bed to squeal in protest against the added weight. He started to chortle to himself. His maniacal laughter sounded deranged, like the bellows from some hideous childhood nightmare. It was the laugh of a man gone mad. Margaret's mind raced. She had to do something. Perhaps she could distract him somehow.

Slowly she turned onto her back and moaned softly into the darkness of the room, "Kev, honey, is that you?" Her voice was barely above a whisper in the tone of one still half asleep. Her answer was swift and painful as something flew through the shadows of the room and scorched the bare skin on her thighs. Then Kevin was there in full view, standing over her with his belt in his left hand held above his head, his right hand returning from the bedside lamp he had switched on. She barely had time to notice before the belt again bit hard against her skin. It burned with the ferocity of the Arizona sun. Without thinking she rolled over onto her stomach and grabbed for the far edge of the bed. He lunged at her and the bed sprung them both to the floor. Margaret landed heavily on her side facing the underside of their bed. Kevin careened off the wall and landed with a thud somewhere behind her, cursing and searching for the belt he had lost in the fall.

Margaret could feel the buckle digging into her hip and she quickly pulled it out and pushed it under the bed as far as she could before he grabbed her shoulder and pulled her to face him. His eyes were bloodshot and half-closed and his breath reeked of cigars and whiskey. He stared at her for what seemed like an eternity, his eyes filled with rage. He grabbed fistfuls of her hair, rested his unshaven cheek against hers, and slowly relaxed his grip. She almost believed that he had passed out, until he spoke to her.

"You're so beautiful," he slurred raggedly into her hair. "You know how much I love you, right?" He sounded like a child and pulled back to acknowledge her response. Margaret nodded in silence as his hands disentangled themselves from her hair and began to roam in earnest over the rest of her body. She looked at

115

the lace curtains fluttering in the breeze from the vent below and closed her eyes. Although they had hung in her childhood room they still had the starchy, clean look of much newer drapery. They appeared to be in pristine condition, but like other things in Maggie's life, they harbored a secret. As a teen, influenced by her peers she had decided to take up smoking. She was having one in her bedroom when she heard her mother on the stairs and in her haste to pitch the butt out the window, the cigarette had caught the edge of the curtain and burned a nasty hole clean through. Her mother, a long-time smoker, was not suspicious when she entered the room, but Maggie positioned herself at the window anyway, while her mother asked her what she wanted for dinner. After answering she spent the next three hours repairing the hole. Maggie carefully cut a strip from the bottom to the rod, painstakingly hemmed the edge and re-hung the slightly slimmer version. No one ever knew about it.

Kevin was finished with her and pulled himself slowly onto the bed. Maggie rose from the floor several minutes after him, pulled her nightgown down and limped to her side of the bed. He was already snoring by the time she lowered her pounding head to the pillow. She cocooned herself in the sheets, but it did little to warm her body. She felt cold, frozen, and the very surface of the sun would have done little to warm her, let alone a spring Arizona heat wave.

She could be pretty. In the bathroom mirror she catches glimpses of a pretty young girl, but when she tries to focus on that image it melts away into a tired, hard-looking, middle-aged woman. One with no regrets and no dreams.

It wasn't always like this. Margaret had inherited an exceptional business sense and love of precision and process from her successful father, and in college she had thrown herself into business and accounting courses with passion. She was driven both by the expectations of her parents and her own ideas about how she could use her abilities to change the world. Her friends joked that she would make CEO by graduation the way she was going, but fate had another destiny in mind. The moment she discovered that she was pregnant, she swore to herself that she would never leave him, that she would try her best to make things work. Kevin had been her only love since high school and he too harbored large dreams, obscured now by the passage of time and his love alcohol. He was enrolled in a pre-med program that had not been easy for him despite his high grades. By the time they discovered the unexpected pregnancy, Kevin had decided to move into an easier and faster medical technician program. He claimed that it would allow him to learn the same things, just give him a diploma a lot sooner, and despite the protests of Margaret and his family, he made the switch.

An above average family up-bringing on the right side of the tracks secured the match. That, and the unexpected news of a pre-marital pregnancy. Neither family would stand for any kind of scandal and the wedding was hurried under the illusion of many months of planning. The society players were there. She had never been so happy, so in love and full of joy as that day. Sixteen years ago. That 20-year-old, carefree kid had disappeared. Now Maggie spent the majority of her time at home tip-toeing around with her fingers crossed.

Maggie stepped gingerly into the shower and tried her best to wash away the memories of yet another brutal night. She'd become so used to it all. Sometimes she thought that perhaps it wasn't the best way to cope with things, but it wasn't the burden it once was. She had long ago come to terms with the fact that this was, indeed her life. She had made the choices that brought her to this place and she would make the best of the consequences those choices afforded her.

It was almost a game, like street vendors with playing cards in a battle pitting the mind against a talented sleight of hand. Find the queen. Keep your eye on the cards. The beatings were frequent, but not severe, she told herself. He was smart enough to attack areas that would not be easily noticed, since he too needed to keep up appearances. She was never seen with a black eye or reddened throat. A closer look might have revealed the true color of her bruised thighs, carefully hidden beneath nylons and tailored suits.

117

The 8th rib on her left side, broken awkwardly in a skirmish years ago, had not healed properly and caused a small dimple under knit tops, so she kept to blouses and bulky over-sized sweaters. She could not grow nails on her big toes over burn scars inflicted during one of the worst episodes, so she simply never wore open-toed shoes. The cover-up was an art. Her family and friends were totally unaware of the hell to which she was chained. A hell that she'd learned to manage. She could put up with anything. She understood that for her, things were as they were meant to be.

Margaret stepped from the shower feeling numb, but normal. She had dealt with the demons and would never consciously relate the events of the evening to herself again. It was over. This was a new day. She toweled vigorously, reddening her normally pale skin, then slipped into her bathrobe. She meticulously mopped up the water from the floor and the steam that lay on the mirror and faucets. It was nearly 7 am and she had a few things to take care of before her shift began at the bank. She looked forward to the days that she worked.

She paused in the hallway outside her bedroom and heard Kevin's soft snoring. He would likely sleep until after she left for work. She continued down the hall to the spare room where she kept her clothes and chose a comfortable skirt suit, dark nylons and flat shoes. She laid the clothes on the bed and paused to look at her reflection in the full-length mirror.

The room behind her had been intended for the nursery. They had purchased this house immediately after the wedding when things were still new and wonderful. She had been so excited about the pregnancy, despite the hassle it had caused with her parents and the fact that she was forced to drop out of college to have the baby. It was one of those strange gifts, that you didn't know you wanted until you got it and, suddenly, you couldn't imagine life without it. Kevin had been so thrilled. He was all puffed up, the proud, soon-to-be father. They made plans decades into the future for themselves and their family. The miscarriage had been devastating to them both. Now she wonders if it simply was not meant to be. They had never used protection and she had never become pregnant again. The doctors told her that nothing was wrong with either of them physically. Eventually they just stopped talking about it. Stopped hoping. If it was meant to be, Maggie believed, then it would be. Still, every time she entered this room she thought of what it might have been like to be a mother. What her children would have looked like, or what they would have grown up to become.

Unable to continue her studies, even after the miscarriage, due to strong advice from her husband and parents, Margaret had dedicated herself to helping Kevin achieve the best from his work. He was never one to put very much effort into anything. He was always charged up at the beginning of a project, but quickly lost interest. Maggie worked hard learning everything she could through Kevin's studies. She found the material and ethics of life and death situations intoxicating, and by the time Kevin graduated she was equally qualified to take on a position in the field. He found work immediately with the Arizona Fire Department and quickly learned that there was more to the job than the actual work. He had aspirations of promotion, but was a poor politician. Margaret was not. She took charge of the campaign to move her husband forward. She threw herself into volunteer duties and was Kevin's social coordinator. They were at every event that would provide visibility for him, and eventually things came together. After only two and a half years, he was named the section leader for the West End. Kevin both resented and respected his wife's abilities, and the enormous help they provided him. Margaret was exceedingly proud of the results her efforts had garnered, and the reputation she had fostered in the community.

Grabbing her clothes from the bed, Maggie slid out of the room and down the back stairs into the kitchen. The sunshine was brilliant this morning and it made her smile to herself. The temperature would be steadily rising outside – the heat wave was expected to continue for another three or four days – but her home was air conditioned and well-ventilated. She popped bread into the toaster and put the kettle on. She set her favorite mug, a gift from her sister, adorned with multicolored hearts, and a saucer on the counter, and got the milk from the fridge. She filled the saucer and opened the back door.

"Right on time, as always, Fred," Maggie cooed to the large orange tomcat stretched out in the sunshine on the welcome mat. Fred purred and immediately began rubbing her legs in earnest.

"Hungry, are you?" she asked. Fred gazed at her with the expression of dignity and pride reserved for royalty and meandered down the steps into the garden. Maggie followed, laughing at his air. Kevin would never allow her pets in the house, so when Fred showed up unexpectedly in their garbage cans a year earlier, Maggie had set about making him as close to a pet as she could. She made a place for him to sleep in the shed at the back of the yard and each morning he was given a saucer of milk on the patio, away from the windows and doors of the house. In good weather, when Kevin was at work, she and Fred would spend hours in each other's company in the yard. He seemed to sense Kevin's discomfort with animals and had never made an appearance in his presence. Maggie found it remarkable that they had managed to keep things going this long.

Out of sight behind the hedge separating the walk from the patio, Fred paused expectantly and mewed his impatience.

"Yes, your highness." Margaret bowed gracefully before setting the saucer down. He purred loudly in appreciation, giving her leg one last rub before lapping up the milk. She scratched behind his ears and was calmed by his contented vibrations. She couldn't imagine a morning without Fred. He was the closest friend that she had and she was grateful for it.

It wasn't that she was antisocial or unfriendly; she just never formed strong attachments. It seemed right that way. Actually, she never felt that she was missing out on anything and preferred to keep acquaintances rather than friends. Acquaintances share only the most superficial parts of themselves, the always positive and smiling surface stuff. Friends, on the other hand, share everything and she could never burden anyone with her problems. It was just easier she thought, for everyone.

120

Fred, of course, was the exception to the rule. Maggie realized that she had been dawdling a bit with him this morning and in the distance she could hear something familiar that took a moment to register. The whistle from the kettle was screaming in the kitchen. Damn! She raced around the hedge. How long had it been going off? How could she have forgotten to remove that whistle stopper? She hurried to the door, but stopped dead at the bottom step. The whistle had stopped. She stayed perfectly still. From inside the kitchen came a barrage of noise. Slamming, smashing, thudding, and then silence. She heard Kevin stomp across the floor and the door slam at the bottom of the kitchen stairs. She held her breath and waited a few more moments before opening the door.

It was amazing the damage he could do in such a short period of time. The milk carton had been flung against the refrigerator and the contents were now pooling slowly on the floor. The instant coffee container had been thrown violently from the counter and there were crystals of java everywhere, the crumbled tin just visible under the table. There was a dent in the cupboard under the sink, likely the victim of an enraged foot, and in the middle of the room were the remains of her mug. She ran to the broken bits of porcelain, her bare feet caking up with milk and coffee. It was beyond repair, but she carefully picked up the shattered pieces and held them in her hands. Turning each piece over and over, looking for the next one in the pattern. She flopped onto the floor, gingerly holding the tiny pieces in her hands, and began to cry.

It startled her. Margaret couldn't remember the last time that tears had blurred her vision and stained her cheeks. What's the problem? It's just a cup. It's just a cup... It had been much more than that. A carefully chosen gift from her little sister after the miscarriage. It had been a very sweet and touching memento from Olivia, who was only seven at the time. Margaret hadn't realized until this moment just how much it meant to her. She glanced at her warped reflection in the stainless steel door of the fridge, before doggedly beginning the clean-up. Somehow she knew that if she remained on the floor, clutching the remnants of that gift, she might never find the strength to get up again. Something inside

121

of her had broken with that cup. Deep down in the depths of her heart and soul, she could feel it.

As she was tying the garbage bag, full of soggy paper towels and coffee, the phone rang. She dropped the bag immediately and had the receiver in her hands before the second ring.

"Hello," she said breathlessly, listening to the sounds of the house, hoping he hadn't heard the phone.

"Hey!" a cheerful voice responded. "How's my big sister on this fine and glorious spring day?" It was Olivia. Margaret's face softened into a smile.

"Liv!" she gushed, "I'm good. You sound like shit though, what's up?"

"Nothin'," Olivia responded, her voice sort of rough. She coughed slightly before continuing, "Just a little bit hung," she confessed and then yawned loudly.

"A little bit hung, huh?" Maggie's voice took on the tone of a mother about to chastise her naughty child.

"Oh, Mags," Liv drawled through another yawn, "I had good reason to celebrate last night."

"Oh? And what is that, exactly," the older sibling demanded. Margaret always smiled when Olivia called her Mags. That was how she learned her name as a child. Margaret was much too demanding for a toddler and the nickname had stuck between the two of them only.

"I'm done," Olivia stated with barely contained excitement.

"Done?" Maggie inquired.

"Done, Mags!" her sister replied. "I aced my final exam yesterday. I am done! Bring on the summer!"

"You know, Liv," Margaret began, "I spoke to Mom yesterday and she told me that you weren't finished your exams until next week."

There was a momentary pause on the other end of the line. Margaret already knew what was coming. Olivia had a tendency to be less than honest with her parents. She had a unique relationship with them, born strictly from her own exuberance for life and need for freedom. Margaret could never have pulled the kinds of stunts

122

that Olivia had in her first eighteen years, let alone gotten away with them. Fourteen years her junior, Olivia had been an unexpected addition to the Naismith family and Margaret had always had a special bond with her much younger sibling. Eventually, Olivia became the child that Maggie never had and she loved her zest for life and adventurous spirit more than Liv would ever understand.

"Mags," Liv responded in exasperation, after regaining her composure, "Mom must have things a little mixed up. I told her that I would get my *results* next week." The impish tone of the sarcasm in her voice made Margaret laugh out loud. Olivia couldn't help giggling as well.

"I see," Maggie laughed. "So, what's in store for the world this week, courtesy of Miss Olivia Naismith?"

"Well," Olivia said excitedly, "a group of us are heading to the canyon to do some rock climbing and camping out for the week. One of my roommates has an uncle doing a dig out there and we will be staying with his team. It is going to be so fun!"

"Hmm… I can see why you would want to avoid sharing so many details with Mom. What do you know about rock climbing, anyway?" Maggie couldn't help but be concerned for Liv's safety.

"I've been practising on the climbing wall at school for the last few weeks and I picked up all my gear yesterday. It will be a blast! There will be plenty of experienced climbers with us and I know my limitations, Mags, so don't worry," Liv finished with a note of genuine affection.

Margaret sighed in resignation. It wasn't like she could talk Olivia out of it anyway, and she would likely have an incredible time. Adventurous she was, reckless she wasn't.

"When do you leave for this little adventure?" Maggie inquired, shaking grinds of coffee from her robe.

"Tomorrow morning." Olivia slurred through another yawn. "I want to see you before I go; can you fit me into your busy schedule?" There was a hint of sarcasm in Olivia's request. Margaret, though never too busy to spend time with her sister, did keep pretty busy between work and various activities.

123

"That sounds great… I am working today until four, so why don't you meet me downtown and we'll grab some dinner somewhere?"

"Great. Why don't you have Kevin meet us as well? I haven't seen my brother-in-law in ages."

"He's on afternoons this week, so it'll be just the two of us," Maggie was relieved that the excuse was genuine. She hated lying to Olivia more than anyone, but she wanted to avoid any relationship that was more than cursory between her baby sister and her husband.

"I swear, Mags, I am wondering if Kevin even exists. He is never available when I am around," Olivia joked. "Or perhaps you are just worried that I will run off with him using my youthful charms." They laughed together.

Margaret could picture her little sister, sitting sideways on a huge lounger chair she had insisting on pulling out of someone's garbage for her dorm room. Even though she went to school in town, their parents had encouraged her desire to live on campus. Their parents had even pulled a few strings to make it so, having had a very trying four years ushering her through high school. They were ready for some peace and quiet and Olivia was ready to soar. The sisters looked nothing like each other. Perhaps it was the age difference, but for all the lanky height that Margaret had inherited from her leggy mother, Olivia was portly and plump. Everything about her was round and though she was only slightly overweight, she looked much plumper than that. Her round face was always flushed and framed by wispy blond hair. She had large brown eyes that took her years to grow into and a smile that lit her entire face. In old family pictures she bore a striking resemblance to their great-grandmother on the Naismith side. In contrast, Margaret was all legs, tall and thin. Her hair was brown and straight, where Liv's held some natural wavy curl. Maggie's eyes were greenish yellow, sort of washed out and bland like her pale complexion, and she had her father's long thin nose. She was rather out of proportion, she thought, but had learned to use fashion, style and cut to her advantage with her mother's help.

Olivia had never indulged in such trivialities, which explained why every outfit she owned looked something like a potato sack. Maggie had tried to talk her into other things, but Olivia was interested only in comfort and cost. It didn't matter. She looked great in that sloppy gear. It totally suited her personality, which was also in opposition to the rest of the family. Margaret was her parents' child, without any doubt. She mostly took their advice to heart and lived the life that they had planned for her. Olivia was the rebel, going her own way and on her own terms from the time she was a tot. For all the embarrassment it afforded their parents, Maggie was invigorated by Olivia's escapades and lived vicariously through her many adventures.

"It's settled then. Meet me outside the bank just after four and we'll decide where to go from there."

"Great. That gives me plenty of time to nap." Olivia yawned loudly again.

"I'm looking forward to it, Liv."

"Me too, Mags. See ya."

"Bye," Margaret said softly. She hung the receiver back in its place and stood still for a moment thinking about her upcoming evening with Olivia. It was exactly what she needed. She resumed her clean-up and took the garbage outside, retrieving Fred's empty dish on the way back in. He was nowhere to be seen, having likely found a sunny spot to doze away the day.

Margaret dressed quietly for work in the dining room where she'd placed her clothes. The job at the bank was a mindless affair but it got her out of the house, and after eight years she'd gotten pretty good at it. The shift manager would be retiring in another ten months and she'd thought about applying for his job. She needed a challenge in her life, something to focus on, something new. She left Kevin a note on her way out, reminding him of her shift at the bank and directions for re-heating some leftovers. She slipped her shoes into a bag and donned her runners for a leisurely walk into work. It took about an hour, but she wouldn't miss the opportunity on this sunny morning, despite the heat. She would have her sister drive her home after their date. She felt a twinge of

125

rebellion as she left the house, still heartbroken over the loss of her sister's gift. She saw herself slam the door shut on her way out, craving an outlet for her frustration, but the cost... the cost was unthinkable. Instead, Margaret pulled the door gently until she heard the soft click of the lock, turned and headed down the walkway on her way to work.

Chapter 11

Simon

Grier was dead. His eyes, empty and cold, stared blankly up at the ceiling, and his face, at least the mask he still bore, possessed a macabre hollowness with the mouth slightly ajar and the lips curled back into a meek smile. Margaret had managed to resuscitate him momentarily, doing so probably for fear of her life more than anything else. Carl, Kayla, Alan and Simon hovered over her as she worked to bring him back from death's door. Pete was ordered to remain in the main room and watch the hostages. After several cycles of CPR, when it was just becoming clear that he was gone, shockingly Grier's eyes had opened, blood trickling down his chin. Then his body rose slightly off the marble and they all had the premonition that he was going to stand up, flick the dirt and blood off his suit, and ask them what the hell they were looking at, so startling and quick was his convulsion. It was, however, Grier's final effort to suck down into his lungs what would be his last breath. His eyes frantically searched the faces that hung above him for some help, some reassurance that he was going to be alright. He locked onto the eyes of Margaret and spit out some barely intelligible words, "Thake tho thoney." Then he was gone. Kayla sighed. Save for that one sound, the rest of them were still. Silent.

"Take the money?" Kayla said, echoing Grier's words. She looked alarmed initially but as Margaret continued to work on the lifeless body, her attitude quickly shifted to indifference.

"Sounded like that, didn't it?" replied Alan. He had stepped back when Grier spasmed; besides that, his expression remained unaltered throughout.

"Screw him. Load his body into the back and let's get on with it," Kayla said, unaffected by the death of their leader.

To Simon's surprise, she was immediately backed by Carl, who piped up saying, "Kayla's right, let's get outta here, casualties of war my friends, casualties of war."

Carl was thrown off balance when he had discovered that Grier had been shot. For the first time in many months, he was without comment. He'd stood still beside them all as Margaret hammered Grier's chest and performed C.P.R. in the regular rhythmic fashion of a veteran paramedic. He hadn't seen this coming, but now that it was upon them all, he felt compelled to reassure them of the plan's inevitable success. Carl understood that in the wake of Grier's death, Simon would be the next best person to lead them to freedom. And so, after only a momentary pause in conversation, he placed a hand on Simon's shoulder.

"Well, dear boy, we are slaves to your intellect; you have only to ask and thy will be done."

Simon met his eyes, returning Carl's calm gaze.

Alan nodded at Simon. "I love a touch of irony." He grinned.

"As do I," Kayla agreed. "As do I. We're on board, what's the plan?" Her eyes expressed both relief and concern.

With Carl's verbal support, any thought that Simon could not fill the void of Grier's death was dismissed. Simon would give them the best possible chance at escape. The bloody melee with the college kids had certainly changed the dynamics of this job, especially knowing that one kid was dead and another was dying in the main room even as they spoke. Time was a commodity they could not afford to waste.

Simon knelt on one knee beside the body; on the other side of him sat a bloodied and exhausted Margaret Sawyer, the teller. She'd done a remarkable job. She had given it everything she had to bring him back from the brink, as if Grier was some relation to her, even if it was only to hear him mutter the words of a money-grubbing, sociopathic killer. Simon looked contemplative, thoughtful and reflective, formulating the best possible way to proceed. They all knew this and so they obliged him with the time and silence he required. Finally, he rose and issued a series of short commands.

"Alright. Here's the deal." Simon spoke directly to Kayla and Alan. "Cuff Margaret to Grier; she's right-handed so cuff her left hand. We'll need one of the hostages, his name's Patrick, Will can point him out. Bring him back here along with all the women's purses you can find. Cuff him to Grier's other hand. OK? Got it?"

Margaret, as exhausted as she was, looked startled by the words she was hearing. Had she not done everything she could to save this dying man? Simon, seeing her growing despair and bitterness, knelt down very close to where she sat slumped against the wall. "Margaret. You can help everyone here, especially yourself. I know about the bruises."

Margaret pulled down awkwardly on her skirt.

"I know that someone, most likely someone you cannot escape, hurts you. And I'm offering you an out, if you'll help us." Simon's words were clear and measured.

For Margaret, this was all too much and she felt hot tears roll out of her eyes and others begin to form.

"You know this man is wearing a mask. I need you to take that mask off with extreme care and put it on the man that my associate here will bring back. I know you are an expert at applying make-up, and the job you do will allow everyone to get out of here safely. No one else will be hurt. Margaret; we are thieves, not killers. Before you begin I want you to put this on."

Simon took out his knife and cut away at Grier's shirt, exposing the tight black Lycra skin. He cut the suit at the midsection, then turned Grier on his side to access the back. Simon pulled the top portion of the Lycra off Grier. Carl held Grier's legs down.

"There's enough money in here to restart your life," Simon said, pulling the lycra top right side out. Carl positioned Grier on his back close to Margaret, then mopped up Grier's blood in the shirt they'd taken off of him.

Margaret's eyes swelled at the mention of the money: shocked and appalled by the suggestion.

"Take off your jacket and your blouse." Simon instructed, motioning for Kayla to help her.

Margaret was too exhausted to protest. Kayla drew a quick breath when she saw a deep ugly bruise on Margaret's back. A black and purple nebula of pain. Margaret touched her own shoulder protectively, embarrassed by the mark.

"Just for a second," Kayla assured her.

With the blouse off, Kayla lifted Margaret's arms up over her head and Simon pulled on the heavy dark black Lycra top. Although the suit hung somewhat off her smaller, frailer bones, once her blouse and jacket were back on, she looked surprisingly normal, twenty pounds heavier but still fairly proportional.

"You have nothing to lose, Margaret; if you are discovered you can tell everyone that this was forced upon you; if you decide you cannot live with the thought of being free from the one who abuses you, you can come clean. If, however, you see this as you should, as a chance to start your life again, this suit will allow you to do so. The bank is insured; it's nobody's money, Margaret. It's freedom. You can think on it while you are applying the mask to Patrick. Like you, he is innocent in all of this. If the police discover that he is a fraud because his mask is coming off or looks in any way unrealistic, you can be sure that he'll be shot and killed. Do the best job possible, for him. For everyone."

Simon stood up slowly while Kayla slid the plastic tie around the wrist of Margaret's left hand, binding her to the dead body below. He seemed for a moment to hang there, considering his next words, analyzing their options, weighing out consequences.

"Sebastian and I will go into the back and get loaded up; let's not forget we have this thing planned out way beyond the point we're at now. Pete will stay top side and watch over the rest." Simon's orders were just that, there was no mistaking that he was now in command. The others accepted it. They knew his instructions were meant to save their lives.

"You two," pointing to Kayla and Alan, "once you're done setting Margaret up, I want you to walk out the side doors and fade. That was the plan, I don't see why it should change now, except for the obvious," Simon said, glancing down at the dead man that used to be Vincent Grier.

Alan nodded his agreement, as did Kayla.

"Alright, go, go, go," Simon said as he marched off in the direction of the vault with Carl.

Grier

11:24 am. Grier felt himself floating a long way off. What sounds there were seemed to echo in a canyon miles below him. His body felt weightless as if in a dream, but all around him was a vast ocean of emptiness, so much so that he felt even if there were light, the shadows that existed here would swallow it, reducing it to a faint glow before devouring it entirely. It felt not altogether unpleasant. It was time to sleep.

Then the darkness gave way to sensation, time to wake up, and as he felt consciousness return so too did the pains of his utterly wrecked mortal body, broken and bloodied as it was. Light came flooding into his eyes as he looked up and out of them once again. Then the memory of the gunshot found him, filling him with the knowledge of his imminent doom.

"*Who is this woman?*" his mind inquired.

Behind her and to the sides were the familiar faces of his companions. They looked shocked and bewildered, as if they had been startled by something, but by what he could not imagine just now. The money! They had to get out with the money, but somehow, he didn't think they had a chance, so long as he lay on

131

the floor dying. He tried to move, to rise, but found that he could not. Why had they bound him here? Was this a mutiny of some sort? Then he felt the whisper of consciousness begin to falter; his eyes grew heavy but did not close. I must lead them. And with a Herculean effort he sucked down both air and blood into his lungs to issue his orders. He felt as though something was pulling him down into himself. There were so many words to put by his tongue just now, and then he fancied to look once more upon this unknown woman; this must be my savior.

And so Grier sputtered his last words, "Thank you honey," through his bloodied throat and mouth.

He could sense fluid in his throat. Water, he thought, but I'm not thirsty. Then the light faded and was gone. He could no longer see, although he didn't think that he had closed his eyes. Time to sleep, was Grier's last thought. Lights out.

Harry

11:26 am. The plastic pulled at Harry's skin; with the fat stubby ends of his fingers Harry could feel the worn edges of the tie on his wrists. Surely he was well over halfway through the blasted plastic by now. It was exhausting work for the rotund security guard who considered the walk from his vehicle to the bank's staff room and back again at the beginning and the end of his shifts to be a major part of his daily physical activity.

Harry sniffed at the air. He'd always had an acute sense of smell and there could be no question that what he smelled was blood. As a child, he was constantly tasked to prove the unfathomable accuracy of his barrel-like nostrils. His peers had him touted as some sort of evolutionary throwback. He remembered being able to actually smell the difference between Coke and Pepsi, a feat that earned him not only a moderate amount of respect but also a few bucks every now and again. The day that his dog Bullet, a childhood companion, had died, he'd come home from school and into the house. He remembered his mother's expression when he asked through his stinging tears when Bullet

132

had passed. His mom had no idea; she'd let the dog out for a pee an hour or so earlier. Harry had smelt death that day for the first time, and now, bound and partially blinded on the floor of his workplace, he could smell it again.

The tension in the bank was palpable, the words clear and clean. The frenetic, disbelief in the voices of the much younger, much more chaotic thieves was unmistakable. Shock, as surely as if an electrical charge had passed through them. Harry could feel their rising momentum, could almost hear the scales of choice slide tenuously back and forth as these new ones, the young ones, decided how to proceed. And in the firefight that followed, Harry knew that those youthful voices would end up silenced, not that he was sorry for them – after all, they too had come to take what was not theirs –but Harry felt something tight swell up in his chest; it felt like remorse. The death of the young brought him back to his brother, taken too soon, too young, too innocent. Damn them! He'd make them pay.

In the aftermath, Harry could only pick out certain words of conversation because the noise from the hostages peaked into a crescendo of pleas, grovels and sobs. If he had been ready, he should have ripped open the plastic tie when the guns were being discharged. That was the time, the perfect instant when he could have plied all his muscle in the interest of freedom. In the interest of vengeance and retribution. The melee ended so quickly that Harry had only the time to curse his indecision. Was his life to consist of anything other than regret? He was uncertain how this question would be answered, but he knew that one possible response lay buried in a small holster about twelve inches above his left ankle.

Looking across the bank lobby, he could see one thief, pacing, breathing irregularly, fidgeting, scanning left then right, towards the street then back down the hallway towards the vault. The other had disappeared from view. As the moans and the cries of the hostages began to subside, two figures emerged from the hallway. One moved around the room, at one time very close to Harry, picking up the purses and bags that were strewn around the floor.

When she came close enough, Harry could see that this one was a woman: he didn't think she looked like one of the customers and she most certainly wasn't with the bank. Whoever she was, she seemed to be assisting these criminals. He wondered if she was being coerced into their service? It wasn't enough that they cleaned out the vault, they now wanted the dribs and drabs from the purses? It didn't make sense. Were they losing their minds? Losing their grip on the severity of the situation? The only course of action for them that Harry could fathom would be to exit and run, but then again, nothing these people had done up to now made much sense to him. The other figure stood close to the one who had been watching over them. They spoke. Too low to hear. One of them buckled over. Then he pointed into the middle of the group. They grabbed one of the hostages, a man as far as he could tell, and the two of them, slowly but purposefully, walked towards the back hallway which led to the vault. Already a woman had disappeared down that corridor, apparently someone who knew first aid, but she hadn't returned. Perhaps she'd been killed or, worse yet, violated and tortured. The thought of which bolstered Harry's resolve and, sensing that eyes were away from him, he once more began to work the already frayed plastic against the air ventilation grate behind him. They hadn't left the bank and he'd make them pay for their arrogance, their stupidity.

Tony

11:24 am. Tony looked down into Conrad's eyes. One was a red blot, the orbit filled with blood, the other perfectly green against a puddle of white, looked fearfully up into his own. Clara knelt beside Tony, holding tightly to his arm; Tony got the impression that she would have climbed into his jacket if it had been a possibility. The wound in Conrad's shoulder was remarkably clean on the front but at the back, well, the bullet seemed to have taken out his entire shoulder blade on that side. The pressure that Tony applied to the wound only seemed to force more blood through that gaping hole.

"Is it bad?" Conrad coughed.

"Not too bad…" Tony replied, surprised at how easily the lie came.

"What a fuck-up, a complete fuck-up, I can't believe I dragged you guys into this," he stammered, his eyes blinking rapidly, trying to stay focused.

"Forget it, you had no choice, remember?" Tony consoled him.

"I'm such an idiot, I'm gonna die, am I gonna die?" Conrad asked incredulously.

Tony looked away for a moment, Clara seemed to hang on the edge of this question as well, waiting for Tony's response. His integrity demanded that he tell the truth and in a similar circumstance, Tony felt that he would very much like to know that the end was approaching.

"I don't know." It was all Tony could say, staring down into that one emerald iris while holding in what felt like Conrad's heart with his hands.

Conrad took the reply for what it was; an omission of truth. "Tell my sister that my will is under the mantel in my old bedroom." Conrad coughed, and more blood squeezed through Tony's fingertips. "This is it."

"Stay with us, Conrad. Come on. You can do it." It was the first time that Clara had spoken since they were in the small lobby. She'd been quietly weeping, watching Conrad bleeding out, dying, and now that she'd spoken, her words seemed to touch off in her a reserve of resolve and she wiped away her tears with her free hand, unable or unwilling to dislodge the other from Tony's arm.

Conrad closed his eyes, for a few moments before opening them again. "You two really outta get together you know. Everyone knows that you guys are in it." They knew what he meant.

Clara's new-found resolve melted under the weight of his words. She turned into Tony's shoulder. "You may have something there Conrad. Clara's a diamond alright," Tony confirmed.

Conrad smiled slightly; he'd always relished making his friends uncomfortable with the truth, and this he'd done one last time.

Tony felt the tears well up in his eyes, great drops of remorse and sorrow, of anger and frustration. They fell upon Conrad's bloodied shoulder. Conrad took in six quick accelerated breaths and, offering nothing else to them, exhaled that air in one long extended sigh. His chest did not rise again. Tony turned to Clara and wrapped her convulsing sobbing body up into a tight package bundled by his massive arms, shielding her as much as possible from where they were and what they'd seen.

A few moments later, they were searched and their hands were bound together in front of them with sturdy plastic slide ties. The one who had killed Conrad escorted them into the back with the other hostages. Another man ran to the front door and secured it. They were seated together, leaning up against a side wall, and hoods were placed over their heads. Outside, Tony knew that the car would be running; parked as it was in a no parking zone, it would soon attract attention, if the shots hadn't already done so. Someone else had been wounded; he recalled hearing them shout for anyone with medical training while he and Clara watched Conrad breathe his last. Somehow, in the back of the bank like this, hands secured, next to Clara and blinded, Tony felt relatively calm. He still held Clara; he brought her under his arm after they'd been seated. The plastic tie pulled awkwardly on his wrist but it was worth the discomfort to have her close. Clara's body moved every now and then through her tears. This was, he realized, where he needed to be. With Clara. Silently he thanked Conrad for his final words. Within him, Tony felt the stir of emotions that he'd buried shatter the bonds that had previously bound them.

"We're gonna make it," Tony assured Clara, keeping her steady, lending her strength with his powerful arms.

Patrick

11:27 am. The hood pulled awkwardly at Patrick's throat, then was loosened with some assistance before being removed. Patrick looked into the eyes of a dark-haired young man of medium build and height.

"Patrick?" asked the man, his voice a mixture of composure and purpose.

Patrick hadn't heard this man's voice before but he resembled another customer in the bank he'd noticed this morning. Yes, he was nearly certain that this was the man who seemed to be staring out the windows towards the sun to the right of the two security guards. He already knew about the woman, the pretty one who had tossed the keys to the front door of the bank across the room into the waiting palms of the thieves. Patrick supposed that it was possible that there were even more of them. It was extremely fortuitous to place people in the bank prior to the arrival of the main thieves, to deal with many of the eventualities that might occur during a heist such as this.

Patrick nodded in return.

He easily pulled Patrick from the floor and helped him steady his feet.

"This way."

It was an order to be sure but it was not uttered with malice. Patrick followed the instructions, moving towards the back hallway. He wondered what was to become of him, wondered why he was singled out. Did they think he knew too much? He would assure them of his ignorance and then he hoped he'd be led back out amongst the others. He felt isolated and alone without the throng of hostages strewn about him.

Once in the darkened hallway he could make out one of the tellers; she was sprayed with blood, kneeling down beside the body of one of the thieves. He was quite obviously dead. His shirt and jacket lay to the side of him and for reasons Patrick could not possibly fathom, the dead man was bare-chested. As he approached, Patrick could see that the woman was removing what

137

at first looked like the man's skin from his face, but upon further inspection was in fact a fascinatingly realistic mask.

"Sit here, on this side of the body," his escort commanded.

Patrick did as he was told, although it felt good to walk, if only for those few moments. His legs were cramped and achy. Once he was seated, his escort cut loose the plastic tie which bound his arms. It was a painful relief to be able to pull his arms forward once again and he rolled his shoulders a couple times, stretching out his cramped muscles. His freedom didn't last, however, as his right hand was fastened to the left wrist of the dead man.

"Margaret, this is Patrick. Patrick, meet Margaret."

Patrick looked at Margaret; she looked awkwardly layered in her skirt and blouse. It was probably the effect of having her blouse pulled out. All around her lay the contents of the women's purses; Patrick noted that none of the wallets were opened. A pile of make-up cases rested next to Margaret where she knelt. Her right arm, Patrick realized, had also been bound to the dead man. She caught his glance and nodded shyly before returning to her work.

"Patrick. Here is the deal…"

There were a lot of words in the speech. Words like "need" and "dead" and "safety" and "shooting," phrases like "best for everyone" and "no other way" and "the power to help" and "only you." It was an eloquent plea: simply put, they needed Patrick's help and apparently all he'd have to do was don the mask the dead man wore and put himself in a position to be seen by the police when they arrived. He'd only need to be seen momentarily for their plan to work. For this he was being assured that everyone in the bank would be released, that everyone would be unharmed, and that this would all be over in the next forty-five minutes. Patrick could not help but think of his reunion with Melissa, her shining face, looking inquisitively towards the door of the restaurant for some sign of his arrival. In another forty-five minutes she'd just be arriving. It was too much to hope for given the circumstances, but, for an instant, he savored the thought of walking through that door and telling her everything of the last few hours, few years, few minutes. Abruptly, he was pried from his fantasy. His life was in danger. He remembered the bomb.

"What about the bomb? Is it real?"

"The bomb has been defused for now. You needn't worry."

Any doubt that Patrick harbored that the bomb was a hoax faded away under the gaze of this man, whose response revealed not only the fact that there was a bomb, but that it indeed was to be used at some point during the robbery.

Patrick sighed heavily. "Alright. I'll let her do this, only because I believe it will save lives."

Patrick sat on the cold marble floor beside the dead man. He prepared himself to be transformed, in order to save not only his life, but also the lives of all of those hostages in the main room. This has to be enough. It will be.

A few moments later, his escort returned, carrying over his shoulder the body of a young man. The body of a kid, one of the would-be thieves who had entered not knowing the hell they had stepped into, until it was too late. A few seconds afterward, as the body and man disappeared around the corner, another man, his chaperone into the back, appeared carrying over his shoulder a second body, another young man shot down, they too disappeared around the corner towards the vault.

Margaret had expertly pried off the mask and was about to complete the transfer when the two undertakers returned and stepped over them, returning to the front room of the bank. "It will be easier if you lie on your back."

It was the first time she had spoken and Patrick was startled by the gentle tone of her voice. He was reminded of his mother, her voice would lull him to sleep as she spun magical tales in the late-night hours while the world slept. Patrick pulled himself down into an adequately comfortable position near the head of the dead man but away from the blood, his right arm hanging awkwardly a few inches off the ground, held aloft by the dead man's hand which rested underneath his own. He pushed away his disgust and fear. No one else would help if he refused. No one else would rise to the challenge of the day. He knew this. And so, he settled in.

"How's this?" he asked.

"Fine. That's fine."

Patrick felt a wave of doubt rise in him as she placed the mask over his skin; it felt slick and cold against his face. He was slightly claustrophobic but didn't think that was the problem. He was about to play a dangerous game of charades in which the police would think him the enemy. Perhaps it was time to say no, to refuse to help. Just then the corridor echoed with the footfalls of someone returning from the vault.

Patrick lifted the mask from his face and looked at his "friend" from before and another man as they approached. The one in the front, a large burly fellow, disappeared down the hall towards the front room. His "friend," his acquaintance, paused beside Patrick and bent down in order to talk to him. Patrick could see in his eyes, not desperation, not fear, only conviction and faith.

"My associate has explained what needs to be done?" he inquired.

Patrick nodded.

"I see that you are having trouble with it all."

Patrick wasn't certain if indeed he could see, but it was the truth.

"Know this, Patrick. I can guarantee that if you do this, if you don this mask and we are able to place you in a position, a safe position where you can be seen clearly by the police or the FBI, or whoever, as soon as that is done, I will tear that mask from you myself, in order to reveal your true identity. You will have saved many lives. You see..."

The young thief paused, weighing the amount of information that he was willing to reveal.

"You see," he continued, "if they do not see this face, we will be forced to stand our ground and fight our way out, and many people will suffer. However, I know that once they see this face, they will be gripped by a fear so powerful, they will let us go and try to capture us away from the bank. Not a single shot will be fired or drop of blood spilt. I assure you."

Patrick understood that he believed the words he was spouting and they did in truth pacify his angst somewhat, but he had to know, "Who am I becoming?"

"I'm not going to lie to you. You'll look like a very dangerous man."

"That's not good enough. I want to help these people. I want to live but I can't do it blindly. Could you?"

The question hung in the air.

"I want to say yes, Patrick."

"But you can't."

"No. No, I can't. Not with certainty."

Patrick sighed.

"I'm not the man that you are," the thief admitted, uncomfortably.

Patrick looked into his eyes. Something there. Compassion? Restraint? Regret. The eyes, windows to the soul, could not disguise it. At least they had that in common. "OK, I'll do it."

"Thank you, Patrick. Now you just sit back and Margaret will do her magic."

Patrick shook his head at the absurdity of his situation. He wanted something, he was giving so much, he needed something in return. "What's your name?"

The eyes darted away for a moment, then returned. "I'm Keith, Keith Mallory," he said, rising once more to his feet.

"You could be." Patrick said.

"What's that?"

"I said, you could be."

The thief looked down to the floor, playing out some scenario in his mind, before abruptly walking away. Patrick put his head back and closed his eyes. Margaret once again placed the sticky mask over his face, manipulating it in order to fit his eyes and nose and forehead. He could hear her fiddle through the various make-up cases, then he heard it, a long way off it seemed at first. Like the echoing sounds of a dream. The sound grew in intensity. A second, then a third, then a fourth, then it was impossible to

141

distinguish how many sirens he could hear. Margaret paused in her search for the appropriate cover-up to listen as well. Then there were tires screeching and people yelling outside the walls of the bank and still more sirens approached. Patrick heard Margaret take a deep breath, then redouble her efforts. Turning him into someone: a criminal, an outlaw, a killer.

Alan

11:23 am. Alan was the first to react to the sound of the gunshots and so was the first to see Grier, lying wounded on the floor. Coming around the corner with some trepidation, having Kayla and Carl hot on his heels, Alan briefly considered the possibility that Grier had merely ducked down to avoid wayward shrapnel. The blood that spilt out of him quickly abolished that hope. Alan was shocked but not fazed; he told Carl and Kayla to remain with Grier while he scouted the main room. There was the possibility that the bank had been breeched and that Simon and Pete were captured or killed. On the very fringe of his contemplations was the chance that Pete had simply snapped and went on a bit of a shooting spree, removing his silencer and passing judgment on the hostages they held.

His fears abated quickly; it took only a few moments for him to realize what had happened, as impossible as it seemed. There was a bloody body lying in the middle of the floor, halfway between the teller stations and the front door. Close to the teller wall lay another man, bleeding and being tended by a young man and a young woman; both, he was certain, had not been in the bank when they had arrived.

At Simon's request Alan picked up the automatic that had killed Grier, then quickly re-locked the front doors of the bank and pulled the dead body around the corner of the teller station, out of view of the front lobby windows. In the corner, by the open door of one of the side offices, Alan picked up the second firearm. Too light. Turning it over in his hand revealed the Viper label. A starter's pistol. Pete stood over the two others who were tending to the second victim. The thin thready breathing of the victim likely meant that there would be a second body very soon. They were obscured enough by the desks and partitions of the bank that they could remain in place without fear of being seen. Pete stayed in the front so that he might maintain some sense of order. Alan proceeded back down the hall to where Grier was lying, with Kayla, Carl and now Simon with one of the bank tellers in tow, a woman who apparently knew first aid. He'd seen the wound and the blood and he didn't harbor much hope, but that isn't to say that he didn't have any; after all, there was always a chance.

Watching her work, seconds turning to minutes, Alan resigned himself to the fact that Grier was dead and no amount of chest compressions or air ventilations was going to bring him back. Then Grier had regained consciousness. Alan took a step backwards into the wall when Grier heaved up and drew that final breath. The gurgled words were incoherent to his ears; that is, until Kayla repeated them. The blood that swelled in Grier's mouth prevented any kind of proper pronunciation. What did it matter? Then he was gone, and they all looked to Simon; in truth Carl would have been in his opinion an equally capable leader merely for his inspirational qualities; however, Simon had proven to be adaptable and intelligent and they would require his psychological intuition now more than ever. Alan had never been comfortable with Grier's plan for Simon, and although he'd voiced his opinion along with Carl and Kayla, Grier had refused to budge. He couldn't help but observe the irony of the situation. Besides, he and Kayla were scheduled to exit, to ride off into the sunset, their tasks completed in accordance with the original plan.

Simon's words once again impressed the others with his genius. Without the face that Grier wore to go behind the words of the criminally fanatical band they imitated, their realism and plausibility decreased exponentially. The group that they were attempting to emulate, the Mallory brothers and their entourage, operated very much as a patriarchy, whose few chosen sons were incapable of action without the presence and commitment of their leader, Clay Mallory. A fact that was well known by criminal and cop alike. Without an interactive Grier as Clay Mallory, they lost all credibility. And so Simon's intention to remove the mask and place it on the face of a hostage in the bank by the name of Patrick was simply genius. The fact that Simon knew the man's name meant that he had developed, in the short time they had been inside the bank, a relationship. The acute aptitude of Simon's skills meant that Patrick would most likely comply. The reason for this submission was irrelevant. Simon had done what he did best; control and manipulate.

Kayla deftly made her way through the hostages, grabbing all the purses she could find while Alan busied himself with getting Patrick onto his feet and down into the hallway where Grier and Margaret waited. When Alan laid eyes on Patrick he knew the motivations of this man would be anything but selfish, sitting as he was, soothing the hostages around him with his quiet reassurances.

Pete had been surprised by the news that Grier was gone, buckling over slightly at the waist before swallowing down his sinking feeling. He recovered quickly enough to point out Patrick. Alan pulled him onto his feet with ease before leading him down the back corridor. He'd removed Patrick's hood and introduced Margaret. Time was a commodity that he could not afford to waste and rather than wait for Simon to return from the vault, Alan took it upon himself to reveal the plan, the only possible avenue any of them had for escape. Patrick, to his credit, sat and listened, quietly considering Alan's every word.

"We need you to help us, Patrick. This man is dead. In order to ensure everyone's safety when the police arrive it is necessary that this face be seen. Otherwise this bank will turn into a shooting gallery and many people will be hurt or killed. The only way to proceed is to make it appear that this man still lives. Margaret has agreed to transfer the mask from him onto you. You would only have to be seen, nothing more. This face must be seen; only that will stop the police from breeching the bank. There's no other way. Only you have the power to help us; only you can do this thing and give everyone in the bank a chance, a chance at life."

Alan looked into Patrick's eyes; he seemed to drift for a moment, looking down at the dead man before him. Perhaps he wasn't getting through, perhaps Simon had read him wrong, but then the eyes quickly snapped back into focus and when Patrick voiced his concern about the bomb, Alan felt sure that he would do it – a pervasive sense of duty and honor demanded that he must. There really are heroes in the world, thought Alan.

Margaret

11:28 am. The last ten minutes were a blur. Had she really done all that? What had possessed her to become involved? It had been a decade since she had looked over the medical textbooks. What about the bruises, had everyone known for all these years and just been too scared to say anything to her? Was she the laughing stock of the bank? When she went home, was she what they all sat around discussing in the staff room? Margaret remembered the eyes of the dead man opening, just when she was reaching her physical limit; the muscles still burned in her arms and shoulders and her knees were aching from shifting positions, from the head to the chest, again and again and again. More bruises to add to the tally. And now, now she was in the middle of it all, the suit she wore filled with money; she'd been in a daze when they had pulled it over her bra and replaced her blouse and jacket afterwards. Freedom? They had no idea of the complications of her life; freedom was a word she'd cherished as a child but found that its truth eluded her. Words like love and compassion, honor and respect. There were so many words that existed only as a fiction for her.

She'd been sure that she heard the dead man thank her, although the woman had supposed that he'd uttered something else. The look in his eyes, the expression on his face told her that her first impression was right. He had thanked her and then died.

"Thank you, honey."

145

And now, now she sat, make-up brush in one hand, the other securely fastened to the same dead man, applying a mask to the face of a man who like her had the courage to take his own life and the lives of the other hostages in the bank into his hands. Was that what she had done? For the first time in many long years Margaret tapped into a reserve of purpose and vision, a treasure trove filled with dreams and desires that she'd long ago been forced to bury for fear of their destruction. Every verbal slur, every fist that beat against her flesh, every alcoholic kiss, every violation of her person had been another brick in the impenetrable wall that separated her from herself. Somewhere in the last few minutes that wall had bent and crumbled under the weight of her actions.

"I need you to talk," she nearly whispered into Patrick's ear.

"To talk?" he questioned.

"If I'm gonna make this work, I need to see how your mouth moves as well as the facial expressions you make. I've never done this before so I want to be certain that I get it right."

"I understand," replied Patrick. "You have a lovely voice."

Margaret could feel her skin flush. The old Margaret would have said nothing and dismissed the compliment, but the new Margaret, rising like the phoenix out of the ashes of her persecution, found the strength to say, "Thank you."

They had both heard the sirens a few moments prior, but had said nothing. Suffice to say, that as the sounds had intensified Margaret felt certain that by now the bank was completely shut off from the rest of the world. She wondered what Kevin would do when he found out what was going on. He might wish for her death. She tried to push the thought away. She imagined him and his bottle of vodka in the living room or in some deadbeat bar downtown yelling at the police on the TV to open fire. Like the way he yelled at the TV when he watched football. Angry and disgusted.

A phone started to ring somewhere close by. It was the phone inside the manager's office behind the teller stations. As

Keith picked it up, both Margaret and Patrick could hear clearly his half of the brief conversation that ensued.

"Hello."

Pause.

"We have sixteen hostages; no one has been hurt yet. Call us back in ten minutes for a list of our demands."

A longer pause.

"Well, Rutherford Mills, Chief of Police, if you want the hostages out safely I suggest you call back in ten minutes."

The phone crashed its way back on the hook.

"I thought he was under investigation by the city," Patrick muttered.

"Last I read, charges had not yet been formally laid against him," replied Margaret. She'd been following the story for several weeks along with many other Phoenix residents. It seemed that finding witnesses to testify against Chief Mills was extremely difficult.

"I hear he's a dirty shirt; the papers have been lambasting him for a month. Possible mob ties to the Pisanni family: drugs, prostitution, extortion, a little bit of everything," Patrick continued.

"Well, let's hope he doesn't do anything stupid in an attempt to salvage his reputation."

"I hear you."

"OK. Give me a few moments to attach the jaw line on this side. In the meantime, Patrick, think of a story you can tell me when I need you to talk again."

"Hmm. I think I can come up with something."

And once more they fell into silence, Margaret delicately laying and attaching the sides of a mask to Patrick's face and Patrick wondering where to start his story, a story he was all too familiar with. A love story. Outside, the police put up the last of the barricades. There were already a few pedestrians watching the scene outside the bank in spite of the hot, hazy, noonday sun and more would soon arrive; it was a certainty: nothing brought out the people like a dose of real-life human tragedy.

Chapter 12

Rudy

Police Chief Rutherford Mills awoke to the ringing of his bedside telephone. Shelly did not stir. She'd struggled with the midnight phone calls when Rudy made detective, but had developed over time a tolerance for them. Like the tolerance that existed in their marriage. Rutherford, or Rudy as he was more commonly called, grabbed the phone and pressed it to his ear.

"Mills here."

Pause.

"A situation? I understand, I'll be there in thirty."

He hung up the receiver and righted himself in his bed; on the far side of their king-sized mattress lay Shelly, her breathing rhythmic and deep. She was still sleeping soundly. Why the hell shouldn't she be? Probably got her fill with that pretty boy personal trainer, Brad. The marriage was so in title only. They both needed something the other possessed. It hadn't been like that in the beginning. He still remembered their first few years together, a perfect combination of mystery, seduction and personal gratification. It faded quickly. Quietly. Now they lived off each other like parasites. Shelly's need went straight to his financial success, not that his income as the Chief of Police garnered him an exorbitant salary, mind you. It was his extra-curricular activities that were making him rich and powerful. He reached up and wiped the sleep from his eyes before standing and making his way over to his walk-in closet. He would have loved to throw on some sweats but there was a "situation" that demanded his attention.

It was James MacMillan on the phone. A "situation" meant there was trouble, the kind of trouble that could not be discussed on the phone over a line they knew was tapped. With the heat coming on, his business "associates," especially those in his drug and prostitution rings, were getting restless. Any one of them could bolt and turn states evidence if he didn't keep a constant vigil over them, more threatening than reassuring. If he had to guess... tonight... What the hell time was it? He stepped back out into the bedroom from his closet and looked towards the clock on his end table. 3:58 am. Shit. Been asleep for just over three hours. This was not good, especially with the added pressure of the press. Someone had leaked the internal affairs investigation to the media. Now his every move, his every word was available for public scrutiny. If he had to guess, it would be Ferrara Parr stirring the pot this evening, or morning, whatever it was. Maybe a couple of his best girls got picked up and he wants an early release, get them back onto the street before the end of the night and the city's perverted slide back into their business suits and pencil pushing day jobs. There was still money to be made, even at this ungodly hour, in the trading of human flesh. Especially with the youthful energy that Ferrara's girls were known for. Rudy had experienced the quality of their work first-hand on more than a few occasions. One of the perks provided for his protection.

He returned from the closet, gray suit pants, button-down blue shirt and a smoke-colored silk tie. He considered for a moment waking Shelly as he left, out of spite. Turning on the lights or slamming the door. But he quickly reconsidered. The more beauty sleep she got, the better she'd appear on television that afternoon and evening. She needed his money to support her wide and varied tastes and he required her social graces. She was

149

an exceptionally beautiful woman, to be sure, and the camera could not help but be drawn in her direction. Appearing next to her was a sure-fire way to win the support of the public in addition to avoiding the more pointed questions he would be asked if he were alone.

He hurried down the stairs and out the front door, grabbing his car keys on his way out. He craved a coffee but a cigarette would have to suffice. He clicked his car alarm off and climbed into the silver BMW 530i. He'd be downtown in his office in exactly twenty-five minutes at this hour. He'd banged his head against the brick wall of the daily traffic jams when he was green, a rookie on the force, but now that he was in a position of power and authority he made his own hours, choosing when to come and go. His doctor said that his promotion had lowered his blood pressure by ten points. He wasn't about to give that up. Ten points was a heck of an improvement, especially when he also carried around an extra thirty-five to forty pounds on his chest and gut. Fortunately, he was a tall man, and the weight, although noticeable, wasn't yet repulsive or winning him jibes at his physique, at least not that he knew of. Then of course there was the smoking to add to his condition. He'd stolen his first cigarette out of his aunt's purse when he was fifteen. He'd coughed only once. He found that he had a knack for it. "*Stick to your strengths*," his father used to say. Some people killed themselves staying healthy and in shape; others lived life to the fullest. That was him: live his life now when he can, not later when he's an old man and nothing works.

Three years ago he'd had a "*flutter*". The doctors called it a minor heart attack. As if. He'd be dead if he'd had a heart attack; it had killed his father and his father's father and would, he was sure, eventually kill him. Genes were tough things to contend with. No, no. He was quite certain, he'd only had a flutter, everything was going to be alright and for God's sake, there was simply nothing wrong with his lifestyle that demanded any changing. Besides, that had been three years earlier and hadn't he been the picture of health since? Aside from the occasional bout with the flu or a virus of some sort or another. Yes, yes. A model of health. Rudy thumbed another cigarette into the ashtray as he pulled into the garage at HQ. Phoenix City Police Headquarters. His home away from home.

"*Look at that,*" he thought to himself, looking at the discarded butts. "*Only had three on my way in tonight; I must be slipping.*"

He quickly ran out of smokes sitting in his office listening to the evening's event outlined by his right-hand man, Assistant Director of Operations James MacMillan. The proverbial shit that he was told was hitting the fan wasn't so proverbial after all. The situation was rank and there was no way around it.

MacMillan finished talking. He sighed once before shuffling into one of the brown leather high-back chairs that graced the office and awaited Rudy's response. It had been a good twenty minutes since he had begun explaining the events of the last several hours and he'd never once stopped pacing about the room, such was the level of his agitation. This was a serious threat to the prosperous empire that Rudy and he had built up over the years. He'd sent enough assholes and gangbangers to prison in the last decade to know that he'd meet a torturous and putrid demise if he ever saw the inside of the local pens. Rudy had come in and sat pretty much exactly as he sat now. Slumped slightly in his chair, cigarette burning out in an ashtray that desperately needed to be emptied. Each butt a tombstone in a desert of ash. And when Rudy Mills got quiet, people got nervous, and rightly so. The few "*problems*" that had appeared in the years following his rise to power had either quickly submitted or found themselves in a deep sandy grave outside the city.

"You know..." said Rudy after several moments of reflection. "This guy, he's brought this upon himself. Malcolm Shaw. He's dug his own grave. We've done everything we could to help him see things as they should be, as they are."

"No question there," replied MacMillan.

151

"A good cop though, not like the others; Shaw's got something special." Mills spoke momentarily with reverence, respect even. It wasn't so much that Mills was thinking about sparing the young officer; no indeed, he had decided quite quickly that this one, especially after tonight, needed to be silenced; but there was something about this man that reminded him, like an echo from the past, of himself.

MacMillan, picking up on the cadence and tone, and feeling that Rudy might go soft on this guy and give him some breathing room, felt forced to add, "You know, I heard him talk once about your wife."

Rudy waited.

"He said she was a hot ride."

"He didn't."

"He did."

"Well. We will have to make him regret his words, won't we?"

Seeing MacMillan twitch so easily, allowing him to sense for a moment that he might leave it alone, it made Rudy smile. He wondered if this wasn't what friendship was all about.

"What's so funny?" MacMillan asked.

Rudy raised his hands as if it were nothing. "Well," he said, "let's get busy. We've got a body to bag for the morning news."

For the first time that morning, MacMillan grinned. James was not the sharpest knife in the drawer, but he was vindictive. MacMillan had told Rudy about busting his old shop teacher on possession of a narcotic substance, ruining his career. James had planted the drugs, his first foray into corruption. In that case, James had said it was peace of mind. Justice, MacMillan professed, had many faces. Rudy knew then that he'd be useful.

As with any new officer assigned to the force, Rudy and James had carried out an extensive background check on Malcolm Shaw. Their sources were many and extremely well informed; such was the nature of information when it was paid for and paid for well. Of course the Academy would have carried out their own kinds of checks, their own kinds of psychological examinations. It was an odd mix of emotions and experiences that made a police officer, a combination of aggression and restraint, a tenuous balance between moralistic conscience and wholesale ruthlessness. It was no easy job. They would immediately become the enemies, whether it was warranted or not; they would be scrutinized, jeered at, slandered and spit on, but they would, if trained well, hold to a code of conduct. The code gave them the strength to battle through impulses that told them to fight back, in order to uphold justice and honor. It's a special kind of person who becomes a cop.

Malcolm was an excellent candidate. He had grown up in Chicago, on the periphery of the east side housing projects and general squalor. He'd attended and passed all of his high school credits, playing both football and basketball for the Jackson High Jaguars. His athletic abilities at one time even garnered the review of two college scouts, one from Buffalo State, and another from Chicago U. The excitement of these prospects soon faded, when both schools stopped all correspondence and communication with the Shaw family. This was odd, especially given the impressive numbers that Malcolm was producing in both athletic fields and, sensing that there was something more to the story, Rudy and James rolled up their sleeves and dug deeper. Eventually, they accessed Malcolm's student file. In it, a social services and psychologist report. An altercation between Malcolm and his high school girlfriend, Jinny Burns. She had appeared one day at school after the two of them had broken up from their long-term relationship with a black eye and a swollen lip. She told her guidance counselor that it had been Malcolm. The principal got involved and then social services stepped in; he was suspended from all extra-curricular activities. The police were notified but no charges were laid and no police record existed with his name on it. There was also, in the same file, a confession by Jinny some months later that it had in fact been her uncle who had hit her. But by then, the damage was done. Malcolm had lost the interest of the college scouts and his grades had spiraled from slightly above average to mediocre and less than satisfactory. Another kid, at that age, might have fallen prey to self-pity, might have turned to drugs to escape the reality of his life's misfortunes, but he was not another kid, and something inside demanded he make something of himself.

Malcolm moved to Phoenix the day after his high school graduation, he had a cousin that worked for the Phoenix City Public Works Department who helped him get settled. Two weeks later, he applied to the Arizona Law Enforcement Academy.

"We've got him easy," said James once he'd read through the report.

"Happy day," Rudy said, smiling over the folder that contained the carefully documented notes of the counselors and the principal.

"Of course this will never do; it just doesn't fit in with the rest of it," said Rudy, referring to the confession about the uncle.

"No, I quite agree, let's shred that little tidbit."

"Agreed," was Rudy's cold reply.

They had sat in his office, the same office, and destroyed Jinny's confession. That was three and half years ago. Time well spent.

"I'll photocopy the rest of the file and make sure it's returned as silently as it was removed," said James, flush with excitement.

It wasn't often something so damning, so clearly unjust was discovered, like some buried treasure. He relished this kind of tragedy. The hero, Malcolm Shaw, dragged into an incident in which he had absolutely no part. Accused and subsequently punished for a crime he did not commit. It was unsettling how one lie could ruin a man, not only once, but be poised to ruin him a second time as well. James felt quite certain that there was no fate, no destiny in this world. In fact, he felt it was entirely more plausible that fate was a man that looked just like him.

Rudy thumbed open the middle drawer to his desk and withdrew from its shrouded interior a small remote control. Pointing it towards the sidewall, decorated with a painting of a tiger in a green, tangled storm of vines, roots and trees, he keyed in the code and a portion of the wall, the size of a doorway, clicked and pushed open. Resting on the floor of this secret nook sat a mid-sized gray safe in which emergency money and other important commodities could be housed, and perched above it was a large tan filing cabinet. Rudy stepped around the corner of the desk and moved easily over to the cabinet, replacing the remote in his drawer and locking it. MacMillan stood and walked over to the cabinet with him. He loved it when they went into the files; something about the set-up in Rudy's office reeked of espionage.

Rudy scanned the folders quickly, deftly pulling out the Shaw file.

"See that this goes to the appropriate sources when the time is right," he said, handing it over to James.

"Not a problem; it's been a while since we leaked anything. The vultures are circling for something juicy." He grinned.

Rudy nodded and closed the drawer. It was an impressive collection of information: some of it was being used in a variety of extortion scams; however, most of it sat silent, waiting for the name on the tab to screw up in some way or another. Rudy kept all of the files here except for one – one he considered too sensitive to leave in such a poorly protected area. No, no. That one he kept in a safety deposit box, in a vault, in a bank out of state. He'd added to it over the years, a taped conversion here, a handwritten memo or a signature there. Indeed, it was what he considered one of his prized possessions. It protected not only him, but his accumulated wealth as well, and if he ever went down he was absolutely certain he'd be vindicated because of the information that it contained.

"Well, all we need now is to bring Sanchez up to speed. He'll be reluctant to collaborate but I'm sure we can get him on board, especially in light of the money he's lost tonight." Rudy pushed the hidden doorway closed, watching it seamlessly click into place, revealing nothing of its existence to the naked eye.

"You know," said James, "this might be our best opportunity to off the old man. Simpson is itching for a chance at his turf and might be more co-operative."

Rudy sighed and took in MacMillan. He was a squat man, relatively unpleasant to look upon. His rolling jowls framed a face that was both fatter and whiter than any other in a city such as this, a city of sunshine. His stature, at just over 5'5", made him the brunt of many jokes and jeers, and he took every comment he heard personally. This actually, was a quality that Rudy felt redeemed some of his more annoying attributes. On top of his head his thinning light brown hair swung neatly from left to right in an embarrassingly obvious attempt to cover the freckled and pock-marked skin of his ever-advancing forehead. The last thing that he and James needed right now was a newcomer. The removal of Sanchez, the boss of the drug division that they operated, he was sure, was only suggested to him because of the toxic relationship that they shared. They hated each other, openly. MacMillan and Sanchez. Rudy felt like a school teacher trying to keep them from tearing each other's throats out. That's why it had been over 7 months since their last face-to-face. Rudy took care of the business personally on that end. It was an inconvenience, but James had spent the additional energy to forward their interests in other areas and they had prospered from the arrangement.

"Now is not the time for change, my friend; you know this as well as I do."

James shrugged. "You're right. Just let me know if that prick gives you any trouble, I'd be happy to…"

"Yes, yes. I know," interrupted Rudy. "Perhaps you can get me the report that was filled out this morning, while I call the old man. And I'd like you to have a face-to-face with Daniel; he shouldn't be too difficult, he's really short now. What is it? Two months till he collects his pension?"

"More like six weeks. Ingenious that, pairing the two of them up right from the get-go. As for the other items, I'm all over it, boss."

MacMillan shuffled out of the office leaving Rudy to contemplate the flurry of activity that was about to take place, all the gears that were about to be greased in order to bring down a single man, an innocent man whose only fault was doing his job and doing it better than anyone else. He picked up the phone. "It's me. We need to talk; meet me at Fran's in fifteen." Click. It was done. Rudy would have his face-to-face with Sanchez at a greasy spoon just around the corner and then everyone would be brought up to speed. Another man would have trouble sleeping at night he knew, but not him; he slept like a bear. You had to have a conscience in order to be affected by it.

When Sanchez arrived at the diner, in his button-down shirt and black suspenders, Rudy knew what had to be done, having read over the report turned in not more than four hours earlier. It seemed their man Malcolm had inadvertently overheard a few choice words while relaxing at a downtown nightclub. He had then seen the same suspect deal a few doses of "product" to some patrons at the club. This was nothing new to him, and would have most likely been ignored if it were anyone else, but this was Malcolm Shaw, straight and narrow, clean and pristine. Whatever the reason, Malcolm tailed the suspect through the late-night city streets until he pulled up to a warehouse in the industrial district. He penetrated the lax security and got an eye full. Malcolm called in the cavalry. The DEA impounded over 35 million dollars' worth of ecstacy and a few scant million dollars of heroin. The manufacturing equipment, worth over 3 million dollars, was also taken into custody. One of the biggest drug busts in state history. Of the people who were arrested, however, the original suspect did not turn up. It was not uncommon, in a raid so quickly organized and executed, for people to slip through the cracks and past the barricades. But this fact, this unaccounted-for suspect, would be the impetus for the tragedy that would befall Malcolm Shaw in the next few hours, most likely while he slept peacefully at home. And all of his intuition and instinct couldn't save him.

Rudy slid the report over to Sanchez as he sat in the booth. "Read that," Rudy ordered, sipping his coffee and shaking his head.

Sanchez reached forward with his gnarled bony hand and clasped the report. He was only sixty-six, Rudy knew, but he looked like he was well into his eighties. Wearing the suspenders as he did showed the frailty of his shoulders. Meetings like this were certainly not the norm, but when their hands had been forced, this was the easiest way to connect without attracting attention. Sanchez sat in the same seat that MacMillan sat in when they ate breakfast or lunch at the diner; if the old man knew, Rudy felt sure that he would have pulled up a chair. Men were about to be destroyed. Rudy felt compelled to stay silent for the time being. Sanchez finished reading the report and grunted. Judging from his weariness, he'd obviously been up for some time: news of his operation taking a hit like this would have come as swiftly as his anger.

"You know who matches that description," Rudy said.

Sanchez leaned back in his chair. "Yes. It's him, my stupid nephew."

"As bad as things seem right now, I can steer us clear and get everything back into shape, but we need the kid."

Sanchez looked to the ceiling for guidance. Rudy knew that he shared a special bond with his dead sister's only son. He had been grooming the boy as his replacement and while he seemed to understand and value the business, Joe, as all young men tended to be at that age, was reckless. Joe felt immune and invincible. That myth would come crashing down this morning, one way or another.

"Rudy, he's all I got," Sanchez remarked. "What's the plan?"

Rudy sat back and took another hit from his coffee. "This is the way I see it," he sighed. "We have some information on the investigating officer that we could use to taint this entire operation. He's a bit of a hothead, if you know what I mean."

Sanchez nodded his understanding.

"This ain't gonna be easy, Sanch. But I figure if we bring the kid in, beat him with the billies and dump him, we can pin the cop responsible and take some heat off your operation."

Sanchez's eyes darted around the diner. He shifted uneasily in his seat.

"Now, we wouldn't kill him, mind you, but we'd need to make it convincing and serious; he'd definitely have to be hospitalized, but we'd need him to ID our cop friend."

"Maybe he'll learn something…" was all that Sanchez could mumble.

His hands were shaking slightly. He'd sworn on her deathbed, his sister, nine years ago, to watch over Joe, to care for him as his own. How could he do this to him, put him in this position? Sanchez felt his sorrow being rammed into submission by his rage. "One condition," Sanchez muttered.

Rudy, seeing the inner turmoil, answered, "What's that?"

"I do it. No one else. Just me."

Rudy understood that he wanted to protect the boy, to keep hateful hands off of him, especially those hands that belonged to James MacMillan. Rudy most likely would not have let MacMillan at Joe, for fear that his hatred would kill him with a few well-placed, spiteful strikes to the skull.

"Just you. Agreed. We'll need to do this quickly," Rudy added. "Meet us at the hole in thirty, sooner if possible."

Sanchez did not respond. He stood and walked out, leaving the restaurant in a cold, hurried rush. Rudy watched him leave, shuffling along, looking older than he had not five minutes ago. Rudy hoped he could go through with it. He'd have to bring along a few clubs of his own just in case, and MacMillan as well. Not for the physical task of course, but to motivate the old man to get the job done. This was, after all, business.

The car ride was uneventful. James filled in the details about his conversation with Daniel Yves, Malcolm's partner. Yves assured James that on several occasions he had seen Malcolm use excessive force when making arrests or attempting to gain

159

information. The two of them had not hit it off well. To the young, the old always seemed to do things the wrong way or the slow way. Fortunately for Rudy, those judgmental views would solidify Daniel as a collaborator in this case. And who could blame him. Six weeks from retirement, he knew he'd get the most dangerous details on the force if he didn't co-operate. James had a particularly effective way of motivating people.

They pulled up to Clyde's Tavern, parked in the rear after making sure that they were not followed, and went in through the side entrance off an alley lined with garbage bins. Inside and down a flight of stairs, Rudy saw that they were the last to arrive. Joe was sitting in a chair in the middle of a barren room. Pipes and electrical wire lined the ceiling and the cold hard concrete floor was disintegrating into clumps of moldy sand along the edges and in the corners. A large drainage grill, broken and rusted, gurgled occasionally in the middle of the room below the chair. The walls, a bluish tint, were covered in ghetto graffiti. With Joe was Sanchez, looking entirely different in his suit and tie. With him were his personal bodyguards, Tie and Zachary. Four light bulbs draped down from above, casting shadows, deep and dark, onto the floor.

Sanchez stepped forward. His hands, a pale, ghostly hue of white latex, reached out. A resolute look in his eyes.

"Give me the baton."

Rudy's gloved hand reached into his jacket, down to his belt, and removed the black, nondescript weapon neatly packaged in an evidence bag. He handed it to Sanchez. Neither spoke.

Sanchez turned, he glanced at James for a moment, then walked back over to Joe, removing the baton from the evidence bag as he went.

"Joe... On your mother's grave, I swore to protect you."

Joe began to whimper. He sat in a wooden bar chair, his hands tied behind his back. He was not gagged or blindfolded; he was to witness his uncle's wrath as penance. He knew what was coming, but that knowledge served only to exacerbate his fear.

160

"Look what you've done! Have I not cared for you? Have I not given you all manner of independence?" The old man was building up the anger, the spite from inside, the motivating factors, which would ultimately bring the baton cresting over his head and smashing down upon his very own flesh and blood.

"Have I not done everything I could to make you happy?" His voice was rising, a fountain of emotion ready to break.

Joe shifted uneasily in his chair, his whimpers turning to sobs. Rudy knew this would only fuel the old man's rage. He despised weakness. Every whimper that escaped Joe's lips would shame the old man; all this cowering and he hadn't even hit the boy yet. No. It wasn't gonna be pretty.

"You shame me!" screamed Sanchez.

"You shame your mother!" His voice broke in its ferocity.

"You shame our name!"

And the baton arched back over the old man's head and came thundering down, on Joe's legs. The silence was broken only by the bolting forward of Joe's body onto the floor.

Sanchez, with a quickness that belied his age, sprang over the kid and raised the baton again, this time unleashing its speed and fury on Joe's back.

The baton seemed to move quickly from the floor and Joe's body to the ceiling above as it came smashing again and again, over and over.

Rudy and James stared at the spectacle. Blood had come after the fourth strike; they had all heard the left arm shatter, and based upon the awkward position of the left leg, there was a chance it was broken as well. Somewhere in the middle of the attack, the old man, sweat dripping from him, spit trailing out of his mouth, had begun to cry and finally, after what seemed like many minutes, stood upright and let the baton drop from his latex-covered fingertips. It echoed momentarily on the floor before it too was silenced.

Joe's body lay broken and motionless. Blood flowed slowly towards the drains. He was unconscious but still breathing.

"Tie, Zak. Take him and dump him where we discussed." Sanchez rasped through his labored breath.

Rudy and James stepped forward; James took the baton and placed it back in the plastic evidence bag. Rudy stood beside Sanchez. "We'll call the paramedics and they'll have him in hospital within the next half an hour."

Sanchez did not speak. He did not move. He stood there staring at the graffiti. Finally, Rudy turned and motioned for James to accompany him back to the car. They still had plenty to do.

In the car on the way back to HQ neither man spoke. When they reached the precinct they found it under siege by reporters, no doubt looking for the next big break in the investigation. As they parked their vehicle, James turned to Rudy.

"That was the best," James said, his lips curled in a grin from ear to ear.

"Yeah, who knew the old man had it in him?" was Rudy's response before exiting the car.

The reporters crowded around, badgering Rudy with questions, hoping to get anything to lead their morning broadcast. The news of the drug bust would be making headlines, but if this swarm was any indication, the allegations brought against him over the last few weeks were still fueling the tabloids and local television stations. He made his way purposefully through the throng, maintaining as best he could a calm, composed demeanor. The temperature, already at some ridiculous number, inched its way skyward.

"No comment."

Another question.

"No comment at this time."

Three more questions.

"Who put the damned parking lot so far away from the front doors?" thought Rudy.

"I have no comment."

Finally, a question about his legal counsel sent him spinning back, an urgent need to slam the lawyers of the world, whom he detested. Why did he need to pay a battery of lawyers so many hundreds of thousands of dollars just to be advised to say no comment? Fucking blood suckers.

Reporters gathered around him, microphones crammed into his face, cameras and lights filled his view of the world.

"The law is sometimes secondary. We protect the citizens of this great city. That is the job of the police, first and foremost. Lawyers and courts decide the outcome. Sometimes they can bring the full weight of its wrath down on even an innocent man, although speaking from experience I've seen lots of guilty men walk free. It's not perfect, but it's all we've got and we're doing the best we can."

There was a flurry of questions afterwards but he ignored them all. He'd said his piece about the lawyers. He'd shown his contempt for the profession and the public, he was certain, would love him for it. Everyone hated lawyers, didn't they?

Back in the safety of his office, Rudy decided to stretch out on his leather couch as he waited for the information to come in. Over the next hour, James confirmed that Joe had been picked up and had positively identified the man responsible for the beating as Malcolm Shaw. He also confirmed the information regarding Malcolm's sordid past was in circulation. Everything was moving forward as planned. His cell phone rang. It was his lawyer, Kyle McDunna.

"Hello Kyle."

"What?"

Rudy sat up and turned on the television. It was true. The news had chopped his full statement. There he was on television saying, "the law is secondary." And "lawyers and courts decide the outcome." Adding, "speaking from experience I've seen lots of guilty men walk free." This was a disaster. Rudy's mouth went dry, he'd screwed up, but he couldn't be certain how badly.

"What do we do?" he asked, desperate for an out.

McDunna and Mills would hold a press conference that afternoon to limit the fallout from his blunder. Worst of all, he'd have to listen to McDunna's self-righteous rant about what to say and when to speak. Fuck. Television, it was his most powerful ally when he accomplished something on a grand scale, but it could also be his most indomitable foe.

James knocked and then entered his office. "Good news, boss."

"Please, I could use some of that," said Rudy as he straightened up.

"Malcolm is in custody."

"Excellent. And the baton? It's in evidence?"

"Done. He's baked." James smiled.

"Alright, I have to get a few hours of sleep. McDunna and I are gonna attempt some damage control this afternoon, gotta look my best."

"Right-oh, have a good one," replied James as he exited the office.

What a morning, thought Rudy, glancing over at the clock. 11:00 am. He'd been up for seven hours already. He slipped off his shoes and stretched out on the couch at the back of his office. It was definitely turning out to be one of those days, filled with winners and losers. He was teetering on the brink. He needed something to push him over the top. Sleep came not long after that thought tumbled through his mind like a baton hammering again and again against his skull.

"Let's go, chief! We gotta move!"

Rudy sprang up from the couch, opening his eyes in time to see James grab his jacket from the back of his chair and hand it to him. He had barely slipped on his shoes as James pulled him out into the hallway.

"What the fuck's goin' on?" asked Rudy, gaining his bearings.

"Preliminary reports say we've got a robbery with possible hostages in progress at the National Bank," James reported as they jogged down the hall.

They skidded through the maze of desks and headed towards the parking lot where a car waited.

"Hostages?" asked Rudy, unable to contain his excitement.

They approached the car, half running, Rudy searching his jacket for his cigarettes.

"Hostages?" Rudy asked again.

"Looks like," replied James. "You are one lucky son of a bitch, you know that?"

Rudy felt the rising crescendo of invigoration. How was it possible? How did he deserve this? He didn't really care. He'd hit the jackpot. A robbery with hostages? He saves one hostage, one person and he becomes the city's greatest hero! Of course it was a bit of a double-edged sword; if they all died, he'd be finished, completely finished.

"How many?" he asked, opening the car door and sliding inside.

The more hostages there were, the greater the likelihood that they could negotiate a release. If it were only two or three then it would be much more difficult. More than six and he was golden.

"Not sure yet... But they are thinking what with the staff and all, that it's somewhere between fifteen and twenty."

"Fifteen to twenty?" James nodded.

"Fifteen to twenty." Rudy repeated.

James smiled as they weaved through the city streets towards the bank, siren blaring. Rudy straightened his tie and gathered himself for the coming storm. He'd have to take control of the situation immediately and assert himself in the crucible of television. City blocks buzzed by them; the bank appeared out of the front windshield, surrounded by squad cars and police officers taking up support positions by their vehicles. Wooden barricades were being erected. Whatever was to happen, whatever the cost, Rudy set his sights on saving at least one hostage.

Across town in the city hospital, a young man, having been admitted with serious wounds allegedly inflicted upon him by a Phoenix police officer, suffered a massive stroke and died. The

165

fatal effects of a sub-dermal hematoma caused by the vicious assault. Doctors were able to reduce the swelling but it was too late to stop the stroke from happening. The identification of the man responsible for the attack, now a deathbed confession, pushed the charges against Malcolm Shaw to murder.

Chapter 13

Harry

The sound of sirens and the sharp screech of tires provided for Harry the same kind of cover that had been previously offered through the firefight minutes before. This time he was ready. Sweat-drenched and badly cramped, Harry finally ripped open the plastic tie. The relief was immediate. Although he was careful to keep his hands behind his back, he allowed them to separate those few more inches that had previously been denied. The strained muscles in his arms and shoulders heaved a collective sigh as the burden of bondage was excised.

"*Next move, next move,*" he thought quickly to himself.

Harry had been so intent on freeing himself that he hadn't really considered what exactly his next move would be. He'd read enough true action novels and magazines to know that communication between the criminals and the law would start in earnest. They'd try to negotiate the release of the hostages. Maybe they'd storm the bank and kick some major ass. Harry didn't want to miss that, no chance. And now that he was able to sit more comfortably, it would be a hell of a show. If they did breech, he'd pull his own gun and do some damage, yes indeed, some nasty damage. However, now that he was free, at least to make a move for his gun, to remove his hood, he felt the grip of cowardice tighten. He could still be a hero, but yes, he'd wait for a sign, a move from the police or from the robbers that forced his hand. Then they'd pay, that would be the time. It was coming, he was sure of it. No sense in forcing it. Let it play out. Destiny was sweeping down upon them all.

Kayla

Alan and Kayla left through the side emergency exit; the alley was clear, and they walked the short 30 feet to the street in silence. As they neared the edge of the alley, where the sun-drenched sidewalk lay just beyond the seclusion of the sandwiched buildings, Kayla grabbed Alan's hand and gave it a squeeze.

"Good life to you and your daughter, Kayla," Alan said.

"You too." And as they reached the sidewalk, she quickly dropped his hand and walked away from him, the bank, the plan, the life, forever.

Alan

As Alan reached the opposite side of the street, he heard the faint but unmistakable shrill of police sirens approaching. His pace never wavered, and by the time he reached the small underground parking garage and his transportation out of the city, he had counted nine squad cars. It was gonna be one hell of a show. Quietly, he said a prayer for his remaining companions. For them, there was still so much left to do.

"What a ride," he thought.

Rudy

"How many inside?"

It was Bradick. Captain of the Phoenix SWAT teams, and general pain in the ass to the regular uniforms.

168

Rudy looked over his shoulder, but remained standing with binoculars in hand, pointed towards the bank. The perimeter had been sealed nicely as per his orders and traffic had been successfully re-routed with minimal delay. He'd done a great job and he wasn't about to let Bradick step in. Besides, he needed this, needed it very badly to up his political appeal and public opinion.

"They said sixteen," Rudy replied coolly.

Of course if something went wrong, something went amiss, he'd need a scapegoat. Bradick would fit the bill very nicely.

"What do you think, Bradick?" Rudy asked, feining interest.

"I've got my men moving into position now; I'll have a line on this thing in sixty seconds." Then he spoke quickly and dramatically into his headset microphone.

Just then MacMillan walked up to the car. "Chief, we've got the first news crew on site."

"Already?"

James nodded and pointed over to the back of the barricades.

"It's not Allison Brodie, is it?"

James shook his head. "Nope, never seen this one before, channel 9 still, name's Vanessa Greene. She's a looker."

"Good, I hate that Brodie bitch. How do I look?"

James looked him over quickly. "You're good to go."

"OK, bring her in, she'll be the only liaison; make sure she understands our position, will ya James?"

"You got it," replied MacMillan, and he shuffled off towards the news truck parked at the back and the woman being restrained by a couple of police officers.

"We can confirm through heat sensors that there are approximately twenty people inside the bank at this time and that they are centralized around the rear of the bank between the tellers' station and the offices."

Bradick spoke purposefully and confidently. He highlighted the areas where his team had confirmed the presence of people on a blueprint of the bank. Rudy admired his precision. He looked very

169

much the seasoned veteran in his black SWAT uniform, decked out with SWAT-issued communications gear and weaponry.

"Well done, Captain. I'd like you to formulate a plan for a breach of the bank complete with probable casualty rates in the next ten minutes. If we have to go, I want to be absolutely certain we can succeed."

Bradick, nodding, carried his blueprint back towards the command center, a large RV fitted with the latest and greatest tech the city could afford.

Rudy was glad to be rid of him for the time being. He peered through his binoculars. Nothing. It was almost time for his return phone call. Whoever they were, they certainly screwed the pooch on this one. Total snafu.

"Alright, I have her and her camera crew standing by," James revealed, once more coming to stand with him behind the squad car that sat directly across from the bank's large double-door lobby.

"It's time for the call. We'll make a statement right after," Rudy responded.

"You thinking breach?"

"With sixteen… how can we lose?" he confirmed coldly.

"We can't." James grinned. "We'll have the keys to the city when this is all over."

Simon

It was nearly time. Simon walked slowly. Patrick's words rambled around in his head. *You could be.* It was true. He'd found something, someone in this whole screwed-up situation, someone worth fighting for. That meeting had forced him to examine his years in Thailand. Comfortable, but empty. Those years felt hollow now. Wasted. Patrick had hollowed him out with those three words. Simon would not return the same man. And for the first time, he realized, he was happier for it. Patrick had read him straight down to the bone.

"All done?" he queried.

"Yes. It's the best I can do; the lower portion of the neck is still suspect but it's nothing that a collar can't cover," Margaret stated nervously.

"Well done. Patrick. Let's have a look at you…"

Patrick sat up. The work was remarkable. Simon grinned unconsciously. He was pleased. There would be little trouble convincing the officials that he was the man that he needed to be. It was a make-up job worthy of a professional and Simon knew it would most likely save all of their lives. When they saw Clay Mallory, they'd know. He didn't bluff.

Kayla and Alan had left quietly, as per the plan, out the side emergency exit. It was only a few precious moments afterwards that the sirens began to make their way through the busy city streets, tumbling down on their position. They'd had a sufficient amount of time to slip through the seams of the police blanket that was now no doubt fully engaged. They were ready. A few short conversations with the police, a few intense and vocal words spoken in earshot of the hostages, a few meticulous minutes on the bomb, and they would finish this, one way or another.

Except for the ringing of the office phone, an eerie silence fell upon the bank just then. Simon turned from his two Samaritans and prepared himself for the conversation that would follow. This was the cue that would set all other contingencies into motion. Like some great mountain that needed to be traversed, those final few agonizing steps, they were at that precipice, and everything that was to come would happen in a flurry, as speed and time and necessity would propel them to the final conclusion of this job. Time was about to move unfathomably fast and they would have the rest of their lives to contemplate the brilliance of the plan, the genius of its execution, and the bountiful abundance of its reward.

Patrick

Patrick was once again released from his bondage. Except this time he would not be re-bound, he'd be free to move, to run if he wanted, if the opportunity presented itself. Three people were dead

171

at the hands of these criminals; why was he helping them? Why shouldn't he just rip off the mask that covered him? Or better yet, he could remove the mask once he knew he was in visual range of the authorities. He glanced down at Margaret, still attached to the dead man. No. These were good people, worth saving.

The big man with the preacher's voice shuffled him down the hall back towards the main room. "Here. Take this. It'll be part of your performance when the time comes, and don't sweat it, this cake's got no filling."

Patrick took the weapon, cold and heavy. He'd never held a real gun before and was sorry to be holding one now.

"This will all be ancient history soon enough," commented his escort just as they moved into the main room and rejoined the hostages. "Take a seat in here."

Patrick moved into the VP's office off the front room. He sat heavily on the faded leather chair, the gun held loosely in his right hand, and his future grasped desperately in his left. He released the fist. His fingers ached from being held in place too long; his hand yawned out its cramps and complaints. Looking over at a painting in the room, he caught his reflection. The image startled him. Who was he? Who had he become? He reached up with his free hand to touch his face.

"I wouldn't touch it if I were you," came a voice from the open doorway. "Not yet at least."

It was more of a caution than a threat. But Patrick snapped his hand back down to his lap, all the same.

"If it's any consolation, you look better in that mask than the original owner."

Patrick felt a jolt of heated rage, like a flash of lightning in his mind. This wasn't any fucking fashion show, this was life and death, this was heaven and hell, this was a meeting of fate and death and divinity.

Tony

Tony's exhaustion was insurmountable. He'd been kicked around for hours of practice at the six football training camps he'd attended, and yet, those day-long rituals of brutal and merciless poundings could not rival the intensity of his present state. He felt spent. It hurt to move, but moving was a necessity. Clara needed him. Stone was dead. Conrad was dead. Twenty minutes ago they were in a car, talking, listening to the radio, living... breathing. No more. He moved his arms up and down the side of Clara's body, trying to reassure her, at least provide for her the veil of safety, the illusion of security. Her crying had stopped. No small reward for his exertions.

Tilting his head towards the noise, Tony could hear the robbers moving purposefully around the back of the bank. Something was happening. The air felt charged. Like the locker room right before game time, the output of every player, the emotional swing and adrenalin rush of every mind and body, propelled downwards into those instinctual motivations that drove human evolution. Survival of the fittest. He could feel the charge building.

For now, all they could do was listen.

"Don't be a fucking idiot, Will, there are cops everywhere... We ain't getting outta this one, no sir, we ain't getting outta here! I'm telling you, let's just rip this city a new asshole and take our chances when the bomb gets lit."

"Yeah, I think he's right, I'm not goin' in again, no fucking way."

It sounded so much like Conrad, the madness of desperation. Tony, felt certain the wheels were about to come off.

"You dumb fucks think you know what shit I went through in my last stint in the joint? Fucking ingrates. We do this according to plan, we'll light it up when and if the old man says so and not a goddamn second sooner and if I see anyone even so much as look in the direction of the back I'll tear your fucking eyes out with my teeth. Stupid fucks."

173

Someone spit the last words out in disgust.

"We'll wait for the call, there's a good chance we can bleed them a little more, a little longer, we'll just have to show them who they're up against."

Tony couldn't tell if there were three of four voices in the conversation.

"You got that right."

"Fuckin' right boss, fuckin' right."

On cue the phone rang. Tony couldn't hear any of the robbers while this exchange went on. They all hung, as he did, on every word of that brief phone conversation. The tension was palpable.

"OK, Mills, listen carefully. I have sixteen hostages. I have an arsenal of automatic weaponry, which I am prepared to use, and I have a bomb which could, if set off, wipe out this entire city block. Don't fuck with me. Others have fucked with me before, don't be a fool. You're dealin' with the Mallory brothers. I'm warning you, one red laser light penetrates a single bank window and we blow the bomb, got that Mills?"

A momentary pause proceeded the demands.

"We want a city bus, unmarked, out front in ten minutes. The bus will take us to the Feldman airfield; once at the airfield we will release all but five of the hostages. We want a Learjet gassed and ready to fly. I know there are three presently on the ground at the airfield so don't try to pull any bullshit delaying tactics. We will instruct the pilot where to go once we are airborne. The other hostages will be released once we land at our destination.

"You have ten minutes. Don't try anything. Get that bus parked outside or the blood of these hostages will be on your hands."

The call ended.

Tony's mind was whipping with possibilities. He nudged Clara. If they had to move quickly, he'd need her ready.

"Clara," he whispered. "Clara, we are gonna have to move, and I mean soon."

"So I hear," she said, shifting away from him slightly. "I can't see anything."

"Stretch your legs and tense your muscles a bunch of times, that'll get the blood flowing back into them. I can make out dull shapes, but I've heard enough. Hold still, let me see if I can get some slack on this hood."

Tony leaned into Clara's shoulder; his hood, he could see from the light emanating from below his chin, was loose. After a few moments he had it above his nose and off of his right eye. Clara did her part by pinching the fabric between her chin and shoulder.

"I can see now."

Tony heard someone coming from the direction of the offices. "Stay still," he whispered to Clara. It was a man; he walked out, through the hostages, and stood purposefully, quietly in front of the double lobby doors. In one hand he held something metal, perhaps the detonator for the bomb, and in the other he held a gun. He stood there, staring out the front. For an instant, Tony felt like the man might bolt, make a run for the lobby: he stood suspiciously taut, knees slightly bent, ready to sprint. But then he turned and walked slowly back towards the offices. As he turned Tony saw his face. He saw the terror that burned in those eyes. Something was very wrong.

Margaret

Margaret had been moved from the back. She'd been lifted gently to her feet by the biggest of the robbers. The act of lifting her seemed as effortless as lifting a briefcase; this one had some strength in him to be sure. She was tired. She felt the pins and needles of her confinement in her feet as she was guided back into the main room with the rest of the hostages and placed in a remote corner of the bank, close, she noticed, to Harry Truman. Judging from the stains on his shirt, he undoubtedly stank of body odor and she was glad to be away from him, at least some small distance. They'd never gotten along. Not since an episode in the staff room when he said he'd smelt blood. A ridiculous comment. No one was bleeding, and of the three other women in the lounge, she might not have been the only one menstruating. It was a particularly heavy flow that day and she'd been horrified by his callous comment. She'd left immediately. He was a strange man, that much was certain.

She was bound with her hands in front of her body, a far more comfortable position than when they first took the bank. Looking about, she could see the bodies of her co-workers and customers, their arms stretched behind them; her shoulders ached just looking at them. She was also glad to be without the hood that many of the other hostages wore; she supposed that since she was now privy to their intentions, her vision needn't be obscured. Whatever the reason, she felt more in control than she had in the beginning. She tried not to think about the money. There it was, strapped to her body, perfectly disguised. A sum of money that could set her free, once and for all. She'd once thought that there was no sum of money, no amount of financial freedom that could win her that prize. That had been this morning, but now, now that reality was baiting her with a future, and a means to set that future in motion, she entertained thoughts of independence.

She watched carefully as Patrick made his way to the front of the bank. She was proud of the work she'd done; he was very nearly a spitting image of the dead man. At the same time she was terrified, waiting for the whispered whiffle of the single, silenced bullet that would kill him. But none came. And moments later, she saw him turn and head back towards the office, mission accomplished. She heaved a heavy sigh of relief. It had worked.

The telephone rang for the second time.

"You've got eight minutes to produce the bus. If at eight minutes you have not provided our transportation, we will begin to kill the hostages. One hostage every minute after the eight, until there is only one hostage left. At that time, we will wait for you to breach the bank. When you do, we will set off the bomb. Many lives will be lost; you alone will take the blame. We will only talk again if and when the bus arrives. You have seven and a half minutes."

Click.

"Screw 'em! They ain't gonna deliver, let's blow this place now!"

"Calm down. They'll deliver."

"Yeah, shut the hell up, we're waiting for the *Man* to pull his head out of his ass here, and he's still got seven minutes to do it." The canned dialogue continued.

"Bullshit. That's bullshit. Let's set the bomb."

"Shut up!" The tall, skinny one pushed Keith. He came up hard against the wall of the staff room. Both men pulled their weapons. Training the barrels for a pair of head shots. Slowly and cautiously the big man drew his weapon. Patrick also raised his gun in the direction of the lanky fellow. Quickly and quietly it was three against one; the thin one with the short fuse was outnumbered. The big one, the one who had helped Margaret to the front, seemed less enthusiastic about his choice, but he'd made it nonetheless. There was a bond here, they shared something, the big man and the thin one, that much was certain.

"Lower your weapon." It was Keith's voice, no question about it. Low and smooth. Guiding. "Lower and holster the weapon…"

The shoulders relaxed in the long thin one, the gun dipped, then lowered, and was placed once more in his belt. "Shit… I got a bad feeling about this."

"Let's all relax. Sebastian," the big man finally got a name, "take Will to the back and set the timer, try to calm him down, we are still in control here," said Patrick. His voice wavered in the beginning but soon found its conviction. He was a quick study.

The two left the corridor, heading towards the vault. Once out of earshot, Keith called Patrick over. Margaret was prepared for the next words, having heard them several times while she was applying the mask to Patrick's face. Still, it frightened her.

"You want to waste those two?" Patrick queried.

"God-damn right we should waste them, shoot them both, back of the head, they're liabilities, and I'm tired of nursing their egos," Keith confirmed.

177

"Do it," Patrick said loudly.

With that Simon slid through the maze of exhausted and terrified bodies down through the hallway where Grier had been shot and killed, then resurrected, then died again. Margaret could envision him turning the corner towards the vault, removing the silencer from his weapon in order make a larger impact on the hostages. He fired twice; the echoing screams of bullets vomited so quickly, so brutally from the chamber of his gun, gave Margaret a numbing, spine-tingling sensation. She halfway believed that Patrick, standing at the back of the bank, still wearing the mask she'd transferred, would turn the gun on the hostages and open fire. Instead, he reached into the pocket of the jacket he was wearing and removed a small blade. All according to plan. At least the elements of the plan that she had been clued in to throughout Patrick's rehearsal.

"Presentation is everything," Keith told Patrick at the end of his instructions, as she put the final touches on his mask. She wondered if Kevin knew yet about her predicament. He'd be halfway into a twenty-sixer of vodka over at McBean's, it's where all the guys hang out he used to say... She knew better. McBean's opened for drinks at ten, early bird gets the worm, so to speak. They'd have televisions on. Kevin fancied a younger newswoman from Channel 9, Vanessa something or other. She realized that he probably didn't have any idea where she worked. She giggled, thinking about the absurdity of her life. Patrick, she noticed, was moving quickly, hostage to hostage, up, down, blade flashing. Soon it would be her turn.

Chapter 14

Vanessa

Vanessa stood naked in the window on the 21st floor of the Wiltshire Hotel and watched the first light of day touch the city. She'd been in Arizona for four years, fighting for the spotlight, waiting for a break. She was a star, but it seemed to be taking an awfully long time for people to see that. Four long years. The thought irritated her, but her attention was diverted to her own glorious reflection in the window, illuminated in the glowing morning light.

"Fucking right," she whispered to her image. "Star quality."

Everything was going to change – starting today. She turned from the window and slipped into bed. She had waited a long time to play this game. She knew from experience the danger of it, but that only enticed her more.

"Jack," she whispered sweetly. The figure next to her showed no sign of movement or lucidity. She began stroking his chest, belly and thighs. His body immediately responded, though his mind was still dreamily occupied. She continued her journey across his body until he stirred and she could hear his breath quicken. With cat-like ease, she rose above him. He was now awake enough to participate and his hand moved past her small waist to cup each breast in turn. She was impressed, despite herself. She had not expected this man to be half the lover he turned out to be. Jack Donoghue would be celebrating his 17th wedding anniversary next week. In Vanessa's experience, a man married that long was not a gifted lover. She knew instantly that this was not his first indiscretion. She didn't care. It made her job a little easier.

She lowered herself onto him. He gasped slightly and closed his eyes, arching his back in an appreciative mutual effort. She watched him closely, rotating her hips and using her knees to slide her body along his chest.

"Oh, Jack," she breathed. "Oh, baby."

Jack moaned, arching his back further so that his face nearly disappeared in the pillows. Vanessa reached down and yanked them away, tossing them on the floor. She slid her body down onto him, rubbing her breasts on his chest, thrusting her tongue into his mouth. She had his full attention now.

She pulled back and slowed, watching him. He had the glazed look of pleasure that told her the ride was nearly over. She stepped up the pace. His head twisted from side to side; his hands squeezed each nipple tightly. She screamed as the orgasm shook her, moving her hips suddenly to drive him home. He gasped and spasmed.

She slid off of him slowly. Panting and sweating beside him.

Jack got up and went to the bathroom. At 43, he was in amazing shape and despite herself, Vanessa watched the sinewy muscles in his legs as they carried him across the room. His whole demeanor projected control. As executive producer of Channel 9 News, he was a seasoned veteran who demanded respect. His power had intimidated her when she first arrived as a copywriter four years earlier. It was that same commanding presence that drew her to him now.

She heard the shower start and looked at her watch on the nightstand. Almost 7:30. She hadn't realized how late it was. Time for another day in the trenches.

"We should have done this sooner," Vanessa mused, stepping into the steamy shower with Jack. He wiped the suds from his face and took her tanned body into his arms. He looked at her for a long time before bending to kiss her lightly.

"You are stunning," he said, nuzzling into her mussed, thick auburn hair. "I am glad we did."

"Me too," she whispered, sliding out of his arms and into the stream of warm water. She heard him leave the bathroom and realized she had been holding her breath. Damn. A few deep breaths and she was on the way to winning the battle with her guilt. She could justify her behavior. It was just easier when the feelings were reciprocated. There would be no relationship. She had no time for such triviality. This was business.

"This would be much easier without my Christian roots," she said out loud to herself. She filled her palm with shampoo and began to massage it into her hair. The curls she wore naturally belied the length of her hair that came to her elbows when wet. She swept it up and her mind swirled with the suds around the drain.

Vanessa Greene had been born Karen O'Shea to second generation Irish immigrants in a small rural Pennsylvania community. The only remnants left of the youngest tomboy child of Annie and Colin O'Shea was the rich red hair and the name of the county she grew up in. Greene County. She kept the name as a reminder of a place to which she would never return. A childhood – dead and buried.

Always the rebel, Vanessa was adventurous and inquisitive. It was no surprise that she landed in the career that she did. She learned in early adolescence to use the gifts that God had given her to charm her way out of anything. She was a natural beauty and, though many tried, she had never accepted the love of any man. Her dreams were far too large to be crowded by relationships. At 17, she convinced a married man to run away with her and they left Pennsylvania for New York the summer she graduated. They were not long in the city when she detached herself from him and landed a job fetching coffee for reporters at the *Times*. From there she learned all that she could about the business, took night school courses and cultured professional relationships in the tiny bedroom of her shabby apartment. Always careful, she spent her nights with particular men who could help advance her ambitious career plans. They were either married or equally ambitious so there was never any worry about the relationship becoming anything more than a business proposition. It was far from foolproof and she'd been burned a few times – New York was a tough learning ground. All in all she had no regrets about the path she'd chosen. Everything was going according to plan. She adopted a new name, Vanessa Greene, and a new backstory, an orphaned child of middle class parents determined to make it on her own. An orphaned child, had no where to go for Christmas or Thanksgiving, they had lots of free time around the holidays, and they needed guidance, the kind of fatherly or motherly advice that editors and station managers liked to dole out. However, during her fifth summer in New York, working at a local station as a copywriter, everything very nearly, fell apart.

Throughout her time in New York she dutifully sent periodic correspondence to her parents, informing them of her successes. She provided them with a post office box number for return mail, but paid little attention to the gushes of bad grammar that returned with all the news from Greene County. The last thing she expected on the eve of her 24th birthday, when she returned home with her producer for a nightcap, was to find her parents in the foyer of her apartment building. Horrified, Vanessa was too shocked to properly contain the situation, and before she could regain her composure, her father was amiably shaking the hand of her date and making introductions. It was a disaster that destroyed her credibility. She was forced to pack up and leave New York for parts unknown. In Phoenix, she met with Jack Donaghue for a low-level copywriter post and here she had been reborn. He had offered her the job on the spot, never checking into her background in New York. She hadn't communicated with her family since and legally changed her name to avoid ever having to deal with similar situations.

"I'm heading out," Jack called from outside the bathroom door, startling Vanessa out of her musings.

"OK, Jack," she responded, rinsing the suds from her hair, "I'll see you at work."

"Try not to be late this time," he suggested. The water pounding on her head had masked the sound of the bathroom door opening; "Status meetings are always at nine sharp." Jack pulled back the curtain, winked and smiled. Vanessa leaned out and kissed him quickly, playfully biting his bottom lip.

"We could both be late, you know," she said provocatively.

"Yes, we could," he responded, despite her grip on his lower lip, "but darling, I fear that if I do not leave you now, I never will." He pulled away from her and gave her another playful wink.

"Get out," she laughed, pulling the curtain closed between them.

"See you in an hour," he called as he closed the bathroom door behind him. Vanessa rinsed the conditioner from her hair, turned off the water, and grabbed a towel. She was famished. She would have to make time for room service.

Vanessa arrived at the station at 9:08 and ran through the halls to the meeting, already in progress. Everyone stopped talking for a moment when she burst in apologizing and making up an excuse about traffic. Jack shot her a stern look and pointed to his watch. She smiled and took her seat.

"As I was saying," Jack continued, carefully taking a swig of coffee, "we are all very proud of Allison and wish her luck in her new ventures with CNN." Everyone turned to Allison and clapped as they offered their collective congratulations.

Allison Brodie had been the anchor at Channel 9 News for five years after a long run in the field with the station. She had recently been offered a position as a features reporter for a national affiliate. The promotion was as much a feather in Jack's cap as hers. He had groomed her from the beginning, much the same way that he was now working with Vanessa, and their patience and hard work had paid off with this recognition. Vanessa's congratulations were less than enthusiastic. She and Allison had been sparring with each other since Vanessa's arrival in Arizona. They were similarly minded: starkly ambitious and competitive to the point of near physical confrontation. Underlying the battles a strange sort of respect had formed. Vanessa suspected, but could not confirm, that Allison too had slept with Jack. Promotion or not, Vanessa felt confident that she was the better lover and what Allison had done in five years, she would do in three.

"OK, everyone." Jack tried to bring the meeting back to order and returned to his seat, flashing a warning look in Vanessa's direction. She slid back into her shoes under the table and avoided his eyes. "Allison will be moving off the desk for her final few weeks here and onto the street. For the moment, David will handle the desk duties alone. No decisions have been made about a replacement at this point, so just hang tight for a while."

There had been much speculation about whether Jack would move people around from inside the station, or bring in a new face for the main desk. Vanessa was pleased that no decisions had been made. Though it was unlikely that she would be given the coveted desk position, she hoped to at least move up from the puff pieces that she had been delivering for the past year. She wanted some hard news for a change and felt more than ready for it. The fact that Allison was not being replaced immediately gave her hope that she still had a shot.

Jack was handing out the day's assignments and Vanessa paid little attention until she heard her name.

"Vanessa, I want you to interview Mrs. Ito of the Japanese American Historical Society. They are having an event at the old internment camps to educate Japanese Americans on their history here."

"Nice," Vanessa coughed.

"Try not to get too excited," Jack responded coolly. "This could be a great story for you. It's racially charged; maybe it could lead to a series of reports."

"Yeah," Vanessa agreed half-heartedly. "No problem."

"OK, folks," Jack addressed the room, visibly angered by Vanessa's attitude. "Let's get out there."

Everyone rose and filed from the room. Vanessa gathered her papers slowly, pouting as she tried to think of some way to spice up this puffy report.

"Vanessa," Jack was flipping through his own pile of paper, "hang back a minute." The remaining reporters in the room hurried their exit, recognizing the tone in Jack's voice. When the room emptied, Jack rose and walked its length to close the door.

"What the hell is with the attitude lately?" he started.

"I am tired of these soft pieces, Jack, and you know it," Vanessa spat.

"We have been through this before. You will get your chance. You just have to be patient." He spoke like a father to an insolent child.

"Jack," Vanessa said in exasperation, "don't give me that shit. I don't count patience as one of my virtues. I want a shot, some real news!"

"Look, I can't help you right now. Maybe in a few weeks when Allison is gone and things have settled down a bit we can look at changing the menu for you. Until then, Vanessa, I don't need your attitude."

"Aw, Jack, I may not be happy about it, but I am still giving you quality stuff."

"Just see that it continues." Jack held her gaze for a moment, looking every bit the part of the powerful producer, and then left the room. Vanessa quashed the urge to send her paperwork across the mahogany table and settled for crumpling the edges in her fist. A few minutes later she was dodging interns in the hall looking for her ride.

As usual, Vanessa's sidekick was milling around her desk waiting for her. Larry Finley was a 37-year-old lackey who drove the truck and operated the camera for Vanessa. He had never been married, probably had never had any meaningful relationships, and as far as Vanessa could tell, had zero professional aspirations. Hardly the ideal fit for Vanessa. He was capable at his job, but lacked imagination. To make matters worse his obvious attraction to her was a constant annoyance. She had pleaded with Jack many times to replace him, but to no avail. He was a fixture around the station and rumor had it that he was related to the ownership in some way. As far as Vanessa was concerned, that could be the only explanation for his long tenure there.

"Well, hello, gorgeous," Larry drooled, "you are looking wonderful, as usual, today." Vanessa's skin crawled and she couldn't help the look of disgust that came over her. She didn't even try to hide it anymore. Larry seemed completely oblivious.

"Larry, for Christ's sake," she snapped, pushing past him to her cubicle. "How many times have I told you not to talk to me that way. Are you capable of maintaining some semblance of professionalism?"

"Oh, cranky today, I see," Larry rambled, appraising her through his horn-rimmed glasses. "I heard that you had a little run-in with Jack this morning, but don't take it out on me." He feigned hurt, but his eyes remained focused on her breasts.

"Larry," Vanessa sighed, "go start the damn truck."

"Anything you want, hot stuff." Larry bolted from the cubicle, barely avoiding the sponge brick that Vanessa hurled in his direction. Jack had given her the gag brick a few years earlier when her temper had caused some minor damage to a vending machine. She stepped out to retrieve it when Larry was out of sight and placed it back in the top drawer of her desk.

She finished her coffee, reviewed her e-mails, and tried to focus on the task at hand. Jack had provided her with enough research and background information to go straight to the interview. It was annoying and entirely too efficient of him. She had no excuse not to have the story ready quickly. Jack knew her very well. She knew Larry would wait in the truck until she got there regardless of how long she took, so she decided to stall a bit longer and tour the station. It was part of the job. There was always something going on and she needed to keep her ears open to the gossip to stay in the loop. Especially now with so much up on the line.

A half-hour later, having found little new information, Vanessa decided to make her last stop at Kelly Sullivan's desk. Kelly had been working as Allison's assistant for a little over a year, and she and Vanessa had formed a strange attachment. They were nothing alike. Kelly was sweet and innocent, completely loyal to Allison and dedicated to her work. She was recently married and starting her 6th month of pregnancy. Vanessa liked her immediately and, though Kelly was slightly intimidated by Vanessa and her reputation, the feeling was mutual.

"Hey Kelly," Vanessa said as she swung around the corner, startling Kelly in the process.

"Oh shit, you scared me."

"Sorry, Kelly, I didn't mean to startle you. Your alright?" Vanessa asked.

"Yes, I am fine, thanks," Kelly confirmed, reaching across her console to turn down the scanner volume. "I haven't seen you in awhile. Where have you been hiding?"

"Nowhere exciting," Vanessa whined. "What about you? Allison keeping you busy?"

"Busy? That's an understatement. She has me on these monitors for days waiting for a story good enough for her to take on. I've started talking to my husband in police code." Kelly laughed and shifted in her chair, her hand across her swelling belly. Vanessa laughed as well. She could imagine Allison's urge for a good live story to add to her personal achievements before she left for national exposure.

"I swear," Kelly continued, "if nothing noteworthy happens soon, she may insist that I rob a bank for her or something."

"Well, don't worry, Kelly, something is bound to come up. So, how is the baby?" Vanessa inquired, placing a hand on Kelly's abdomen. She was fascinated by Kelly's stories about the pregnancy.

"Getting big," Kelly sighed, "and already running my life. I am in the bathroom every fifteen minutes. As a matter of fact, I am dying to go right now, but Allison will kill me if I leave my post. Vanessa, can you listen to the monitor for a few minutes for me?" Kelly pleaded.

"Of course I will. You go on," Vanessa responded quickly.

"Oh, thanks. I'll just be a minute or so," Kelly gushed, easing slowly from her chair and waddling down the hall.

Vanessa sank into the chair, careful to keep her weight balanced to the front to compensate for the settings preferred by her pregnant friend. She turned the volume up slightly, feeling sorry for Kelly, listening to this boring babble all day. She was wondering how long Kelly might be when she heard a frantic call. Immediately she switched from speaker to headphones. The female dispatcher sounded frightened and repeated the code in progress. Vanessa grabbed the manual and flipped through it until she found the definition.

"Holy shit," Vanessa said to herself. This was her story. Fate put her in that chair at that moment. She was giddy. When she saw Kelly coming down the hall she quickly changed the channel on the scanner. It would sound the same to Kelly and give her the time she needed to get her ass to the scene. She removed the headphones, grabbed the scrap of paper that she had scribbled the address on, and bid a hasty farewell to her friend. As she rushed out to the truck, the image of Kelly lowering herself slowly into her chair forced a surprising pang of guilt, but she quickly pushed it aside. This was her opportunity. This was the best chance she might ever get. Fuck Allison Brodie. She already had her break. It was her turn now.

"Larry!" Vanessa barked, jumping into the truck. He had been napping and her sudden appearance caused him to hit the lever that brought the driver's seat upright, sending his head onto the steering wheel, sounding the horn.

"What the hell?" He stated, rubbing his head and re-setting his glasses on his long nose.

Vanessa thrust the scribbled address into his face and did a quick check behind her of the van's contents. Everything was in place. Vanessa was satisfied, but they still weren't moving as Larry continued to moan about his head.

"Drive, Larry!" Vanessa demanded.

"What's going on?" Larry asked, fumbling for the ignition, looking confused by the edge in Vanessa's voice.

"Just shut up and drive," Vanessa said flatly, reaching into her bag for her phone.

"OK, OK, I'm driving," Larry muttered as the engine sprang to life. He placed the scrap of paper that Vanessa had given him in the visor over his head. The National Bank of America, 1st Avenue and Taylor. Larry cast a quick glance at his passenger and decided not to ask any more questions.

Vanessa's mind was racing. She had to do this right. She opened Maps on her phone and found the intersection. She was trying to picture the street. She needed something close by. Of course, the Piazza Petrullio wasn't too far from the bank's location, three or four blocks at most. Perfect. She rifled through her bag until she found the number for Mrs. Ito. Quickly she dialed the number and checked her watch. 11am. This could work. The phone was ringing. One. Two. Come on. Four. Five. Larry took the corner of 14th Street and 7th Avenue a little tight and nearly sent Vanessa out of her seat. She glared at him and reached for the seat belt. Six. Finally a click and the answering machine at the Ito residence picked up.

"Come on, come on," Vanessa whispered to herself as the message rambled on. She could already hear the police sirens and knew that they were very close to their destination. Finally, the long beep sounded and Vanessa started to speak calmly, hiding her growing excitement.

"Hello, this message is for Mrs. Yuka Ito. This is Vanessa Greene from Channel 9 News. I believe that our station manager has discussed with you our desire to run a story about the plans you have for the historical preservation of internment camps and the Japanese American Historical Society. I would like to set up a meeting for today, if possible. It is," Vanessa paused for a moment to check her watch and quickly recount the morning's events, "11:00 am and I would love to meet you for lunch, say at 12:30. Do you know a restaurant called the Piazza Petrullio on 4th Avenue?" Larry started to protest the lie and Vanessa held up her hand and glared at him. "Please call me on my cell phone at 602

555-6729 to confirm. Thank you and I hope to hear from you soon."

She hung up the phone as they turned onto Main Street. A line of black and white cruisers had already taken position in front of the bank, but the street was clear otherwise. They were able to pull the van up into the melee before being flagged down by a uniformed officer. Vanessa's heart was pounding in her throat. She looked at Larry; he was grinning from ear to ear, like some toy clown. She grabbed the direct line headset to the station.

"I have to talk to Jack," Vanessa demanded, when an intern picked up the receiver. "No one else but Jack." A few moments later Jack's voice came over the radio.

"What's going on, Vanessa? Where are you?"

"Jack," Vanessa was breathless, "I made plans to meet Mrs. Ito downtown on 4th Avenue and when we passed 1st and Taylor the place was crawling with cops. We're in front of the National Bank of America on 1st Avenue. I'm not certain if it's a bank robbery or a terrorist attack in progress. There might be hostages. We are the only news crew on the scene. Not sure how long that will last." Vanessa looked at Larry, who was staring at her with his mouth open. She slapped him on the shoulder. He laughed briefly out loud and made his way to the back of the van to get the equipment ready. "What should I do?"

"Don't worry. I'll talk you through it. I want you to get ready to go live on air. Set up your shot and put Larry on the line."

This was it. Live on air. Sweeter words were never spoken.

Chapter 15

Patrick

Patrick moved quickly. His job was simple. He enjoyed doing it. He moved from hostage to hostage cutting their hands loose. He instructed each hostage, "Stretch your arms but don't get up or touch your hood." He added, "It'll be over soon."

Freeing the bluish hands and allowing the hostages to roll their shoulders and move, even slightly, gave him tremendous satisfaction. He was responsible for liberating them; he was the quiet shepherd watching over them in their hour of need. He still wore the mask and he found that a little unsettling; Keith had promised he would remove it when he returned from the vault, but it wasn't soon enough for Patrick. His task occupied him enough to keep thoughts of it at bay. Halfway through the severing of the plastic ties, several shots hissed out in the stillness of the bank. Even silenced gunfire wasn't so silent in the stark vacuum of the bank. He froze. Everyone froze. Patrick breathed. Slowly inhaling. Slowly exhaling. Those shots weren't part of any plan that he knew of. He looked down at the knife and quickly got back on task. Stay focused. Free these people. He had worked through two thirds of the hostages. Only a few people remained bound, a security guard, two men in business suits and Margaret. Patrick saw three men creep into the main room from the back hall. Two were unrecognizable, but he surmised quickly that they were two of the now maskless robbers. In fact, putting the pieces together in his mind, they had to be the two robbers, the big guy and the skinny one, that Keith had offered to take out. No doubt, they were meant to blend in with the other hostages. Well planned, thought Patrick. The other was Keith, who beckoned him over before joining the other two sitting against the sidewall of the offices. Patrick obeyed.

"Let's get that off," Keith stated quickly, reaching up from his squatting position. Patrick knelt beside him. The other two moved further into the room. The mask came off in three pieces, almost disintegrating in Keith's hands, making Margaret's work all the more remarkable.

"That's better. Good as new."

"Feels better." Patrick nodded.

"How far did you get?" asked Keith.

"Only four left, including Margaret."

"Great. Sit tight, I'll finish up." Keith said, moving to stand.

Patrick made a motion to sit, then reconsidered. He wanted to say something to Margaret, and he felt that this might be his one and only opportunity.

"No, let me finish. I want to thank Margaret."

Keith considered his request.

"OK, just stay put over there when you're done, though. Got it?"

Patrick nodded his understanding and stood once more. He noticed that the big man and the skinny guy still remained fairly close together. It was disturbing how different they looked.

Harry

The shit was hitting the fan. He'd almost been uncovered. Someone was moving from hostage to hostage, and the sound was unmistakable. They were cutting the wrist ties. Luckily he was stationed in a fairly remote area of the bank and would be one of the last if not the final one released. In his mind, Harry imagined how he would allow the robber to turn him slightly in order to reach the plastic tie behind his back, how he would grab the hand that was behind him while his torso pitched forward letting him reach into his pants for the waiting gun, then how he would do a quarter roll, in order to lie on his side as he fired the pistol point blank into the robber's brain. It was flawless. He'd seen it done a thousand times on the cop shows and in the movies. In his mind, he played out the same scenario over and over. Each time he heard the quick slice of the blade through plastic, his mind quickened. Soon he'd be discovered, soon he'd be a hero. In his heart of hearts, he knew he awaited more likely the butt end of a pistol as his secret freedom was revealed. He'd been listening to everything that had transpired between the robbers, the factions and how they'd been divided. The cold-blooded murder of their own. Why would they hesitate to kill him, given their brutal, lethal tendencies? No, sir. In their shoes, he figured he would kill the fat security guard without so much as a second thought. But these were his shoes he was wearing... always one size too big, he'd never been able to fill them, to fill anything in his life, his house, his job, his dreams. No matter how fat he became.

Harry counted the shots as he heard them. One. Silenced gunfire? Two. Yes, definitely. Three. Not in this room. Four. But somewhere close. Five. There's a rhythm to the firing. Six. Like someone shooting at a target. Seven. Probably a ten-bullet magazine. Eight. An automatic pistol. Silence. Harry strained to hear, but no more shots came. A magazine usually holds ten bullets... wait a minute, thought Harry, if it's the same gun from the killing, well that would explain the two missing bullets. Harry grinned slightly under his hood, he was pleased with his deduction. Harry saw the knife wielder get back to work, his shadowy form traveling to the next batch of hostages. Only four or five hostages left. It was only seconds now before he was exposed. Then, inexplicably, the blade-slinging killer returned to the central area before Harry's cunning was revealed. It was to be only a momentary reprieve; Harry could see, through the cloth of the sweat-soaked hood he wore, the same knife-toting bastard walk quietly over in his direction. Harry's heart raced. His glands worked overtime and pumped even more fluid out of his body. He felt flush, the blood streaming to his muscles, begging for action, pleading for movement. The fight or flight response shot into his barrel chest and he felt the vise grips of certainty bear down on him. He was going to die... he was going to die. His mind released itself, the images of heroic deeds and practiced combat fled, leaving behind a mind so terrified, so hopelessly unprepared for death that for once, finally, he, Harry S. Truman, was able to act.

Simon

Simon moved back towards the hostage holding area. The bomb was primed. Both Carl and Pete had shed their alter egos and now walked silently behind him in their full civilian guise. The masks and clothes were left draping over the bomb, along with the discarded remains of the real Mallory boys. A menagerie of twisted body parts and artificial skin littered the floor of the vault. The bomb detonator fit anonymously into Simon's left palm, an easy click to unlock followed by a three-quarter squeeze to release. There was no timer: although the job had been painstakingly coordinated, a timer wouldn't allow them the kind of flexibility they required. It had been a point of debate several weeks ago; some argued that the bomb would force them all to stay on task, on schedule, but Simon had convinced them, with the help of Carl, that a preset timer eliminated too many options. Of course, Grier had been the last to give in to their logic. His plan, his baby, needed nothing but six warm bodies with a grade ten education, he'd proclaim, especially after someone had screwed up in those tedious weeks of preparation. Glancing down at his watch, Simon smiled briefly. They were seven minutes past where they should have been. Everyone would have been vaporized by now, had they not banged away on Grier's ego till he relinquished the idealistic insanity of the timer. Simon realized Grier's death had relaxed him. He was in control, he was calling the shots and that calmed him.

He'd been dazed in the vault when Carl told him about the second bomb. Simon couldn't believe what he was hearing.

"A second bomb, what for?" Simon had questioned when he'd ascertained that Carl was speaking the truth. Sure enough, there in the second briefcase was another explosive device, except this one... this one was ten times as deadly, ten times as destructive as the first. "The first bomb." It sounded ridiculous. Talk about overkill. Grier had really screwed them over this time: it was one thing to get plugged in the throat halfway through a foolproof plan and quite another to bring in something like this on the sly. Something that could kill everyone in the building.

"He didn't think you'd like the idea... I'm sorry, Simon, but you're the only one that didn't know" was Carl's reply. "He figured on setting the initial explosion off; it would provide the noise and the smoke to drive out the hostages and cause general hysteria with the crowd and cops. He'd been agitated about being detained by the police. If the police had a secure perimeter, it was very possible that everyone could be detained, and possibly, however unlikely, caught."

Simon nodded as Carl spoke; certainly the adage of not killing the messenger was being invoked. Simon's stomach dropped a couple of inches. A second bomb – this was turning out to be one big joke.

"So he suggested that as we all left the bank with the hostages on the tails of the first bomb, and made our ways to our individual escape routes, he would detonate the second bomb in order to assure our flight to freedom," Carl continued, looking sheepishly at Simon.

"It made sense to us, Simon. We all agreed."

"So, if it made such great sense, why didn't anyone tell me?" The agitation in Simon's voice was unmistakable. "I want to know how this ingrate," he pointed and kicked slightly at Grier's body just to the left of where he was standing, "how this genius convinced you not to tell me?"

Pete fidgeted with his hands. Finally he pulled out his gun and polished it on his jacket. Over and over. He was losing his edge, Simon could see. The anxiety eating away at his resolve was gaining ground, advancing, marching forward to that dangerous precipice where Pete would finally, fatally, act. Simon wanted to say forget it and just hustle up to the front, putting everyone at ease, but he waited instead for Carl's response. He had to know.

Carl looked conflicted. He placed his hand on Simon's shoulder and confessed, "He said he was gonna kill you and stick you in the vault with the body parts, that you were fodder for the forensics team."

Simon's face whitened. He could feel it, the color drain like a plug being pulled, circling around and around and around until it was gone. He felt gutted. He'd given up so much, sacrificed so much, to help Grier, to help them all.

"We fought him on it, after you'd arrived. But he'd threatened to bag the whole job if we dissented. We all needed this job, Simon... I'm sorry."

How could he, of all people, have been so blind to their intentions? He could feel the weight of this revelation come to bear mercilessly on his shoulders. Of course he wasn't told about the second bomb; he was the one person in this band of misfits that had any moral fiber, any conscience about the safety of others... There was no question in his mind, he was the one person who would have fought to the bitter end against the notion of a second bomb. Pete could be turned he knew, Carl not so easily. Kayla? *"Watch your back,"* echoed through his head. *"I'm hoping for one deviation,"* she'd said. Alan, too?

Simon looked down at the body of Grier, rolling him over from his face-down position so that he could see the man who had planned his execution.

"You lose," Simon concluded.

He felt his finger twitch, the gun now positioned loosely over Grier's body. He saw him, standing in his living room in Thailand, the smug aura of Grier's arrogance filling the peaceful confines of Simon's life. He saw the wide-eyed adrenalin junkie getting ready for the push in the van this morning. He saw a mentor, a friend... a mortal enemy. He saw the others, Pete, Carl,

Alan and Kayla, talking in hallways and kitchens. Simon recalled a few sideways glances, a head shake, a nod. Had it all been about him? About the plan? He remembered the connection he'd made with Kayla and the sadness in her eyes just last night. How? Simon couldn't remember when he started shooting but by the time he was done he'd pumped his entire magazine into the lifeless body, shot after shot, bullet after bullet. The bank stirred with the whispers of silenced gunfire.

"Shit man, he's FUBAR," Pete said, looking down at the remains.

"Time to end this," came Simon's reply, ejecting his empty magazine and replacing it with a fresh one. His face once more flush and full, his tank re-filled, his resolve cemented in survival. Simon led them out of the vault towards the main room.

"How is it activated?" Simon asked.

"The detonator, it's dual channeled, same detonator as the one you've already got boss, just flip the switch on the bottom."

"Easy enough," Simon sneered. 'Let's light it up."

Rudy

Rudy hit the pavement, hard and fast. The "shots fired" alarm was raised over comms. Rudy could see, towards the back of the barricades, people ducking a little further down. Many of them ended up on their knees, which is where they should have been all along. After several quiet moments, heads began to poke up from behind the perceived safety of car doors and doorframes. The silence, coupled with the quickening of everything around him, told Rudy that his adrenal glands were working overtime. Easy... easy... he told himself. His pulse rate slowed.

He thumbed his walkie-talkie. "Captain Bradick, I want a report on those shots."

"Yes, sir. Stand by."

James beckoned him over to the large TV truck just on the edge of the barricade. Shots fired meant that any life saved was a bonus, for the public could never refute the possibility that some hostages may have already been killed. Rudy approached James who stood with a sharply dressed, beautiful young reporter. Oh what he wouldn't give for a full body search on this one.

"Chief Mills, this is Vanessa Greene with channel 9."

"A pleasure to meet you, Chief," she stated with confidence.

Mills shared a sideways glance at James, who tossed a similar glance back at him.

"OK. Listen up, Vanessa," Rudy started, glancing up at the cameraman. "First things first. Turn that camera off or you're out."

The camera dropped down; the cameraman looked relieved; apparently the camera was as heavy as it looked.

"Good," continued Rudy. "I like channel 9, but I hate that bimbo they've got anchoring, I don't know how you're here so quickly or how you got yourself into this position but, honey, this could take you places. Now, you and only you will be my direct link to the media. I will filter all my information to you before I go public with it."

Rudy paused for effect. He waited. The generosity of this deal demanded some kind of appreciation, and yet Vanessa just stood there with the same intense stare that she wore a moment ago.

"OK, you know what? Forget it. Maybe you're not the right person for this…"

"No, no. I know what you need, I can do it for you," Vanessa stammered.

"Oh, you think you know what I need?" Rudy was becoming impatient; he didn't appreciate slow reaction. "OK then, Ms. Greene, tell me what I need."

Vanessa

Vanessa saw her opportunity slipping away; she knew that she was taking a chance, that he had been fishing earlier for thanks, for adulation she was unwilling to give. She was nobody's pawn. She was a player and she was about to prove it.

"You need this. You need a hostage to walk out of that bank alive. You need to take full responsibility for the success of this job. Only by taking full control and thereby full credit for the work of the police today can you assure yourself of some much-needed public support. Support that has been waning lately. In addition," Vanessa continued, feeling more confident than she had thirty words earlier, "in addition, you need a media spin that will make you look very much the hero regardless of how many lives are saved or lost. And that, Chief, is exactly what I can give you."

Rudy leaned back, to his full height. He was impressed. He slapped James on the back and pointed to Vanessa. "Finally, a bitch with balls."

Vanessa cringed inwardly at the comment. She was in.

"OK, Vanessa. They have eighteen or more hostages. And they have been successfully identified as the Mallory brothers. They are all known felons, they are heavily armed, and they have a history of using explosives. This situation is extremely volatile, as you might imagine. You have a three-minute head start. I go to the rest of the media in the time it takes to piss."

"Got it…" Vanessa stated.

"Larry, let's set it up over here," Vanessa commanded. "And get Jack on the two-way headsets ASAP."

Rudy

Rudy turned away from the reporter and started back towards the bank. Bradick waved them over.

"What's the situation, Captain?" Rudy demanded.

"There were sixteen confirmed heat signatures but the heavy shielding around the bank's vault prevents us from making an entirely accurate assessment. Our intel confirms that eight shots were fired from a silenced weapon approximately two minutes ago from somewhere inside the bank, most likely the vault area; it's the only area that would explain the specific intensity of the acoustic signature."

"Let's hope they're just shooting off steam," Rudy interrupted.

"We can confirm only fourteen heat signatures inside the structure after the shots. I've got Alpha Team at the front of the building ready for a frontal assault and Bravo Team in the back and on the side. We've got snipers covering the front and the back of the structure and Charlie Team in a helicopter awaiting analysis of a rooftop entry."

Rudy was pleased. Bradick's report was concise and intelligent, if a bit Hollywood.

"Well done," Rudy said, wiping some sweat from his brow; the sun was approaching its zenith. His shirt was soaked through under his jacket.

"As per your communications with the terrorists, we are readying two city buses in order to transport the hostages to an airstrip where they say most will be left behind. The hostages they do take off with will be released when the plane reaches a non-extradition country."

"That's bullshit and you know it," MacMillan piped up.

"Yes, I agree. I say we breech. Pull back Alpha Team and put them in the buses; as they start to come out for the buses, we send in Bravo from the back and side and squeeze them in the middle." Rudy needed this. He needed it badly.

"It's risky. At least four heavily armed robbers. Those Mallory boys have a history of blowing shit up. I'd say you're looking at a possible eighty percent hostage casualty rate," Bradick informed him.

"It's a risk I'm willing to take." But if your boys fuck it up, it'll be the end of your career not mine, thought Rudy. "OK. Work this out, Bradick. Let's save some lives."

Bradick moved away quickly to his command center to organize his troops. This was it, a full-fledged breech into a totally hostile civilian center, exactly what they were trained for. James and Rudy were left alone at the frontline of the barricades, looking into the darkened, shadowy center of the bank.

"Nice score on the reporter, James, she fits the bill perfectly," Rudy acknowledged.

"Yeah, our lucky break I guess," James replied.

"You buy that shit, James? Eighty percent casualty rate?"

"Wishful thinking if you ask me. Surprised Bradick hasn't had to change his shorts yet; this has to be a wet dream for him," MacMillan sneered.

Rudy smiled, laughing quietly.

"Hell, he could have said ninety-nine percent and I still would have gone breech," Rudy revealed, adding, "Heroes breech, politicians buckle."

"You got that right, boss," James agreed.

"Just gotta get one. That's all I need James, just one lucky duck."

Larry

Forty feet behind Rudy and James, on the top of the TV van, Larry was manually adjusting some ultra-sensitive sound equipment so that when the action unfolded they could get the best audio and visual feedback in the city. He hadn't expected to record anything of consequence, but he had. He knew it was the kind of thing that could either get him killed or give him his 15 minutes. He climbed down off the roof, leaving the job incomplete.

"Vanessa, get in the van right now. I need you to listen to something."

"Larry? We're on in three minutes, can't this wait?" she protested as he dragged her into the van.

"Van. Now. Trust me."

The look in his eyes told her it was something serious... Something very, very serious.

Simon

Simon watched Patrick; he was kneeling close to Margaret, his back was turned, but Simon could imagine the things Patrick was saying to her. He owed Patrick at least as much gratitude as he surmised was being imparted to Margaret. He'd worn the Clay Mallory mask and played Grier's part with selfless guile.

201

"You could be," Patrick had said. Simon played that clip over in his mind. Of course, he was right. He had it in him to be a better man, but never the thrust of resolve. Now, in the face of Grier's manipulations, of the group's collusion about his death, of Kayla's vulnerability and desperation, he was ready to be the person he imagined. Yes, the after effects of their dialogues would, he hoped, guide him back to a life worth living, back into the world. Patrick had almost completed his job; it looked like two on the ground to his right and the fat security guard with the loud bowels were the only ones left to be released. It was time for Simon to put the final act into motion. He went into the small office that looked out over the bank and dialed Mills. The bus was due in 60 seconds. Simon doubted seriously that they would get it, but his crew at least had to provide the illusion of a frantic escape. He picked up the phone.

"Mills here."

"OK, Mills!" Simon screamed. His voice was a thundercrack against the silence. "Where the hell is my bus?"

"On the way; we ran into a little trouble..."

"Bullshit! You stupid Pig, you have no idea... no idea what's goin' on in here do you? Blood has been spilt. Maybe I should just call CNN and tell 'em how you've got trouble getting a goddamned bus down here in order to save some lives. Get me my bus or more of these precious patrons go down. The bomb is ticking, Mills. Ten minutes from now. Ten minutes." Simon's voice trailed away but it was still projected far enough to reach the ear of every anxious body in the bank.

Simon stepped back out into the main room. He glanced towards Carl and Pete, winking once in their direction. Pete gave him the thumbs up, then looked over at Patrick who had begun to stand once again, presumably to complete his task. Simon's gaze fell upon Harry, the fat security guard – there was something not quite right. Something about the way the man had shifted that caught Simon's attention. Looking across the bank at that picture, the knife in Patrick's hands moving now to the closest prone hostage, the fat security guard, still hooded, sitting propped up against the wall, his hood sweat-soaked, his arms, his shoulders pulled back behind him, something… Simon's eyes took it in, there was an abnormality, an itching bite that begged Simon to scratch, something was off… Then Simon realized.

"No!" he thought as he yelled urgently at Patrick in warning, "Get down!"

And on the edge of his senses he heard, outside the bank, a city bus rumble to a stop. Patrick turned in his direction; Simon could see behind Patrick that Mr. Fat Ass was moving now, rolling on his side and fumbling with his pants, his free hands moving up his pant leg. On the edge of Simon's conscious mind, he saw the grill of the air vent in behind the security guard and surmised how he was able to free himself. Simon brought up his gun and yelled to Patrick.

"Get down!"

Simon could see the panic in Patrick's eyes, the flash of fear as he dived for the floor. Simon squeezed the trigger and bullets ripped into the wall above the security guard's head. Simon didn't have a clear shot at him; Patrick's diving body was in the way, and then Simon could see and hear the bullets from Harry's weapon discharge and by the time he found cover, it was too late. Life, Simon grieved, is devoid of justice.

Chapter 16

OUTSIDE THE NATIONAL BANK

Vanessa

"This is Vanessa Greene reporting live from The National Bank of America on 1st Avenue in downtown Phoenix. I've just spoken to Police Chief Rudy Mills, who confirmed only moments ago that there are at least eighteen hostages inside the bank, the result of a daring mid-morning robbery gone wrong. Chief Mills reports that the perpetrators have been identified as the Mallory boys, a group of four ex-cons led by the notorious Clay Mallory, who in addition to their drug, assault and robbery convictions have been found in possession of large amounts of explosives. We'll have more on these dangerous and deadly individuals in the coming reports. The police have secured the block around The National Bank of America and are preparing to open negotiations with the armed and dangerous Mallory boys inside. The city SWAT teams have been mobilized and the FBI has been alerted to the threat. We'll have more on this harrowing development in the moments to come. Stay tuned to Channel 9 News for up-to-the-minute updates from the scene of the robbery. This is Vanessa Greene reporting; back to you, Allison, in the studio."

"And cut," said Larry. "They are reviewing and playing back the footage of Clay Mallory's trial thirteen years ago. He's the professed leader of the Mallory boys. But they'll have us back on in about three minutes with an update."

"Good work, Larry."

She still couldn't believe what she'd heard only moments before her broadcast. Mills and MacMillan, both of them nattering at each other, joking about the lives of the citizens inside the bank, lives they'd both sworn to protect. She had them cold. No question. But she'd play it out. She'd use Mills to get the inside scoop about the bank and then afterwards, afterwards she'd nail him to the wall. She'd probably be anchor by then. She hoped the hostage situation went on for days – more coverage, more exposure. Every minute in front of the camera was a weight on the scales that would eventually tip in her direction. She'd taken the tape of the recording. Larry wanted to erase it, the idiot. She told him she would. Larry was an easy man to control; Vanessa felt sorry for him, almost.

"It's Jack on the line."

"Great," she said, clicking channels on her headset.

"Hello, Vanessa here."

"Great work so far, honey; you're packing them in. What have you got coming up?"

"Well, I was thinking a sweep of the bank, a zoom into the interior coupled with a description of what might be going on inside."

"That's great, we'll give a five-minute window to include all your information; keep it tight and focused. About three minutes in we'll start up a dialogue with Allison here in the newsroom; she'll ask a few questions and you just go ahead and answer them as best as you can."

"Not a problem," she said, looking back towards the bank. All of a sudden, gunshots rang out from inside the bank, and she instinctively ducked. "Something's happening here, gunshots, can you give me a live feed?"

"Coming to you in twenty seconds."

The connection clicked dead. Vanessa ran over to Larry. "Did you get that footage, those shots?"

"You bet, baby doll."

205

"Great, we are on in fifteen; let's walk it over to the bank as far as we can get."

"You got it. Here we go... Five, four."

The rest of the count was silent and the red light, the oracle on the side of the camera that indicated you were talking to the entire city, maybe even the state, flicked on. Vanessa felt the strange vertigo of exhilaration as she began what would be her greatest broadcast to date. In the news business, timing is everything.

Patrick

Patrick turned, hearing Keith's yell. Outside, through the front doors he saw a large city bus arrive on the street. Keith had his weapon in hand and was bringing it up into firing position, waving frantically at him to move.

"Get down!"

He froze. For an instant, he didn't know what to do – dive to the side, in front, or duck and roll – the sudden burst of adrenalin made him want to jump, but he realized something was wrong, very wrong, and then he heard the weapon discharging, like before, the sound somewhat familiar; he could see the flash from the end of Simon's gun and could hear the bullets ripping by. Down, he told his body, down, DOWN! Patrick could feel himself in the air, his hands out in front, could feel the feet kick up, and he could hear a new sound, a sharp concussive sound, from behind, from the direction of the security guard he still had not released. Patrick sensed the filling of the air around his body with bullets, felt the draw of air necessary to propel them forward, smelled the acid discharge in his nostrils, too close, too damned close. His eyes focused on the ground, he was coming down. He tried to think, should he roll or slide or stay motionless... what should he do?

In his mind, he's at the Danbury house; he opens the front door. On the couch in the living room, Khan panting hello. Down the hall, a cork pop from the kitchen; in the background, some music, Bob Seger, no the Eagles. In the kitchen, Melissa smiles over the counter, pouring the wine...

He felt the explosion of pain in his foot; he could see the blood spraying out from his left ankle. It felt like it had been ripped off.

"Arrrggghhh!" he cried.

Then the pain was gone, his body was numb. He landed with a thud on the floor.

"Safe," he thought.

Melissa hands him his glass of wine, then grabs a third glass from the overhead cabinet. She fills it and hands it past Patrick. Behind him a hand reaches out and takes the offering. He smiles and turns. Keith nods to him and clinks glasses with Melissa. He holds up his glass to Patrick. Patrick smiles, pushing his glass towards Keith's. The stemware shatters and red wine explodes in slow motion all over him. Looking down, Keith's glass is gone. Instead, he's holding an automatic. "You could be, you could be."

He was still in the bank; on some level he knew this. But he felt sleepy; he could only see out of one eye, which was strange and he reached up to rub his blocked eye, to clear whatever might be covering it. But there was no eye, just a hole, he could sense, and a lot of liquid.

Melissa comes to him, dish towel in hand, wiping his face. Laughing. Smiling. So beautiful. She kisses him softly on the lips. Keith's gone, the house is gone, light surrounds her. Just Melissa and the light. She tastes delicious. He bends in to kiss her again.

"I love you, Mel..." Patrick said. And he was gone.

Rudy

"Shots fired! Shots fired!" was the call on the SWAT radio that Bradick had geared up to his vest.

Mills and MacMillan rose from their coverage behind the lead squad car and peered towards the bank, when the flurry of sound had faded.

"This is getting outta hand," Mills said. He was pissed off that the city's SWAT teams were unable to get a camera into the bank. Buncha weekend warriors who couldn't wipe their own asses without a training manual. What a fucking joke. It was time. Shots were being fired; a team was in position in the bus; the sun was baking everyone in a black uniform; it was time.

Looking through the opaque glass into the interior he could see some movement and hear loud voices. Something was going on inside. He'd be left to the wolves if he breeched and found all the hostages dead. No question, that would be it, retirement, to a non-extradition country of course, but he wasn't ready to trade in his loafers for sandals; there was still a filing cabinet of people to bleed.

"It's time to breech," Rudy said matter-of-factly to Bradick.

"Are you outta your mind? We haven't established a visual of the target and have no idea what's going on inside, except for the occasional discharge of semi-automatic weaponry."

"I'm the senior ranking officer on site and it's my call, you cowering piece of shit. If we wait any longer, there may not be ANYBODY to save." Rudy was straight and direct. Bradick seemed stunned, turning to look at the bank. Mills took this opportunity to scan the crowd at the back; he could see Vanessa trying to make her way closer.

"You've got thirty seconds to decide, whether I order this city's counter terrorist team into action or you do," Rudy said clearly.

"I don't need thirty seconds. But for the record, I'm against this maneuver at this time." For all the confidence and bluster Bradick had shown over the last five years on the job, at the moment of truth, in the line of fire, his voice was cracking.

"Noted," came Rudy's cool reply.

Bradick turned to his walkie-talkie, "All teams, we are a go, Normandy One, Normandy One, over."

The buzz of static.

"Alpha Team copies."

"Bravo copy."

"Charlie Team copy, roger that."

Rudy glanced over at MacMillan; his eyes were riveted on the bank. He wouldn't miss a single shot if he could help it. Rudy knew he'd been turned down by the SWAT division three times; that's a lot of training down the drain, but then it was probably disappointments like that that made him such a ruthless bastard and consequently, an excellent second. Rudy would have been lying if he said storming the bank in full body armor with a machine gun strapped around your body didn't sound appealing, but then he'd have to deal with the heat. Talk about a sweat factory. Thanks, but no thanks. Not to mention the enemy fire coming your way. Nah, leave it to the brain-dead professionals. Besides, he had front row seats; it made him feel more involved, closer to the action.

Bradick clicked his walkie-talkie on. "All teams advance, repeat A.T.A., All Teams Advance." He moved back to the command truck after he'd given the order, no doubt the helmet cams would provide some great footage and he could direct the teams from there. This left Rudy and James behind their squad car, peering into the bank as they watched the city's SWAT pour out of the bus. As per their hasty plan, Alpha would take on the frontal assault coming from the two exits of the city bus. Simultaneously, Bravo would penetrate the bank from the side alley entrance. They would meet somewhere in the middle. From the corners of the bank, on the roof of the bank and adjacent rooftops, Mills could see the strategic placement of supporting fire – this was gonna be textbook, and all he needed was one or two citizens to keep their heads down. A few SWAT members had now disappeared into the front of the bank, taking cover as they went. The key to the city would be his, and then he realized, this street, 1st Avenue, would actually be the parade route when they celebrated his heroism. Maybe he'd even get that Vanessa tart into the sack when all was said and done. Rudy grinned at his good fortune. Then the street was enveloped in an ocean of dust and smoke and shards of glass and steel. The percussion of the explosion threw both him and James back several feet, and popped out their ears.

"Those bastards," yelled Rudy; "how the hell am I gonna save our asses now?"

"What?" screamed James, starting to stand.

Rudy just shook his head and stood up, wiping the glass and debris off his jacket and pants. Then through the smoke... unbelievable. The most beautiful sight he'd ever seen.

"Thank you, thank you, thank you," Rudy muttered as he watched the hostages stream out of the bank in all directions, along with SWAT members. The street was a sea of people, smoke and chaos.

Harry

"This is it."

"This is it."

"This is it," Harry repeated to himself as the assailant rose and fell with the knife blade, occasionally glinting in the sun, edging closer and closer to him. He had already decided that slumping to the floor on his side would be his best bet and the quickest way to access his weapon. As the perpetrator rose and stepped fatefully in Harry's direction, Harry slid awkwardly to the ground, pulling his arms from behind his back and reached desperately for the gun in his ankle holster. He heard someone yell something to the man who had turned his back on Harry, the fool. Then the wall above Harry's head and to the side burst and buckled as bullets tore into the fine wood finish. Harry's heart exploded. His pant leg was up. He fumbled momentarily with the handle of his gun, the sweat dripping off his palms and his own inflexibility working against him. Then, finally, with a Herculean effort he secured the handle and quickly whipped the gun into firing position. The man was getting away. Harry closed his eyes and squeezed the trigger. By the third shot, he ventured a glance and could see the man with the knife diving for cover; he aimed and fired. Hitting the man's shoe. The blood spattered and the man let out a cry. Harry felt a confidence and satisfaction, like finally getting his VCR to work or finding two puzzle pieces that went together. He fired again, each time gaining certainty, until finally, just before the man was obscured from view, he fired one last bullet, and watched as it entered, with a sharp zip, the back of the man's skull. Harry rolled and shifted to his left and found momentary cover behind the half wall that led to the side offices. His first kill. He was giddy. Opening his magazine, he counted the remaining bullets. Not enough. Not nearly enough. His first foray into combat left him only three remaining shells. Cursing his wastefulness, he caught the sound of a possible breech approaching from the front lobby of the bank. He could hear the pitter-patter of feet and could hear the panic in the criminals' voices as they screamed for everyone to run. Harry stayed put. He wanted to be carried out, a hero's exit. Then everything was a black, gray cloud of smoke, dust and debris. Silence. Like an old Charlie Chaplin movie, people moving through the black and white frames of his vision. The bomb had ruptured his eardrums. He rose and fell. He rose again, this time using the half wall for support, and stumbled for the door through the smoky carnage of the bomb blast.

Tony

Tony held Clara still. He had released some of the tension he had used to shield her physically from the events unfolding in the bank. As though his hold on her would protect her spirit, which had been severely shaken by Conrad's death and their subsequent incarceration. He'd heard the conversations. Voices filled with jagged edges, followed by the gunshots of the execution. Clearly these were demented and villainous souls. He watched the rise and fall of the man with the knife as he released all the hostages, telling the still hooded Clara what he was witnessing. When their turn came, the relief was immediate and his aching wrists were thankful. Tony was able to pull the hood back down partially before the man releasing everyone turned towards them. He didn't seem to notice or care that Tony's hood was loose. When he had

211

moved away, Tony once more lifted the hood above his right eye in order to see. After Tony was certain that they were not under surveillance he loosened and lifted the corner of Clara's hood so that she too could see. Clara was somewhat revitalized, having her hands released.

"I don't feel like we're gonna die," Clara muttered.

"No, I think you're right. If they meant to kill us, they'd leave us tied. Besides, I've got a summer job starting Tuesday." Tony nudged her.

"Somehow I think Starbucks would survive without you…" Her voice trailed off.

"Not a chance. Nobody makes a meaner grande latte."

"I'm ready to run."

"Me too, Clara. Me too."

Simon

Simon saw clearly the explosion of Patrick's right eye. His stomach rolled and convulsed. Tears welled in his eyes. He bit them back. Simon felt himself drifting away with Patrick's death. He saw Patrick reach up and grab at his bloodied eye socket, bringing his hand away red and viscous. Then his head fell once again to the floor; there was no question, he was dead.

Simon slapped his own face. Trying to snap back to reality. He turned to Carl and Pete. "Fat ass has a gun, he's killed Patrick and is holed up south side east, third desk from the front."

"What's the plan?" Carl asked.

Now that both Carl and Pete were fully in their civilian gear and the hostages were free to move, adjusting their hoods and such, moving them out on a mission like this was ludicrous. Simon's urge was to encircle and kill the security guard, but they were all ready for the bomb. Decision time. Avenge Patrick's needless death, or proceed with the plan?

"We have to blow the bomb."

Carl's relief was immediate. Pete looked disappointed.

Simon peered out the front doors of the bank. The city bus sat idle there, doors open. He hadn't been able to study the bus or even see the exit of the driver; he was certain the bus was wired but if they never intended to use it, it didn't matter much.

"That's our cover, gentlemen; let's hear it for public transportation," Simon said, pointing at the bus, thumbing open the safety on the bomb toggle.

"We all ready?" he said, sliding back down into cover with Carl and Pete.

"Ready."

"Good to go."

He was about to put his earplugs in – both Carl and Pete had already done so – when he heard an unfamiliar sound. On the edge of his senses he could hear the muffled sound of movement. Boots, a lot of them. Simon edged himself up to the counter top and peered towards the front of the bank.

"Oh shit."

"What's up?" Carl inquired.

"We got ourselves a breach in progress, front door, looks like ten to twelve out of the bus."

The side door in the staff room sounded; they were pouring into the bank. All exits would be penetrated.

"We gotta do it now," Simon voiced, pushing his earplugs into place.

"We're with you," Carl said.

Simon inhaled. Checked the toggle on the bomb switch, then screamed, "Everybody run! Run for your lives!"

A couple seconds later he squeezed the trigger. The bank, the bomb, the bloodied bodies, the battalion of breeching SWAT, the beleaguered hostages all rippled in the waves of the blast percussion and then were engulfed in a sea of smoke and debris.

Vanessa

"Are you getting this, Larry?" Vanessa implored.

213

"Ladies and gentlemen. Ladies and gentlemen, if you just tuned in this is the scene at 1st Avenue where gang of ex-con known as the Mallory boys have taken over The National Bank of America and could be holding up to twenty hostages. As the result of an explosion from the bank, glass and debris are strewn about the street and a cloud of smoke is filtering through the front doors. Now, moments before the blast, the city's SWAT teams had begun to breach the interior of the bank; there is no telling what in fact has happened to those men and women or the hostages inside. This is incredible. I see some movement. Yes, some people are staggering out of the bank; they look like civilians from here, probably some of the hostages; they look dazed, but are making their way out of the bank on their own. Yes, yes, now I see some SWAT team members coming out of the bank; it looks like they are calling for aid of some kind, oh yes, I can see blood on some of the civilians, as well as the SWAT members; some now are being escorted. This is unbelievable. Again, a bomb was just detonated inside the National Bank in downtown Phoenix, and now we count five, no make that six people coming out of the bank being tended to by emergency personnel; it appears that their injuries are not of a life-threatening nature. Yes, yes, it looks like some emergency staff are going into the bank with stretchers now, being beckoned inside by members of the city's anti-terrorist SWAT force; smoke is still billowing out of the bank, but I don't see any flames. Oh my God! Oh my God! There are gunshots now being fired inside the bank; from our vantage point you can see the Special Forces personnel taking cover to the sides of the bank entrance; I can still hear shots being fired. More hostages are coming out of the bank now; they are running; three, no five more out of the bank, and now I see, yes, two special forces members carrying a colleague, possibly wounded, definitely unconscious – the body is limp. Oh my God! A SWAT team member has just gone down at the side of the entrance of the bank, wounded perhaps by a bullet from the many gunshots we are hearing; the inside of the bank must be in total chaos. They are moving in and dragging the wounded personnel away. Look now at the entrance, someone is crawling out of the bank, coming out of the doorway of the double doors, they have a uniform on of some kind… it looks like, like a security guard, and he's got a gun! Ladies and gentlemen, a wounded security guard has just appeared out of the entrance of the bank and he's got a gun in one hand; he seems to be wounded in the leg, yes, yes, there is blood coming from the leg, you can see the smear of blood as more smoke clears; this is incredible. Now emergency workers are moving in with SWAT coverage to help the guard; one can only assume that he was at least partially responsible for some of the shooting that we heard earlier. Here come more hostages, along with more SWAT; the surrounding area is a hive of ambulances and emergency staff, stretchers are emerging; it seems like the worst is over now, it looks like the bank is secure as they call in more emergency staff and are now standing down somewhat. Incredible footage here, ladies and gentlemen. I've never seen anything like this before; our thoughts and prayers go out to the families of those who are involved in this horrible and dramatic hostage situation. Several people have been taken, removed from the bank, not under their own power. We have no word of casualties, but will keep you apprised of any new events or information as it is released. Let's send it back to you, Alison, in the studio."

"We're out," Larry confirmed.

"I can't believe it; did you see that, did you freaking see that?" Vanessa exclaimed, hitting Larry on the shoulder with her fist.

"It's crazy," Larry exclaimed, looking towards the bank.

"OK, OK, keep shooting; I'm gonna go get fixed up in the truck for a minute. We'll be back on again in a couple of minutes I'm sure."

"Count on it," said Larry, lifting the camera onto his shoulder once again and focusing in on the entrance of the bank, not wanting to miss anything.

Inside the truck, Vanessa picked up the phone to call the office. She was pissed off that Jack hadn't contacted her from the studio since they went to her live feed. He should have been hitting her with instructions for the next live-to-air broadcast. But he wasn't.

The only thing she could do was keep at it, and get moving on the next big thing. The security guard. His exit from the bank, wounded no less, holding a gun; that was a powerful image. She had to nail down who he was and what his role might have been. It was time to fish for a hero.

"Hello, Kelly. Are you seeing this stuff? It's craziness. I need the details on the guard, ASAP. Who was he, where does he live, his family's address, anything and everything you've got."

"I hear you, Vanessa. You're doing a great job! But that info has a hold on it from you-know-who."

"That bitch? I don't care, this is my story, I should have first dibs on the follow-up. This hero stuff is killer."

"Sorry, Vanessa. My hands are tied. Did you happen to touch any of the police scanners this morning?" Kelly inquired innocently.

"I didn't touch a thing, except your nail file for a touch-up," Vanessa lied.

"Oh, OK. Well, I have job security to think about and Allison laid into me this morning, once she found out about the hostages," Kelly explained.

"Don't sweat it, Kelly, she's outta here soon and so are you with that belly of yours. Listen, honey, can you switch me over to Jack?"

"No problem."

The ringing of the phone in her ear added to her frustration. She knew exactly what was happening. The story was slipping away, right out from under her; the coverage was being directly linked back to the studio and Allison Brodie was sending out her minions to gather the information she would later report on the air, in some sort of special feature. This was *her* god-damned story!

"Hello, Vanessa," Jack said.

"Hi there," Vanessa said in her best let's-be-friends-before-I-rip-your-throat-out voice.

"Great job on the live feed, fantastic reporting."

Yadda yadda, don't blow smoke up my caboose, she thought. "When is the feed coming back here?" she half-asked, half-demanded.

"You've really wowed us down here at the station…"

"When is the next live feed coming?" she interrupted.

"Well Vanessa, it's not. Alison is on her way down there; she'll be taking over the live feed. It just makes sense. Larry knows to expect her in the next few minutes. Alison's team is putting together a feature on that wounded security guard that crawled his way outta the bank."

"Are you fucking kidding me?"

"Sorry, doll, let's meet tonight. I'll treat you to the usual, gotta run."

Click.

Margaret

Margaret wiped away the tears, averting her eyes from the sight of Patrick's body. He was a good man, a noble man – the kind of man that was in short supply. He'd been a savior to all these people, and who would ever know? He was so hopeful and buoyant about the future, his love of life, his new home. In the brief amount of time that she had known him, thirty minutes perhaps, he'd made an indelible impression.

Margaret was only vaguely aware of Harry crawling away down the dividing wall towards the front offices after the shooting had stopped. She could never return to the bank: if the good Lord saw to it that she survived whatever was to come, she would never be able to step foot in the bank again; too much had happened, too many of her illusions had been shattered.

"Thanks to you, Margaret, all these people are still alive and well," Patrick had said to her in parting. She'd held his hand briefly and given it a squeeze before finally letting go. Alive. Vital. More tears began to well up in her eyes; she pushed the memory of Patrick away, for another time, another place. Glancing over at the central teller stations, she couldn't see the thieves. She surmised that they were about to flank Harry, but outside the bank in a brief silence, she heard or sensed the doors of the bus open. Margaret leaned forward in order to get a closer look and she saw, through the slits in the gate of the half-wall that she was behind, the dark uniforms and shadows of a SWAT police force emerge from the interior of the bus. They were coming in. Step by step, each movement closer, narrowing the options these men would have to react. Her heart hammered against her ribs, her adrenalin stoking the fire of that rhythm. Then from out of the silence came a familiar voice: "Everybody, run! Run for your lives!" It was followed by a deafening blast, a vacuum of force that threw Margaret fifteen feet down the side wall of the bank. Her tumble was cushioned by the money vest she wore and, although shocked and disoriented, she managed to stand without staggering and take a few steps towards the exit. There were others, in the smoke and debris, making their way through the haze. Margaret saw hands reaching up from the floor, other hands reaching out of the smoke, searching for an escape route. Then came the uniformed men, grabbing her, escorting her in a new direction altogether.

"This way, ma'am," Margaret heard as she was guided by her elbow and waist. She offered no resistance, allowing the officer to take her to the sunlight, and the familiar heat and humidity she knew would be waiting for her.

As they moved together, the smoke seemed to swell around them, resolved to hang in the air. It irritated her throat, so she covered her mouth and nose with her sleeve. To Margaret's left, from a crouching position, shot up the startled and damp form of Harry Truman. He must have been hiding, waiting for an opportunity to come out of cover. She knew that in the depths of the bank, right now, the criminals still lurked. The danger, she was quite certain, had not abated. She tried to rush her would-be rescuer, but he became preoccupied with Harry's stammering: "I killed one of them just before the explosion, but there is still one out there."

Margaret was pawned off on another rescuer. The new guy was already aiding one of the female customers towards the exit but nodded that he could take Margaret as well. Her own young helper felt compelled to investigate Harry's story. Margaret turned slightly to watch him disappear towards the back of the bank. Surprisingly, Harry followed him. Probably wanted to show off his work.

Seconds later, gunshots ripped through the smoke and she was shoved out of the entrance of the bank into the open spectacle, a sea of flashing lights, police cars and ambulances. Some people were being treated and others were being whisked away. Police questioned some. As soon as the shots came, Margaret ran. Her feet moved quickly under her; the barricades presented only a minor obstacle as she crawled quickly underneath one, shuffling her way between the parked police cars beyond. Attention must have been diverted back to the bank, because only one voice called out to her. Her panic propelled her through the street and down a side alley, where the silence shocked her into cognition.

"I'm sorry, Patrick," she muttered, remembering the kindness of Patrick's actions and the serenity of his words. She came out of the alleyway onto 2nd Avenue and hailed the first taxi in sight.

"678 James Street, please," she said, sitting heavily in the backseat of the cab as it slipped anonymously into the downtown traffic.

Margaret felt the tears come, but she didn't make a sound. She hunched over her knees and examined the floor of the taxi, letting the tears fall freely from her eyes. She was going home for the last time. She recovered quickly and as the taxi came to an abrupt halt a few minutes later, she glanced out the window for the first time since jumping in.

"I need to make a short stop here."

"This isn't James Street."

"Keep the meter running; I'll be back." And with that, Margaret exited the cab. She was no fool. She knew the turns of fate too well to ignore them. There would be more tears to come, but at least she hoped she'd be able to sleep at night.

Tony

Tony and Clara sat in silence, watching the SWAT team move stealthily from the buses. Tony could sense the beating of Clara's heart, each pulse vibrating through her body, her shoulders, her hands. He knew his own heartbeat echoed the same rush of adrenalin, the sound of it sustaining a dull, distant roar in his ears. This was it. This was it! He was also aware that the robbers, terrorists, cold-blooded killers, whatever they were, sat only a few meters away, behind the tellers' station towards the back hallway. They started to slip inside – still no movement, no indication of panic from those who should have been most concerned. Glancing over, he couldn't see any of them. Tony became aware of footfalls in the lobby of the bank; he counted now six SWAT inside or entering, and droves more coming in support from behind. He pulled off the cloth hood and Clara did the same. Then Tony detected the sound of a metal hinge coming from the back of the bank, behind the tellers' stations: an emergency alleyway exit door? Probably. The front entrance wasn't the only way into or out of the bank. All the exits would be covered. Clara's grip tightened. Her eyes were the size of saucers, a deer in the headlights. To the side, he saw a head flash up, one of the robbers. This is it. This is it.

"This is it," Tony said aloud, unaware that he had spoken.

"Everybody, run! Run for your lives!" yelled a man from the tellers' stations. Tony pulled Clara up off the floor and made two giant strides towards the men and women in black whose weapons were pointed at them. Forty feet to the exit. The SWAT team crouched quickly. Thirty feet. They were just about past the large writing counter when he was blinded by a deep, impenetrable cloud of smoke. The sound of the explosion thundered through his head and he lost his grip on Clara's hand as he was flung headlong into the side offices of the bank.

Coming round, Tony thought he'd been shot; there was tremendous pain emanating from his right leg. Not the knee! Yes, the knee. He tried to move but something was on top of him, covering his backside. He felt a wad of hair that could only be Clara's in his left hand; he shook her head gently and she began to move. He could see very little; the smoke was billowing within the bank, its vaulted ceiling offering no escape from the blast's grayish-black fallout. Clara moved slowly at first, but then sensing that he lay trapped, jumped over to his right side and finally into his field of vision.

"What's on me?" he said.

"It's a section of the banking counter. Can you move?" Clara mumbled.

"I think my knee is screwed; can you budge it, Clara?"

She disappeared in the smoke, and a moment later he felt the tension on his knee begin to waver. Tony readied his muscles for a big push, but she managed to slide it off without his assistance.

"Let's have a look at you," Clara said, bounding back up to his head, helping him roll over on his side.

"I thought I was Clark in this relationship."

"That was my plan." Clara smiled.

Now that Tony was on his side, he could put a picture to the sounds he had been hearing, as the ringing subsided. In the interior of the bank, in the haze of the smoke, he could see the hostages, most of them on their feet, making their way through the smoke, walking into each other, some sitting dazed and bewildered. Others crying. It looked like a war zone. A bombed-out medivac station. Then he heard the calls of the city's SWAT team; directing, assisting, calling out for aid of the broken assembly. Most looked too shocked to understand; a few heeded their instructions.

Tony tested his knee. Definitely a tear.

"Think you can walk out of here?" Clara said.

"Just need a minute," Tony said tersely.

Clara sat down beside him.

Out of the hazy din that seemed to settle in the bank, Tony and Clara watched the comings and going of the hostages, the SWAT and medical personnel. The urgency of the moment was lost to them; they were ignored by everyone – either that, or no one had spotted them yet. A faded picture of two people, a man and a woman, young, exhausted, sitting silently in the corner of the front offices, around them the shattered pieces of the large, marble counter. It was surreal.

Tony watched the procession with detached interest. He was nearly ready to get to his feet for the walk outside. He saw a small woman pass by, escorted by a member of the city's rescue team; she seemed so unfazed, so steady. She looked at Tony; something in her eyes snapped him out of his trance – perhaps her acknowledgment of their presence. Whatever the case, Tony started to rise, with the help of Clara, who rose to her feet to help him up.

"I killed one of them," both Tony and Clara heard through the smoke. Then, just as they made their first few steps towards the exit, the SWAT member Tony had just seen with the small woman passed by them followed by a man in a bank security guard uniform. The smoke seemed to be lifting some, and Tony decided to rest a moment before proceeding. The pain in his knee was intense enough to warrant a short reprieve. As he and Clara stood to the side, Tony saw two men come from the left side of the bank down the opposite wall; they looked as steady as the woman he had seen. They moved quickly and purposefully, but in the wrong direction; they followed the same path as the security guard. Then Tony noticed, in the smaller, thinner of the two men, something in his ears. Cotton? Plugs? Something. Why would a hostage have ear plugs? What the hell was going on? As they passed back towards the tellers' stations, Tony saw the thin one pull something out of his jacket and the bigger man did the same.

"Time to move," Tony stated with a quiet urgency.

"What is it?" Clara asked, sensing the change in him.

"Guns."

Two quick gunshots spiraled out of the smoky gloom.

Tony grabbed Clara and flung her beside the damaged writing desk. More shots screamed out through the murky depths of the bank. Hostages bounded for the exit as SWAT team members took cover and raised their weapons.

Two more shots thundered through the din; a raging firefight was being waged in the bank, back towards the tellers' stations.

The sound of bullets ripping into walls and the falling shrapnel urged Tony and Clara to stay put, but they were kicking hard against their flight instincts. Along the left side of the bank, officers began to move forward into the back.

Three more bullets were expelled, one zipping into the marble counter top that Tony had been buried under.

A body in black hit the floor and stopped moving. A shadowy form moved over him, grabbing his arms; another form appeared and took the legs, moving back towards the bank's entrance.

"Fall back, fall back." Tony heard.

Two more shots sang out in the rear of the bank.

A bullet ricocheted off the side of the table that sheltered them. Tony and Clara sat still. Very, very still. Some bodies in black moved back and disappeared in the direction of the bank entrance. Tony and Clara dared not move. Tony felt pinned down, caught in the crossfire.

Something was approaching; it sounded like someone pulling a suitcase along the floor, one that used to have functional wheels. The sound increased. From the corner of the desk behind which they sat, Tony saw the steel, smoky end of a gun, followed by the sliding bulk of the bank's security guard, the same one he had seen moving towards the back of the bank with a member of the SWAT team. His face was speckled with blood. He glanced momentarily towards the back before resuming his slow crawl towards the front lobby of the bank.

"Got another one," he said, smirking briefly to Tony and Clara.

Tony and Clara sat in bewildered silence – a silence broken by the resonating sound of three quick gunshots. The security guard fired his weapon into the smoke. Tony knew he was firing blind.

The sound of gunshots renewed, growing enough in volume to suggest that the melee was moving unsettlingly close.

"NOOOOOO!" someone screamed.

"You'll pay for this! I swear to God," came the same deranged voice.

Tony felt the swell of Clara's need; with every second her drive to run was mounting. For that reason he grabbed her shirt – he wasn't entirely sure she wouldn't just tear through it if she bolted, but it was worth a try.

"Don't run; we stay put, understand?" Tony cautioned in a whisper.

Clara didn't move, nor did she speak.

The security guard had disappeared. Tony could see the blood trail on the floor that he had left behind. The air around them was acidic and burnt. The smell of gunpowder. Five more shots whizzed through the air. Some from the lobby area, some from the rear of the bank. They were in the middle.

A scream came from the direction of the bank lobby; another person down.

As the smoke settled, the light of the entranceway became visible. From their spot Tony surveyed the bank's interior. A black uniformed body lay motionless in the dust and debris. Then a sound. A single person, footfalls slow and steady, approached the front of the bank. He pulled Clara in tight, hoping that they would continue to go unnoticed. Tony strained to hear; there was something else. Muttering, gibberish at first and as the footsteps came closer, the muttering garbling words became coherent and purposeful.

"Vengeance shall be mine."

"Vengeance shall be mine."

"Vengeance shall be mine," continued the pledge.

Clara's quick inhale caught the attention of the man with the two automatic pistols as he sauntered into view from the rear of the bank. His mantra stopped. He stood briefly, looking at them, guns still leveled towards the exit. It was the same skinny, thin man who had followed the security guard and SWAT into the back. In his eyes, a caged fury. Without turning, he fired three shots towards the bank lobby, maintaining his focus on Tony and Clara. In his eyes, Tony felt the hatred. The tension. Tony also saw behind the man, in the doorway of one of the offices, a glint, a tiny movement of black. Someone was there. The man's eyes squinted slightly.

He wheeled about with blinding speed, firing one, two, three times in quick succession. The sound of a body hitting the floor followed. He whirled around and stepped sharply towards Tony and Clara.

"You can take what you want. Where I'm going, there will be no need for this."

After stuffing his weapons in his pants at the waistline, he unbuttoned and removed his shirt, exposing a tight black top lined with rectangular pockets. Tony thought it was body armor. He pulled the top over his head and shoulders. He tossed the heavy top to Tony, who reached out and caught it, keeping the shirt from hitting him in the face.

"Romans 12, 19:21."

He turned, grabbed his guns, and moved again towards the main entrance, bare-chested, grim-faced. Tony heard his mantra return as he stepped out towards the lobby.

"Vengeance shall be mine..."

Several shots followed his departure; they could hear the return fire zipping through the lobby entrance. They could hear the clink of a magazine as it hit the floor and the timely snap of another magazine as it dutifully filled the void.

Clara and Tony fumbled with the shirt and opened one of the Velcro tabs. Inside, a wad of one hundred dollar bills. Three bundles. Three times a hundred hundreds, three thousand dollars, times however many pockets there were... a lot of money.

"Holy shit," Clara stammered.

"Holy shit," echoed Tony.

"Do you see this?" implored Clara.

"I see it."

Another volley of bullets ensued; still the bullets whistled through the air, only a few feet from where they sat; bewildered and beleaguered.

They worked together, not thinking, not considering, not wondering. A team.

The gunshots continued; again the metal clank of a magazine filled the pause in the firefight. Only to be replaced with a heavy snap, followed by a return to shooting.

The black top hung loosely off Clara's feminine frame. It was entirely too small for Tony's bulky mass. Tony peeled off his button-down and helped Clara pull it over her shoulders. He always wore an undershirt, even on the hottest days of the year. Clara looked better with his shirt on, more natural.

Three more times they heard, from the front lobby of the bank, guns expel their lethal innards. Followed this time by a dull thud.

An eerie silence covered them. Covered the world. The shooting had ceased. Through the din, Tony could hear yelling and screaming outside. He rolled to his feet aided by Clara and walked towards the front. Outside... bedlam.

In the sunlit doorway of the bank, slumped to one side of the threshold, lay the body of the man they'd just encountered. Beside him, another motionless body clad in black. From out of the sunlight came several more SWAT, moving quickly, but cautiously, to the body. Tony directed Clara towards the exit. He raised his hands.

"Don't shoot!"

SWAT entered the bank, assisting their departure. Other hostages came out from the rear of the bank; they too must have taken shelter during the battle. He'd thought that he and Clara were the last. Panic welled up from his belly. What if one of them had seen? Outside the bank, propped up on the tailgate of an ambulance, Tony watched the others. All around him people were being treated; many officers were wounded and being attended to, some more urgently than others; stretchers seemed to move by and ambulance sirens could be heard both approaching for more wounded and departing with the injured or the dead. Tony watched only those who followed them out of the bank. A woman and an elderly man walked out of the bank under their own power. They never looked at anything, just the ground before their feet.

"No problem there," Tony muttered.

"What's that?" Clara inquired.

"People… they were in the bank still."

Clara glanced up at the two being escorted by aid workers. She seemed oblivious to their importance for a moment, glancing back at Tony with that "so what" look on her face. But Tony met her gaze and in his eyes she understood his concern, deep and deliberate. She squeezed his hand.

"I understand."

Behind the first two came two more. One unconscious, being carried out on a stretcher by two emergency workers. The last, a young man, was being directed along with the help of a fire fighter. He looked dazed, shocked by what he'd gone through in the bank. His eyes flashed from building to building, from person to person. Of the four who exited the bank after he and Clara, this was the only one who for a split second made eye contact with Tony. In the brief stare, Tony felt a burning condemnation of recognition. There was something in this man's eyes Tony had seen before. He couldn't, just now, place it. Perhaps he'd seen that same clear expression in Conrad's eyes before his death, or maybe in Clara's eyes in the backseat of the car, quietly yearning. These were not the eyes of a man in shock, as his body language suggested. There was something there… eerily reminiscent to Tony.

"We're clear" was the call as the city SWAT emerged from the bank, holstering and slinging their various weapons.

"Tony," Clara said, addressing him tensely, "Let's get outta here."

Tony nodded. He looked back out at the assembly, the man with the fire fighter was gone. Tony's knee needed medical attention but Clara was right. It was time to leave. He'd get help later. Far away from here. The two of them stood up wearily from the ambulance and began to walk along the throng of police cars and emergency vehicles. Every half step, for half steps were all that Tony dared take, sent waves of pain jolting through his right leg, steadily radiating out from his knee where it had been crushed. Clara's hand tightened over his own when she felt him slowing or when they came in close contact with emergency personnel or the

227

police. Tony and Clara passed by them all. Everyone was too busy to deviate from their duties. Looking up, Tony could see the flock of reporters and camera crews that had descended on the blockade.

"To your left, Clara."

"OK."

They approached the wooden barrier; a mass of media hounds swelled to their right, about eighty feet away. From this distance, Tony and Clara could see that there was a press conference in progress. Their timing could not have been more perfect. Clara slipped under, and Tony with Clara's help stepped over, the three-foot barrier. From there they swung around the side of a city bus stop.

"Let's sit for a minute," Tony suggested wearily.

"I think we should keep moving."

"I need to sit for a minute; my leg's hangin' by a thread." Tony insisted, sitting gingerly on the bus stop bench.

Clara sat beside him.

"Sorry," she said.

"Don't sweat it."

They shared a brief look. Sitting, staring out of the open bus shelter towards the circus of reporters and police, emergency workers and their patients, SWAT and Fire Rescue personnel, moving about, reporting this and that, Tony remembered that in the bank lay several bodies – one of them a friend. Was it just this morning they had awoken together in the infamous Jungle House? A weight was slowly settling on Tony's shoulders. His life would never, could never be as simple as it was just a couple of hours ago.

Simon

Everything, as it had transpired since the police arrived, was plan perfect. Grier would have been insufferable. The bomb blast filled the bank's interior with huge, vast plumes of grayish black smoke while causing only minor damage to the structure itself. The shock wave from the blast had knocked out most of the interior windows and crumpled the center portion of the teller stations. That area was subjected to the greatest force, being in direct line with the hallway that led to the vault. The blast had also thrown the center marble writing table to the side of the front lobby. Simon's ears rang from the auditory assault, but he knew it would be nothing compared to the throng of hostages who hadn't had their ears plugged. In the aftermath of the explosion, Carl and Simon took out the plugs in order to listen for movement, the sounds of rescue, the sounds of freedom. Moans and protests began in earnest as the first few calls for help echoed in the shrouded confines of the bank's main room.

Simon peeled off his mask and removed the teller's jacket. Just another hostage now.

"All clean?" he asked.

"You're a lady killer," replied Carl.

"Good luck," Simon said, shaking hands with Pete and Carl.

"You too."

Simon grabbed the second case and carted it off in the direction of the vault. Carl and Pete remained behind. They needn't wait for Simon's return, but they had to be sure that they blended into the assembly, exiting near the end of the evacuation operation when protocol and routine was the most vulnerable. Comfort would return to the emergency crews, the police and SWAT, and that is when they'd be able to slip out, through the barricades and into the streets. The hallway outside the vault was a charred cinder; the edges of what remained of the doorway hung like scraps of flesh, loose and black. Simon, wanting to avoid entrance into the vault turned sideways and bowled the second case, the second bomb down the right side. Carl had assured him that the bomb would not prematurely detonate, but Simon still expected to be incinerated as he watched the case glide along the blackened floor. When it stopped moving, Simon took a breath. He balled up his mask and wig and threw them into the back alongside the case. He could see bits and pieces of the vault interior through the smoke every few seconds; the bodies, the parts, were strewn about the shelves, the walls, the floor – as if the vault itself had been some kind of huge blender. He looked away, and began to feel his way back down the corridor towards the main room. Hugging the right wall, Simon reached the end of the hall noting that Carl and Pete were gone. He heard the emergency crews assisting some of the hostages. He curled his way around the outside wall of the bank, stepping over pieces of wood and loosened chunks of concrete. He noted that some of the hostages seemed trapped underneath a few pieces of the main teller desk. Emergency crews were helping them. Others were being escorted out under their own power. The bomb had been engineered perfectly; he'd seen no fatalities and still the central chamber of the bank was filled with smoke. Only now was it beginning to thin.

Simon approached the edge of the side offices. Here he would have to move towards the central hallway of the bank in order to turn the corner for the exit. Ahead of him through the smoke, the image fading in and out, he ascertained the form of a large man. A large man in uniform.

"I killed one of them," the large man said to a member of the city SWAT as he passed by.

From behind, not more than six feet away, Simon could see Harry's face as he turned towards the back of the bank and pointed. The urge to kill the security guard prompted Simon to grab his gun. The feel of it, the want of his weapon was persuasive. Simon stood motionless watching them, a city SWAT, who had in his company, Simon made out, Margaret. She looked remarkably unfazed. He dared not fire; Margaret was too close to the two of them. After a few more seconds, Margaret was pawned off and the two of them, SWAT and guard, moved towards the back of the bank. Guns drawn.

Simon remained against the wall. His need to avenge Patrick, a man he had only met hours earlier, was squeezing him, taxing his professional resolve. No, no. It was suicide to pursue the man. Exiting the bank was the only option. Simon strode forward to the edge of the side office wall. For the first time since he had exited the back hallway, he could see the other side of the bank, the vast interior becoming visible. Across the space, Simon saw the damaged central writing desk and the boy and girl who had impossibly entered the bank and killed Grier. Simon looked towards the vault, trying to pick out the dark forms of the security guard and the SWAT officer. Others passed by, moving down the middle towards the exit that sat, Simon noticed, like a haloed archway of light. Everything seemed to be moving towards it. The hostages and emergency crews, the smoke itself swirled and eddied on its way out of the building. A sound to Simon's left, somewhere along the back wall of the bank forced him to turn back towards the middle and there through the din, through the grayish murk, Simon saw two unmistakable forms. Pete and Carl. They should have been out of the bank and long gone. And yet, their silhouetted shadows moved purposefully towards the back of the bank where the smoke was thickest. A few more steps and they were swallowed up again in the haze.

Simon stopped. He knew it was them. Why back? Why? He didn't know the answer, but he needed to find out. Simon turned from the corner and began to move back towards the outer wall, retracing his steps. He felt in his jacket pocket for the detonator. It was there, quiet and cold.

Ripped from the barrel of a gun came two shots in quick order from the rear of the bank.

Simon instinctively dove for the floor.

"Fucker!" Simon heard. Pete's voice.

The hammer fell twice more; two more thundering cracks echoed out, followed by a hollow thump. A body hitting the floor.

The sound of weapon's discharge confirmed for Simon that it was either Pete or Carl firing, perhaps both. The Glocks made a specific noise he'd become familiar with during training.

The responding fire? Semi-automatic. SWAT. And still another weapon, a pistol firing, once, twice. Familiar... Patrick...

Return fire. The sound of it brought back the image of Patrick's panicked expression. Security guard's gun. Simon moved forward and found shelter behind some splintered pieces of board. He drew his weapon and ventured a look at the firefight.

Louder, closer, another gunshot reverberated in Simon's eardrums.

"Deliver us from evil," Simon heard Carl say somewhere out in the bank's main room.

Two shots, then the click-click of an empty chamber. Carl or Pete had run dry and if they were out in the open, it would be a costly mistake.

Crack! The sound of another bullet spewed out of the security guard's gun. Loud, hostile, destined. Thud. Another body dropped. Someone had been tagged.

"NOOOOO!" It was Pete. Deranged. Psychic. Simon knew it could only mean one thing... Carl was dead.

"You'll all fucking die for this! I swear to God," Pete's proclaimed.

Simon sensed they were in the far left corner of the bank, but Pete would be beyond reason. No. Attempting to help him now, the malice in his voice, attempting to dissuade him from exacting his vengeance, was suicide. He'd be too far gone. Simon was happy to have the detonator. Pete would have blown them all to kingdom come. No. Pete was lost. Simon had to lie low. He dared not move back towards the front. That's where Pete was heading. The protection of all their patron saints and bullet-proof vests wouldn't be enough to save them from Pete's blood lust. Pete would be killed, for certain. He'd inflict enough damage to demand it of them.

Several shots screamed through the bank, a deadly confirmation of Simon's thoughts.

The sound of gunfire moved towards the exit. Simon could hear a scream from outside. He heard what had to be Pete's footfalls move towards the front doors of the bank. There was a muttering in the air, the words of which were lost to Simon; he knew they emanated from Pete's mouth. Simon chanced making his way to the same side office wall as before. He'd be sheltered from incoming fire and he'd be able to see the hallway, an advantage he could not enjoy from his present position.

Two additional shots resonated through the bank's interior followed by the tell-tale click, slap, smack of an empty magazine being replaced. Then, three more bullets found life in the burning hot chamber of Pete's weapon. These last metal slugs found flesh; Simon heard the muffled gasps as the body count rose. Pete was close. Very close.

Simon edged himself next to the side wall of the bank's front offices. This was far enough, judging from the last flurry of gunshots. In the distance he could make out the edge of the office, and now, just on the edge of his visual range as more smoke cleared from the bank, the far wall. And there, in the distance between the far wall and his position, stood Pete. He held firmly to two guns, both Glocks. His back was to Simon. He faced the desk where the kids had sat. Squinting through the smoke, Simon saw Pete place his weapons in his pants and quickly remove his shirt. Underneath, the black fabric bulged with wads of hundred dollar bills. He stripped off the shirt and threw it towards the damaged desk.

"Romans 12, 19:21," Simon heard.

Simon imagined Pete's face. Grim. Eyes flashing. Insanity. He grabbed the two guns from his pants and turned decidedly towards the exit. Finally the muttering was coherent. Each word a step towards oblivion. An epilogue of his own final chapter.

"Vengeance shall be mine..."

Pete moved out of sight. It wouldn't be long now, Simon knew.

Pete opened fire with a volley of four purposeful shots, Simon knew he'd be aiming around the edges of the lobby. Send them for cover and then find your mark. It would be the next few bullets that would be the most deadly. He'd pick out the lazy ones of course, the closer the better. Some people think cover means hitting the ground, but nothing's quite as easy to hit as a grown man lying exposed.

"Holy shit," Simon heard.

Two more bullets spewed out of Pete's weapons. They would be lethal. The clank of metal against marble. The sound of an empty magazine hitting the floor. Followed again by the slap of a fresh clip. Simon felt oddly cold for a moment.

Peering across the bank he could see the girl, the young woman who had entered with the other kids, pulling the black money-laden top over her head.

Return fire zipped and zagged through the lobby, shredding wood and clanging steel. Simon stayed low and out of sight; now was not the time to indulge in voyeuristic tendencies.

The big guy was helping the girl pull on his shirt. Simon nodded.

"Good for them," he thought. *"Opportunity knocks."*

The shots resumed in fury. This time, there was no pause, no reprieve. Simon could feel the noose tightening, could hear the thunder of the return fire, and at the end, before the sound of Pete's body slapping the ground, a lifeless heap of flesh in shattered glass and steel, Simon picked out the cannon crack of the high-powered sniper rifle. It was over.

The end of Pete marked the end of the most intense gunfire he'd ever heard outside of a movie theatre. Simon could hear the screams for help coming from outside. There would be wounded no doubt. Pete was an excellent shot. Simon's stomach dropped in a vertigo of angst, fueled by the realization of his singular isolation. Grier was dead, a troublesome death that had ironically saved his own life. Now Pete and Carl had fallen, victims of the job, the life, and Grier's perfect plan. Patrick. Dead. The two young men and all police who had lost their lives. At the beginning, the men, they were impersonating. So much loss. Simon couldn't recall the emergency worker pulling him to his feet. Such was the intensity of his introspection.

"Come on now," the man said, "I've got you."

Simon moved out of the side corner and into the main hall. They turned together towards the exit, clearly visible now. There in the doorway lay Pete's body, bare-chested, riddled with wounds. The fatal shot clearly defined above his right eye. Simon looked away, squinting in the sunlight as he and his escort reached the threshold of the lobby and the oppressive heat of the midday sun.

Simon looked around at the circus that had assembled. Police cars and rescue vehicles everywhere. The city bus long removed, although he didn't know when. Nothing looked familiar. Simon glanced from group to group; collections of people stood, sat and lay administering aid or being administered to. Simon's eyes, searching for his exit, found the battered duo sitting silently at the back of an open ambulance. He caught and held momentarily the vacant gaze of the young man.

"*Good luck*," Simon thought.

"Here you go. Just take a seat here," his escort said, helping him sit on the edge of another emergency vehicle.

"Thanks," Simon sighed wearily.

"What's your name?"

Simon sat silent.

"I'm Darren," his escort coaxed.

"Patrick," Simon said.

"Well Patrick, you've done well to survive this," Darren proclaimed, motioning towards the bank.

Simon could see the entrance of the bank; a few people in black uniforms moved into and out of the shrouded interior. It would only be a matter of minutes before they discovered the case. Simon reached into his pocket and felt the detonator. Safe and sound.

"I need some coffee," Simon asked, looking around at the water bottles and ice packs.

"Coffee?" queried his companion.

Again Simon let him eat silence. It was a ridiculous request. Like asking for an ice cream cone in the Arctic Circle. With the added layer under his clothing, Simon knew he looked flushed and drained. But coffee, that was a mainstay of society, no matter the weather.

"Right, no problem. I'll be right back."

Simon watched Darren move away. Surely there would be coffee somewhere close at hand, but not as close as the water bottles that riddled the area.

This was his opportunity. It was time to leave. This phase of the plan was obviously shot to hell. His pick-up was nowhere to be seen. No. He couldn't wait. According to everyone else, he was supposed to be dead in the vault of the bank; it was little surprise that Grier's plan for him was nothing but a ruse. No. Simon knew he was on his own, but he was no rookie. Simon had had the foresight to purchase a bus ticket for Detroit departing that afternoon and stash it with a change of clothes in a buck-fifty locker at the bus station. His bus was leaving in less than an hour – even more reason to move out. Quickly. Quietly.

Simon stood and turned in the opposite direction that Darren had gone and realized that he was still very much in the center of the chaos. Moving down the side of the ambulance, Simon heard and saw a large gathering of police officers, leaning up against their squad cars, discussing the details of the gunfight. Deciding not to chance an encounter, Simon backtracked to the rear of the ambulance and veered off to his left, flanking the assembled herd of cops.

Ahead of him, Simon saw a scattered landscape of police, SWAT and emergency workers. He moved slowly, but purposefully, through the scene, staying as close as possible to the wounded. They were being tended to, and he knew that pausing momentarily by them made him look like a worried husband, an anxious brother, or a dismayed friend, not what he actually was – a man aching for escape. Each step was an inch towards freedom. Reaching the end of the wounded, only two squad cars separated him from the wooden barricades. Simon knelt before the last of the wounded, a young man, seemingly unconscious. He collected himself. Still kneeling, he risked a brief glance back towards the bank. The doorway, a gaping wound in the fine lines and architecture of the building. The three suits that Kayla had dealt with were being escorted through the debris. Their eyes were wide with shock and awe. They'd been completely forgotten in the chaos. Standing there, motionless, Simon could not help but wonder about the lives lost inside. And these three had been spared. He could taste the bile as it reached his throat. He swallowed it down, uneasily.

"Patrick!" Darren called from a few feet away as he rounded the side of an adjacent vehicle, one hand gripping a white styrofoam cup.

"There you are," he said, moving swiftly over to Simon. "Thought I lost you there. You alright?"

Simon quickly considered his options. He pocketed his right hand and found the detonator. He thumbed off the safety and felt the trigger. A single finger curled about the metal, a perfect fit. One squeeze. One twitch. One contraction away.

"I'm looking for a friend of mine," Simon said flatly. Maybe there was another possibility, but his finger's tension did not abate.

"Here. I've got your coffee."

Simon, nodding his thanks, reached out with his other hand and grabbed the cup from Darren.

"There are some detectives that need to speak to you and then you can get on your way; they are taking statements from all the survivors."

Being questioned and possibly searched by detectives was not an option. Simon wanted to be gone. Five strides and he'd be over the barricade. That close. That far. Waiting with his bus ticket were his passport and plane tickets. He had a first class reservation aboard Northwest bound for Phuket. More than anything, Simon yearned to be away from the bank. Away from the blood and memories. Far, far away. He'd call anonymously. Tell them about the second bomb. Give them time to evacuate the building. No one else would die. The bomb would shield his escape, but how many more people would perish? He squeezed the trigger, testing his resolve. It moved under his finger's pull. Some. Not enough. He was trapped here. There was no other way.

Chapter 17

Rudy

"She's gone. She's off the story," MacMillan revealed.

"That's her loss. I'll spin this one myself," Rudy spouted, pissed off.

MacMillan grabbed Rudy's jacket from the car they arrived in and threw it across the roof of the vehicle into Rudy's waiting hands.

"This press conference will be a cake walk," Rudy said, sliding on the coat.

"Yeah, I hear you; the numbers are impressive."

Rudy pulled his jacket on as he walked over to the podium and the hastily erected media center. With five uninjured hostages and six more in stable condition, he was probably one of the most successful hostage situation commanders of all time. True, three of the cities finest had died, but those were deaths in the line of duty. Not so bothersome in the public eye. Honoring those fallen men and women over the next few months would be a full-time job. To have his numbers, especially given the detonation of a large explosive device, was more than impressive, it was unbelievable.

He climbed the small wooden stairs onto the platform and tilted the microphone up a touch. Lights switched on from various locations and the noise of the throng died down to hear his statement.

"At approximately 9:45 this morning a terrorist cell, known to law enforcement as the Mallory boys, numbering somewhere between four and six people, entered the National Bank. Presumably, their original intent was to rob the bank. Their arsenal of weaponry included an explosive device that was detonated at 11:47 when the city's response team was given the order, by me, to breech the bank and save as many lives as possible. Of the fourteen hostages held inside, eleven escaped with their lives. There is no indication at this point that any of the Mallory boys survived. Three officers were killed in the brief yet deadly firefight that followed the detonation of the bomb. The identification of the shooter is at this time unknown. One of the hostages who escaped, a security guard, is reported to have wounded and or killed two members of the group. Other than that, I have nothing further to report at this time. The building is not yet secure and the hostages are still giving their statements. When I know more, you'll know more. We'll have another release for you in five to ten minutes. Thank you."

The silence erupted with calls from the crowd. Each patient, attentive reporter now an estranged, frantic waving hand. Rudy walked slowly, deliberately from the stage.

"All too easy," he thought, stepping down the stairs in the heat of the afternoon sun to where MacMillan waited. They both moved off to find coffee and something to eat.

"Where's that security guard?" Rudy queried, brushing his forehead with the back of his hand in order to remove the droplets of sweat that had formed there.

"Harry S. Truman's his name if you can fucking believe it. We got him at the command trailer, he's giving his statement."

Rudy grinned – the name of a great American president, what could be better? "We'd better head over there."

"You got it, boss."

They found Harry sitting in the trailer answering questions, the bulk of his statement already given.

Noonez stood and greeted MacMillian.

"He's the real deal," Noonez confirmed.

"Give me the short version," Rudy asked.

"Well, he said that he tagged two inside, one before the bomb blast and one after. Ballistics will confirm the bullets. Said he worked himself free by rubbing the plastic tie on an air ventilation grill. Also, he said that there were only two left after they'd turned on each other inside, some sort of internal power struggle. All of the other statements corroborate his account."

"What about the 911?"

"It came in from Ricky Lam, the shop owner across the street. Lam heard shots and called it in. Best part? Ricky said, and this has been confirmed by all the hostages including Harry, that some kids busted into the bank somehow while this thing was going down, thinking it was closed, with the intention of robbing it."

"Seriously?"

"Seriously. The sound of the shots triggered the 911 call after the kids entered the bank."

Rudy stood and looked over at Harry through the two-way mirrored window, which separated the debriefing area from the rest of the mobile command trailer. Harry sat uncomfortably talking to the debriefing officer, his bulk was not suited for the small chair that he presently over-occupied.

"He's not much to look at. Actions speak louder."

"You got that right, Chief," James agreed.

"Let's take him to the people. Get him ready for a press release, Nunez. He won't have to say much; I'll do most of the talking."

"You got it. How long?"

"Five minutes."

"Five?"

"Five."

Margaret

Melissa took the news much as Margaret would have expected. She was devastated but thankful to Margaret for bearing it; the coincidence of her presence outside this restaurant was all at once unbelievable and fated. She was as beautiful as Patrick had described and judging from her emotional response, she'd held on too, like Patrick. How had he put it? Margaret recalled Patrick's words, his "*truth.*" Margaret saw no ring on Melissa's fingers but with all that had transpired, Margaret knew it was not her place to ask. It felt strange sharing such deep emotion with a woman she'd just met, but nothing about the last few hours was normal. She spared a glance back at Melissa in the restaurant, before exiting. The fresh cut flowers, a memorial to lost love in the midst of their shared grief over Patrick's death. Closure too often is composed of a bittersweet duet between tragedy and despair.

"Not for me," Margaret said to herself, climbing into the backseat of the waiting taxi.

"On to James, lady?"

"Yes, no more stops."

Snap. She'd just remembered Olivia! "Do you have a cell phone I could borrow?"

"Not long distance, is it?"

"No, no. Just a local call."

The driver handed her his cell.

On the radio, news of the explosion at the bank was taking center stage. Margaret dialed her sister... *please pick up, please Livie, please pick up...* the phone rang and Margaret sank back into the seat of the cab.

"Hello?"

"Olivia, thank the lord. Meet me at the house, come quickly!"

"Maggie? What's wrong? What is it?"

"How long until you get here?"

"I dunno... twenty minutes."

"OK, Olivia. Twenty minutes. Please hurry!"

"You're scaring me! What is it?"

"It's everything, Olivia, everything. I can't do it anymore! I won't!"

"OK," Olivia stammered through her tears. "OK."

"I'll see you at the house," Margaret quailed, wiping at her eyes.

"See you there."

Margaret ended the call. She couldn't get into it. It was too, too much. She handed the driver back his phone and then sat back. Margaret listed out the things she'd need to gather up when she stepped through her front door. How do you gather up a life in a few small bags? Surprisingly, and sadly, she knew it wouldn't be hard.

Harry

Five minutes? He was ready to go now. The Chief of Police, the highest ranking law enforcement officer in Phoenix, hell probably in the entire state of Arizona, had just asked to step onto the stage with him. Harry S. Truman. The furthest aspirations of youth were uncovering themselves; after decades of disappointment and shame, his worth, his potential was finally going to be recognized. He had pulled the trigger, he had popped a cap into one of the robbers, killing him. He had survived the ensuing gunfight and had escaped the bank, and the wrath of the explosion that had devastated the bank. He'd planned and agonized over the timing of his assault, he had taken a chance, he had committed himself to a course of action that could have very well cost him his life, but it hadn't. No, no. It hadn't. And now, well in four minutes or so, he would walk out of this trailer and step up to a microphone and tell his tale to the whole city, probably the whole country. His eighth grade teacher, Mrs. Brownie, would see him, a success despite her observations about his work ethic. His ex-wife would see him, the hero, the soon to be rich, made-for-TV-movie gunslinger he'd always promised he'd become; she'd be kicking herself over the divorce settlement now. He'd done it. My Lord, if he hadn't done it!

"Did you hear what I said, Harry?" Nunez insisted.

"Right, right. I got it, man. Follow the Chief's lead and comment only when directed to do so by him. I've seen the news before, junior. Christ," Harry retorted, seemingly tired of this pointless prep. He'd been ready for this since childhood.

"Alright, come with me." Nunez led Harry out of the trailer. Outside, the spectacle had swelled considerably since Harry had gone in for questioning. Lights from a hundred cameras momentarily blinded Harry as police officers and other emergency personnel worked to suppress the assembled media. Overhead Harry could see at least two news helicopters circling the site. Nunez directed him from the trailer to the platform that had been assembled. In the middle of the platform stood a small wooden podium which sagged slightly in the middle. To Harry, the podium looked like a holiday chia pet: even from a distance, he could discern the hundreds of microphones laid upon its surface.

"This way," Nunez directed.

The sun reached high in its arc over the city, a giant spotlight looking down on him, the new center of the universe, the new cover of Soldier of Fortune. On the way to the media platform, several officers nodded in his direction; Harry acknowledged each and every look – a far cry from the looks he was used to getting. Something new was in their eyes, something unfamiliar. Respect. Harry wished the walk would never end; he'd never felt so... so... real, so worthy. They reached the back of the stage and met up again with Mills. He looked ready – clean pressed suit, a few touches of make-up to enhance his features. A woman came immediately over to Harry and straightened his uniform, fixed his hair, and cleaned his face where he assumed he'd been blackened by the explosion or in the aftermath. In all, she'd taken less than a minute to do what his ex had insisted on doing for hours at a time. Efficient. Harry liked efficient.

"This is it, Harry. You ready?" Mills said, grabbing his shoulder and looking him man to man.

"Ready, Chief," Harry replied, dry mouthed.

Instantly, there was a glass of water in his hand and he was taking a sip.

"That's better," Harry said and the glass was gone and he was stepping up onto the platform right behind Mills.

Even in the worst Arizona heat wave in history, even with the high-flying golden sun beating down on them, the lights from the television cameras and the flashes from the photojournalist spiked the temperature a few more sweltering degrees. Harry bore the heat; hell, he'd pass out before he'd step away from this moment.

"This city has survived a violent and perilous siege, but we have emerged victorious. Our citizens have been freed. We did not lie down, we did not bend to the will of these criminals; we stood strong, together, you and I and the city of Phoenix. The SWAT teams, the emergency crews, the police, the media, the great people of this great nation have and will stand tall, proud of the stance and action taken here today. As always, the safety of the people of this city is my primary concern; even one life lost is one too many and we must recognize those who were stolen from us this day, defenders of our freedom, soldiers on the front lines of today's battle against terrorism. But also from the ashes of our fallen, like the legend for which this city is named, we must also recognize the emergence, the resurrection of that spirit in heroic deeds, deeds that speak to the heart of courage. One such hero is this man, standing next to me here, Harry S. Truman, security guard at the National Bank."

A flurry of flashes penetrated the back of Harry's eyes. Looking down at the podium, Harry saw no paper there, no teleprompter; the Chief was winging it. Harry admired his command of language and basked in the praise that the Chief was bestowing upon him.

"Harry S. Truman," the Chief continued, "is a man whom we should acknowledge: not only did he escape the bonds that were placed on him, but he battled in the bank for the lives of the hostages. At this time, I would like to turn the floor over to Harry and any questions that you might have for him. We only have a few moments, but heroism such as his must be recognized and celebrated."

The throng surged with their questions, voices called out from all directions, cameras flashed as Harry walked up to the podium and stood beside Mills, who remained firmly in place, unwilling to share the spotlight. This was tomorrow's front page.

"Is the bank secure at this time, Chief?"

"The bank is still being swept, but all indications are that the site is secure at this time," Mills answered.

"Harry, Harry. Bill Wilson, WBCS. What was the feeling in the bank when the bomb was detonated?"

Harry wet his lips, glancing quickly at Mills, who nodded towards the microphone. Harry took a half step forward and bent down as close as he could get to the microphone.

"We…" Buzzzzzz.

"Sorry," Harry stammered, moving back away from the mike, helping to discharge the feedback.

"No need to lean in; speak in a normal voice, Harry. You'll do fine," Mills whispered.

Harry rested on his heels and started again.

"We felt like it was the end. The blast blew out my ear drums and blinded me; the debris and smoke seemed to hang in the air. It was chaos. I was thrown forward, but being on the edge of the west wall, I was not in a direct line with the bomb's shock wave."

"Well done, Harry. You're a natural," Mills confided discreetly.

"Harry. Betty Thompson, CJLK. What can you tell us about the mindset of the Mallory Gang?"

"Ruthless and organized. They were bent on violence and destruction; they brutalized me and my partner. They killed without conscience. Near the end, they turned on each other. At least one of them was killed inside the bank by the others. I never thought I'd survive."

Mills stepped in quickly just as Harry finished up with his reflection on his chances inside the bank.

"I'm afraid that's all we have time for right now."

Cries from the assembly. They had a thousand more questions for Harry, but Mills wasn't interested in giving them more than a taste of this hero. Rudy couldn't let the spin over to Harry take away from what he did. His early and decisive call to breech the bank had to be the top story.

"Great work, Harry. Just step back towards the stairs and Nunez will make sure you're taken care of."

Harry was enjoying himself. He'd keyed in on the questions and spoken the truth, using the best, most descriptive words he could muster. It was too bad about his flub at the beginning with the feedback on the microphones.

"Chief. Chief." He heard someone in the crowd calling for Mills as he moved off towards the back of the podium.

"Cory Wheeler, JWLT. Is there any explanation yet for the apparent lack of destruction and wounded, especially given that a bomb was set off inside the bank?"

Harry turned and saw Mills step back towards the giant pin cushion of microphones in order to field the question.

"So far, our only information on the bomb itself is that it was low yield and thereby less destructive than it looked. Thank God."

"In other words this was not a suicide bombing," Cory Wheeler persisted.

"No, it doesn't seem that way, but it's too early to tell; as we get more information, we'll let you all know."

"Are you aware, Chief, that the Mallory boys are known for setting off large, highly destructive charges?"

Mills, Harry saw, was becoming agitated with the questioning. His hands, which had been quite relaxed, had dropped behind the podium, clenched into tightly packed fists.

"It is true that the bomb used here does not match up perfectly with the Mallory boys MO and there are some other irregularities as well. I assure you that our investigation will be looking at every possible angle with regards to this group of criminals. Thank you, that is all for now."

Mills turned away from the masses and headed towards Harry. It was clear from his expression that he was not pleased.

Harry had turned towards the stairs when he took in a blinding flash of light from the direction of the bank, and was thrown clear across the platform into the podium, along with Chief Mills. The sound of the explosion came like a freight train, assaulting his senses. Harry opened his eyes and looked through his sunspots. In the direction of the bank, he could see that the lower four stories of the structure hung open as if the building had been savagely unzipped. Black smoke billowed all around, and pieces of the building fell like rain on the assembly, cars, people, pavement. Shaking his head clear, Harry propped himself up on an elbow just as a three-foot piece of concrete smashed into a parked police car, destroying it. Looking behind him, he saw that Mills was unconscious, shaken badly from the impact; it was a wonder they both weren't electrocuted. Harry scrambled onto his hands and knees, while the rain of debris continued. He scampered down from the platform, turned around, and grabbed Mills by the collar. Mills was a big man, but Harry leveraged himself on the side of the stage and pulled him onto the ground, then rolled Mills and then himself under the front edge of the platform. Boom! A large piece of debris rattled off the wooden surface of the platform. Bam! Another few smaller pieces slammed into the wooden stage. Smash! The falling debris was doing a lot of damage; the wooden platform surface wouldn't save them from anything huge, but Harry figured it was better than being out in the open. After several more seconds, the debris stopped. Leaving Mills under the platform, Harry crawled out and gazed towards the bank. Completely obliterated. Through the smoke clouds Harry could see that the first three floors were gutted. The upper stories floated above the massive blast crater, hanging on without the support beams and foundation. It stood there, defying gravity. In seconds the building would go. It had to. Then, as if in answer to Harry's thoughts, he watched the entire building, all eight stories, topple forward onto the street. A series of sharp cracks followed by the continuous rumble of destruction left him gasping for air. The building seemed to lurch forward and vomit its contents onto the street leaving a swath of bent metal and broken glass, of destroyed vehicles and dead or dying people. Reporters came suddenly from the fringes; like rats at night, they crowded around Harry, talking, asking, pleading. They all wanted comments, answers, statements to fill their publications. They had seen how Harry had pulled Mills from the platform. They wanted why, they needed how... Harry didn't know. He just had, was all. He just had. Harry stood leaning against the platform, witness to mass destruction, unable to speak. The smell, the same old smell, from his boyhood – death was close. Harry closed his eyes and gave in to the spinning vertigo of his mind.

Tony

Tony felt the pain from his knee slowly ebbing away. He was ready to move. That's when he heard the clack of high-heeled shoes. Tony glanced over his shoulder and sure enough, not more than a few feet from the bus stop, came a news reporter, camera in tow.

"Shit," Tony muttered.

"What is it?" Clara stammered, opening her eyes for the first time in a few minutes.

"We got trouble, Clara." Tony shifted his weight slightly, helping Clara stand.

"You two were in the bank," the woman said.

"No, no, not us," Tony lied.

The woman, tall and lean, definitely pissed off about something, licked her lips and brought the camera from its dangling position at her side onto her shoulder.

"I know damn well you two were in the bank. And unless you want every reporter within earshot to get a piece of you, you'll give me a little taste of what you experienced inside."

"Fuck you," Tony said. "You can't threaten us."

She looked through the camera lens, ignoring Tony.

"Listen, sweetie," she said. "I know you were in the bank, I know that you're injured, so you couldn't get away all that quickly even if you wanted to. All I'm asking for is three minutes and then I'll call you a cab or a bus or whatever the hell you want so you can get out of here."

Tony bit his tongue. She wasn't going to take no for an answer.

"Give us a minute."

"You got it," she said, brightened by his response.

Tony leaned down to Clara's ear as best he could so that their conversation would be as private as possible.

"This bitch is pushy." Clara's head nodded in agreement.

"Let's do this thing and get the hell outta here," she said plainly.

"Yeah, I'm with you."

"OK, we are good to go here," Tony announced.

"Great," she said, pulling the camera into place again on her shoulder. "Three, two, one… This is Vanessa Greene just outside the National Bank of America talking to two survivors of the death and destruction that took place here this afternoon. They have been gracious enough to give us a few minutes of their time to tell us about their harrowing ordeal. First off, can you tell our viewers what your feelings were, in the bank, as it was being taken over?"

Clara squeezed Tony's hand. An indication of dread? They hadn't been in the bank at the beginning. Nerves about answering in front of the camera? In any event, she did remarkably well.

Her words echoed through Tony's head.

"We all felt like this was it, we were all gonna die. All I could think about was the life I'd planned out for myself, all the things I'd never be able to do and all of the things I wanted to say."

"What can you tell us about the Mallory brothers?" Vanessa continued.

"They were ruthless and brutal. They seemed to know what they were doing, like they'd planned it all out. In the end they turned on each other," Clara answered, smoothly, confidently.

"How do you mean exactly?"

"When the situation escalated, they became divided; a rift formed and they ended up shooting their own guys, that's the way it sounded anyway; our faces were covered. I thought it was the end."

"That's incredible. They turned on each other?"

"That's right. After the explosion, we tried to get out as quickly as possible but the gunfire forced us to take cover. I've never been so scared in all my life."

"Powerful and disturbing. Anything you'd like to add?"

"I'd just like to tell my parents not to worry, and that I'm alright, love you guys."

249

The red light on the end of the camera went off. Tony sighed. It was over. Clara had done all the talking; she'd carried it off perfectly. The woman lowered the camera to the ground.

"That was great stuff, you answered like a veteran," she said, shaking Clara's hand.

"Thanks." Clara smiled.

"Now there are just a few more formalities."

Tony was ready to peel. The cops would start to move out, respond to other emergencies. Tony knew they'd catch someone else's eye, the same way they had with this reporter… No, no, it had to end now. They needed to leave.

"I think that's enough," Tony said, standing up slowly and purposefully, hoping his large stature would persuade this woman to move along.

"Just a few more things, big guy," she said.

Tony moved to the edge of the bus stop, motioning Clara to follow. She quickly moved in beside him.

"Let me just take a few shots of you in front of the bank building; it won't be great at this distance, but it'll still add to the story," she said, moving around them, positioning herself to get the best angle.

It was only fifty feet to Taylor Street where he knew they could score a cab. He regretted taking the rest break and wished he'd listened to Clara.

"And I'll need your personal information and addresses as well in a moment…" she trailed, sensing they thought that the shot would be the end of their duties.

Tony wanted to be away, he knew that Clara did as well. The delay was killing him. Inside, he saw himself walking over to this reporter and planting one square on that delicate jaw of hers. She'd go down hard and be out for a while. But now they were stuck, a few steps from freedom.

"Great," she said, just about ready to switch off the camera.

Tony saw it first: a bright flash of white light coming from behind. For a second he thought he could see his shadow on the bus stop in front of him; strange, with the sun high overhead. He instinctively ducked, dragging Clara down with him. The light was followed by a deafening BOOM, and the reverberations of a long thunder crack. The shock wave pushed them forward along the ground. Six, maybe ten feet. The reporter did not fare as well, awkwardly hitting the side of the bus post. Tony saw, lifting his head, that she was bleeding slightly from a cut on her cheek. She sat herself up however, and grabbed at the camera, which she'd cradled like a baby on the way down. Tony watched her struggle to her feet, fall down to one knee, trying to regain her equilibrium, and pull the camera up to her face. Tony glanced over at Clara beside him; she was already sitting up, shaking her head slightly. He moved to rise from the pavement, but the knee, his knee was sparked anew with reasons to remain down. Clara grabbed his hand; squeezing herself under his arm she got him standing. They turned back towards the bank; the plume of smoke rising now from the torn building made the earlier explosion seem tiny by comparison. The lower portion of the bank, the entire bottom third, was missing. The building seemed to stand on only the back portion of its original foundation; the upper three stories hung open, burnt and twisted. Some police cars and emergency vehicles were smashed and in flames. The debris was falling heavily, destructively, on the assembled aid workers. Tony watched the reporter move steadily forward, camera held high, like some entranced zombie, towards the wreckage. He grabbed Clara's hand and started to lead her away. This was their chance. He pulled Clara a few steps, turning her towards him and the waiting safety of the street. They made it just a few steps before they heard a secondary explosion and the popping sound of failing metal, like a car crash recorded in Dolby digital; they turned and watched the entire building, all eight brick and metal stories, come crumbling down, spewing itself onto the street.

Clara buckled at the waist and vomited onto the curb. Tony pulled her back to her feet and together they turned the corner. A few strides later, they opened the door of a stopped cab at an adjacent intersection and were sped away. Back to the world they knew, back to the neighborhood they lived in, back, back into the world where sights such as this remained far, far away on a television set, one click away from not being real. Tony knew they could never really go back, and he settled into that thought with Clara beside him, a blank stare of disbelief on her face. Tony knew.

Vanessa

Vanessa's intuition had paid off. Originally motivated through frustration and spite she'd grabbed one of the van's mobile cameras and stormed off. In hindsight, it had to be intuition, showing her the way, even when she'd been consumed with a red, vengeful rage. The "borrowed" equipment was paying huge dividends. Minutes after leaving Larry and the van, she'd caught sight of the fleeing kids and cornered them into a decent little interview. She had to be persuasive, but they'd understood and stuck around to answer her questions. The shot of them in front of the bank building had really just been an afterthought, and then it happened… She's finally been in the right place, at the right time. The camera, she knew, had taken it in: the blinding, searing flash of light, the eclipse of cascading thunder as the destruction mounted, followed by the shock wave which forced her to the sidewalk. She'd fallen hard; bruises and cuts along her knees and elbows, Vanessa had fought off the vertigo, scrambling to her feet, and just in time really, to see the visual spectacle that followed. The building, hollowed out by the force of the blast, hung like a giant squared top, the base of which, a blackened, sutured apex of twisted metal and steel, concrete and fire, toppled forward, spilling all eight stories above into the streets and alleys below. The footage was undeniably the most sensational, most unbelievable, most frightening thing she'd ever seen. The sound of the destruction, the silence of the aftermath, the powerful images of such a massive structure, suddenly, violently brought down, like some fatally wounded titan. The images raced through her mind, over and over. She turned back towards the college kids and found the street barren; they'd left, before or after the building collapsed, she couldn't be sure. She turned the camera back towards the devastation and kept the tape rolling as the emergency response crews came back to life. In minutes, the scene was a bustling hive of activity. Vanessa knew she didn't have too much time to spare. She pulled the tape out and left the camera tucked under the bus stop bench. It was too heavy to take with her; someone would find it and turn it in or take it for themselves. It didn't matter. Speed. That's what she needed now. She patted her jacket pocket, making sure the audio of the Police Chief's conversation was secure, and ran down Washington Street West. The studio for channel 11 was only six and half blocks away. All news, all the time. Her price would be exorbitant but they'd pay; once they saw what she had, they'd pay. Not only in nice cold cash, but in a job and a future. Fuck channel 9. They'd screwed her over for the last time. This was her chance. The spotlight would follow her images, would shine on her face, the nation would hear her words. She ran through the hot hazy heat of the day, feeling nothing but elation and excitement.

Simon

Simon's finger relaxed its hold on the detonator. It wasn't time. Not yet. The opportunity to exit the scene might still present itself. He pulled his hand out of his pocket and began to move with Darren through the maze, presumably towards the police checkpoint where he would be debriefed and sent along his way. Simon could see the bank entrance to his right; the broken glass and twisted metal of the doorway was but a fraction of the total devastation that would occur should he activate the second bomb. He could see, through the framing of the bank lobby, picture flashes, the light-illuminated detectives and forensic personnel busily collecting the data and evidence that would explain exactly what had happened in those precious minutes between then and now.

"What time is it?" Simon asked, too weary to look at his own watch.

Darren pulled up his shirt sleeve, "12:57."

"Thanks."

Between then and now, much had changed. Simon had survived; Kayla and Alan too. Reframed, that's what success looked like on this job. But others, like those who had set Grier up for this job, no doubt saw it differently. They'd want to know about their investment. Simon pushed the worry away for now. At least Grier's death had saved them all from the annoying post-job antics for which Grier had become famous. Saved themselves from the bragging and strutting.

"That job was perfection…"

"I planned everything down to the last detail…"

"I even knew what time the mail pick-up was at the post office across the street…"

Yes, the lip service provided by Grier's recollections left a stale taste in one's mouth, a dryness that could only be quenched by distance. It was over now; those lips had finally expelled their last. As they passed between the ambulances, Simon saw ahead of him a hastily erected media platform. In the center of the platform stood a podium that was topped by a giant porcupine of microphones; a crown of thorns to mark the tragedy. Ahead the police contingent increased; they were getting close to the edge of the barricades.

"Have you got a phone, Darren? I really should make a call."

Darren turned to Simon. "A phone?"

"Yeah, I've got to give my mom a call; I was supposed to meet her at noon: She knew I was heading to the bank today. I'm sure she's worried sick," Simon said.

Darren hesitated.

"I'll make it quick."

Darren nodded. "OK, no problem," he said, handing Simon his cell phone.

"Thanks, Darren. I appreciate it, and the coffee," said Simon, taking a sip and starting to press some numbers.

254

Darren sat patiently on the hood of a squad car waiting for Simon to finish. Simon moved a few steps away from him, trying to get out of earshot without looking suspicious.

"911, please state the nature of your emergency."

"There is another bomb in the National Bank on 1st Avenue and Taylor; get everyone out of there. Three minutes. Tick. Tock."

Simon keyed the phone off as he switched hands, stepping back towards Darren.

"Yes, Mom. It was terrifying, but I swear to you, I'm alright."

Simon paused and caught Darren's attention, giving him a quick wink before moving back away. This time with his back turned, he flipped off the battery cover and removed the phone's SIM card quickly slipping it into his pocket. Simon turned back towards Darren.

"No problem, I'll see you in a bit, Mom."

Simon went to return the phone to Darren, but dropped it instead. Pieces of cell phone splintered apart. The battery, the battery cover which Simon had left unfastened, and the entire back panel of the phone. Simon, apologizing repeatedly, bent down to gather the pieces, reassembling it for Darren. Darren was more than a little annoyed, but accepted the phone. Looking to the podium, Simon noticed that Chief Mills had moved up to the platform. He was not alone. Harry, the fat security guard who'd killed Patrick, stood beside him. Simon's teeth clamped together, grinding slightly, unconsciously, from side to side.

"I'm really sorry about that, Darren. I owe you one," Simon tried to console him.

"How's your mom?" he asked.

"She's relieved that I'm in one piece," Simon stated, looking over his shoulder towards the bank and any sign that his warning had been received. Nothing yet. He knew it would take time for the ball to get rolling. A minute more and there'd be some reaction.

"What's happening over there," Simon inquired, motioning towards the bright lights and make-shift podium, stalling for time.

255

"That's the media center. Looks like Chief Mills up there with that security guard. They say he shot two of the thieves before crawling out of the bank."

"Really?" Simon muttered.

"OK, Patrick. Let's get you processed and out of here," Darren said.

"Wait a minute, what's happening now?" Simon asked, urgency rising in his voice.

Darren turned and faced the bank. Crews seemed to be steadily streaming from the building.

"Doesn't look good," Darren said.

"Let's get some distance," Simon said, starting to move away from the bank towards the podium.

Ahead of him, Simon could see in greater and greater detail; the security guard was at the podium now, he was answering questions. Simon couldn't hear him; the speakers were pointed away from their position and the sound of his own heartbeat was heavy in his ears. Word was spreading that something was wrong inside the bank. Simon glanced quickly behind him and saw that the police officers and emergency personnel were clearing the area. His message had been delivered.

"Thank God," Simon muttered to himself, reaching into his pocket and keying off the safety switch for the detonator.

About twenty feet in front of him, the barricades came to an end and Simon could see a large cube van parked across the street. That would be the distance, that would be the place to wait out the chaos. Behind him, he heard Darren slowing; to his right he heard words coming from the microphone – the Chief was back in front of the cameras. Simon ran clear across the street, without looking back to the bank, or to Darren, or the Chief, or to the murdering security guard they now called Hero. He made straight for the far side of the cube van, white and nondescript. He rounded the corner of the vehicle and thrust his hand into his pocket.

EMPTY!

"Shit! What the? Shit, shit, shit!!" Simon cursed.

256

His hands came up over to his forehead, fingertips kneading at the stress and anxiety of the last three hours, three minutes, three years. An eternity. He moved back around the side of the cube van and looked back towards his path. There, not looking towards the van just on the edge of the barricades, he could see Darren stoop over and pick up the detonator. It must have slipped out when he'd keyed off the safety. Darren looked at it curiously for a moment before being overrun by a crowd of emergency workers and police officers. The word was out that there was another bomb in the bank. Darren fell to the ground in the collision, along with two of the running emergency workers. Watching them fall, Simon was unprepared for the detonation of the second bomb, which began with a blinding flash of light. A burning, searching, cresting tidal wave of white ripped through the interior of the bank. In that moment, Simon could see the Chief on the podium walking slowly towards the back of the stage, he could see the outline of news trucks, ambulances, fire trucks and police cars, of people running, faces turned from the awesome intensity of the explosion. The sound then reached him; the crackling, smoldering resonant thunder of devastation raged against his eardrums, the light and sound matching in intensity for a moment before the light faded and the sound, rolling and stretching outwards, engulfed him. Screams were inaudible; the sound of the bomb's destructive force reigned. This was followed by the shock wave; the airy push of the explosion forced Simon backwards onto the sidewalk beside the cube van. Simon rolled quickly back onto his feet and dashed down the street. He glanced quickly at his watch. His bus was leaving in seventeen minutes. The bus depot was nine blocks away. It was gonna be tight. Behind him, Simon could hear the chaos erupt. The confusion and horror of the second bomb blast would take several long minutes to recover from. Even the most experienced of them would need a moment. For others, it would be take much longer. Simon was a block and a half away when the National Bank building finally gave way and spread itself, all eight stories, onto the street below. The sound of its demolition was every bit as intense as the initial explosion had

257

been. What a ride. Darren had been good for something after all. What a ride.

The bus station was nearly deserted. The bus itself, Simon saw, was half empty. He had a change of clothes stored in a locker at the bus terminal, along with his bus ticket, but there hadn't been time to change, only to retrieve his belongings and climb aboard. Adrenalin fueled his flight from the bank, arriving at the terminal with a few minutes to spare. Drenched in sweat from the run, matched with the incredible heat of the midday Phoenix sun, he figured on an hour before his body began to regulate his temperature. He'd wait until he stopped sweating before changing. He'd have to do it in transit in the bathroom at the back of the bus. Not the most appealing spot to disrobe, but it would suffice. Sliding into his seat, he congratulated himself. He'd always been cautious. He'd learned to rely only on himself, no matter what. No matter where. He'd secured the locker, bought the ticket, and planned this escape, never thinking it would be necessary. He'd never mentioned it to anyone.

The engine roared to life and the bus left the station. It would be a long trip, but not unbearable. He had a lot to think about on his way home; so much had transpired in such a short time. It would take weeks to unravel every knot of the experience. Of the nefarious elements that had been pitted against him. How it had all intertwined at just the right (or wrong) moment to make it thus. He was thirty-one years old, on a bus bound for Detroit. Seven had begun the journey, three had survived. Lives were changed. Altered forever. Simon would never, could never, forget the unselfishness and bravery he'd witnessed. "*You could be,*" echoed through his head. He would mourn, he knew, Patrick's loss, a death he was responsible for. That guilt would solidify his commitment to be a better man. Margaret – he would pray for her spirit, beaten and broken as she was. The students – Tony was the name of the big kid; he hoped they would make wise decisions with their newly found wealth. They'd paid heavily for their share. Kayla and Pete were well away by now, he wished strength and long life to them. She was a particular beauty, intelligent and radiant, and Simon thought of her and her daughter. Of all the members in their group, she'd shared what Simon hoped was a genuine truth about herself, and amid all the lies and deceits of the last few hours, Simon held onto her words with more hope and trust than any others. Perhaps it was self-delusion, a way to retain at least some semblance of pride for his skill. He was a reader, an observer of lives, a revealer of motivation and purpose, and in this he had failed most miserably when it had mattered the most. Simon looked out at the fading cityscape as the bus merged onto the highway, heading out of the state, turning towards his future, as open as the desert plain.

Epilogue

The late summer sun was sliding gently into the ocean when Simon returned to his beach house, his day's adventure at the Phuket Airport finished. His Mom and Dad were safely on their way back to Bangkok. From there they were flying to Osaka, Japan. They'd always been fascinated by the Orient and had dreamed of visiting Kyoto and Himeji Castle. They were living out their dreams, impossibilities Simon had heard them discuss over the kitchen table in his childhood home. They'd showered him with gratitude during their week-long visit. Simon let them get away with it, relishing their enjoyment of his gift to them. His incredible luck in the state lottery had secured him a financial windfall which he shared in part with them. Simon sat in his patio lounger watching the sun slowly relinquish its hold on the sky, smiling at the world of adventure his parents were discovering. They seemed younger, invigorated by travel. Happy as ever.

He'd wired them some money a month after returning from the U.S. They called the next day. At first they'd refused. Wary of the money's origin, knowing somehow that he'd been involved in things not altogether legal, not altogether above board. It had taken him nearly two hours to convince them that he had indeed won the state lottery with a few old work friends of his in California.

Simon had scanned the net for a big state lottery pay-off. California, Carolina, Texas and Michigan all had huge jackpots won by groups. Three weeks later, with the money still sitting in their account, Simon asked them to visit him in Thailand. And after a few shorter trips, down to Florida and then to Las Vegas, they felt they had the travel legs for a lengthy, more adventurous journey. The money was a new lease on life, a world of opportunity. After the long and arduous years of living paycheck to paycheck, their travel aspirations had become possible, as had a meaningful relationship with their son.

Simon rose from his chair and moved into the air-conditioned living room. He poured himself a tall, cool glass of fresh mango juice and sank into the couch, grabbing the remote on the way down. The television hummed to life. It was just a distraction. He'd received a letter ten days ago. She'd found him.

Dear Simon,

All's well that ends well. Have package in tow. Remember that look in your eye- I felt it too. Meet me in Hong Kong. Royal Hilton, October 1st. Last name Bank. No joke.

K.

Mysterious. He'd decided immediately after reading it that he would not be attending any reunions. But now… after his parents' visit, he wasn't so sure. He longed for something. Companionship? His life was solitary: peaceful yes, but lonely. He craved intimacy and he'd be lying if he said he hadn't thought about her, about their time together. The late-night pizza and beer. The passionate, beguiling purpose of her involvement in Grier's plan. The kiss on that last night in the warehouse. When she'd warned him. He thought about her often- more often than not. Even in his dash for the bus on that fateful day, he thought of her. He envisioned her urging him to run, to hurry. He'd obliged. He'd made his bus, boarding quickly. He'd slept for much of the two-day journey to Detroit. Once there, he changed tickets for a later flight and rented a car.

The farmhouse they'd trained in was empty. No new tenants were interested in the out-of-the-way compound. He walked the yard. He climbed the stairs of the house to the second floor, where he lay down on the bed, the old farmhouse bed that he had slept in that first week before heading south to the Warehouse. He remembered her most of all. Looking back, he heard her words differently, saw her looks with more clarity. He sensed, as an afterthought, that she must have been one of the few who were against Grier's plan. At least the part that included his murder. Simon closed his eyes, remembering her on that first morning, the smell of her smoothie filling the air. He thought he saw anger and bitterness in her eyes; now in reflection, he realized it was pity and remorse. It had been a test, driving down to the Arizona compound with him. Grier had no doubt masterminded it. If she was going to buckle under the pressure and reveal the plan to Simon, that would have been the time. Somehow Grier would know. She or Simon would tip their hand. But she hadn't told. He begrudged her little at this point. She had a daughter to save, a heavy price next to the life of a stranger. She'd passed Grier's test. Grier's control over her had been stifling, no wonder she was so composed when Grier died. She had been the quickest to collect herself after he fell. Simon hadn't planned on sleeping, but the bed, its comfort, lulled him into a deep slumber.

He awoke with a start. The farmhouse. Standing, he took one last look around the room before exiting. He walked down the stairs and out of the farmhouse through the kitchen. It was over. He'd come nearly full circle. He slid into his rental car and made his way back into the city; the flight to Bangkok left in five hours.

On the news in the airport he followed the developments surrounding the robbery and the destruction of the National Bank of America in Phoenix. It was on nearly every channel, the footage of the explosion playing over and over again; he couldn't buy a pretzel or take a piss without catching a glimpse of it. Whoever caught it on tape would be making a killing off it now. Several news stations mentioned her name, a freelance reporter, Vanessa something or other. Also on the news was the footage of Police Chief Rudy Mills being pulled off stage by the security guard, Harry S. Truman. Simon felt pangs of nausea thinking about how he had killed Patrick. The guilt of Patrick's death had hung over him. His head had begun to clear once he heard that Harry S. Truman had been arrested for possession of child pornography. It had been expensive and difficult to arrange from Thailand, but he'd decided on this course of action over anything more dramatic. Death was too easy an out for the man. Public humiliation; that was the path to his demise. Although the frame up had been costly, it afforded Simon complete autonomy. The blood money was put to good use. Patrick's life was at least partially avenged. Afterwards, Simon had contacted his parents with the good news and wired them the funds. One good deed suddenly became two, and a string began to form. A sense of purpose filled his days, while his nights were filled with thoughts of her.

Of Margaret, Simon had heard nothing. He only knew that she had left her husband and he wished her well wherever she might have ended up.

As for Mills, he was forcefully removed from office, but not before his lieutenant and confidant James MacMillan went down for a slew of crimes including extortion, trafficking, murder and prostitution. MacMillan, a made man had been stealing and protecting the cities most notorious criminal families behind the Chief's back for years. Mills told the press that MacMillan had threatened to kill him and his wife if he didn't 'help out' hundreds of times. The Chief had been collecting evidence for the last few years. Of course public opinion condemned Mills for holding out so long on the injustice that existed in the police force and he was forced to step down. No doubt he'd cut a deal with the DA for his testimony.

The big college kid and his girlfriend never turned up anywhere and no charges, as far as Simon could tell, were brought against them. Apparently they too had escaped. Life was full of second chances.

The only other player that made it out alive was Alan, and Simon had heard nothing about the man since that fateful day at the bank. He was a smart, efficient man. He'd have very little trouble in the world, whichever road he chose, responsible citizenship or opportunistic criminality.

Simon thumbed off the television. Nothing on, as usual. He reread the letter. Why did she have to be so damned mysterious? But he knew it was in her nature to make him work for it. If he brought himself to meet her, he'd have to do so under her conditions. If he didn't, he'd never know what, if anything, was possible.

Simon stood up slowly, placing the letter next to his glass of juice on the coffee table. He stood silently for a moment, weighing in his mind the effort against the reward. He opened the drawer and took out a well-worn business card. *Ethan N. Lo. Quick and Easy Travel Services.* He strode over to the telephone and thumbed in the numbers.

"Hello, Ethan."

"Yeah, it's me, Simon. Fix me up a ticket for Hong Kong on September 29th, will ya?"

"The Royal Hilton. Better book me in for the week."

"Great. Thanks."

The End

About the Author

Mark Swailes grew up in Milton, Ontario. Presently he lives in Markham, Ontario, Canada with his two children and wife. This is his first novel.

Author Acknowledgments

First and foremost I want to thank my incredible wife for supporting my dream.

I want to thank my editors, Nancy Swailes, Debra Hanff and Janet Shorten along with my friends and family who have contributed greatly to the novel over the years. Thank-you to Max Turner and Lisa Denis who helped breathe life into the unique voices in the novel. Thanks to Doug Carles who braved the earliest editions of the story and never backed away from a re-read.

A big shout out to the people in my life that ask about my writing and listen to my thoughts and ideas: Doug and Val Swailes, Rick and Marlene Derouin, Baldev Solanki, Jeff Truswell, Hardy Rideout, Glen Harper, Steve Martin, David and Michael Derouin, Richard Denis, Domenico Capilongo, Trevor Burman, Jason Phone, Jeremy Soonshiong, Steve Hutchison, Kevin Bryenton, Kristin Lawlor, Doug and Jill Rowlison, and my niece and nephews; Madeleine, Michael, Joey and Tyson.

Kickstarter Acknowledgments

Thank-you for taking a chance on me and my novel.

Shane Calvert, Ethan Nicholas Lo, Paul Avbar, John Mitropoulos, Shane Pisani, Doug Carles, Rob Backhouse, Ed Tornberg, Darren Johnston, the Namiesniowski Family, Dr. Kevin F. Brown, Peter Tworzyanski, Anna Patterson, Trevor Burman, Peter Chao, TLA Graphics, the Lee Family, Wayne Tsujiuchi and Ellen Philp, Susan Swailes, the Haen Family, Doug and Jill Rowlison, Richard J. Wells, C.A. Johnstone, Linda and Danny Brown, Rick Derouin, Heather White, Max Turner, Dana Williams, Mom and Dad, the Derouin Family, Debra Hanff and the Katsavelos Family.